Memoirs of Benjamin Franklin; Written by Himself. [Vol. 1 of 2]

Franklin

PART I.

To William Franklin, Esq., Governor of New-Jersey

Twyford, at the Bishop of St. Asaph's,[1] 1771.

Dear Son,—I have ever had a pleasure in obtaining any little anecdotes of my ancestors. You may remember the inquiries I made among the remains of my relations when you were with me in England, and the journey I undertook for that purpose. Imagining it may be equally agreeable to you to learn the circumstances of my life, many of which you are unacquainted with, and expecting the enjoyment of a few weeks' uninterrupted leisure, I sit down to write them. Besides, there are some other inducements that excite me to this undertaking. From the poverty and obscurity in which I was born, and in which I passed my earliest years, I have raised myself to a state of affluence and some degree of celebrity in the world. As constant good fortune has accompanied me even to an advanced period of life, my posterity will perhaps be desirous of learning the means which I employed, and which, thanks to Providence, so well succeeded with me. They may also deem them fit to be imitated, should any of them find themselves in similar circumstances. This good fortune, when I reflect on it, which is frequently the case, has induced me sometimes to say, that if it were left to my choice, I should have no objection to go over the same life[Pg 14] from its beginning to the end: requesting only the advantage authors have, of correcting in a second edition the faults of the first. So would I also wish to change some incidents of it for others more favourable. Notwithstanding, if this condition was denied, I should still accept the offer of recommencing the same life. But as this repetition is not to be expected, that which resembles most living one's life over again, seems to be to recall all the circumstances of it; and, to render this remembrance more durable, to record them in writing. In thus employing myself I shall yield to the inclination so natural to old men, of talking of themselves and their own actions; and I shall indulge it without being tiresome to those who, from respect to my age, might conceive themselves obliged to listen to me, since they will be always free to read me or not. And lastly (I may as well confess it, as the denial of it would be believed by nobody), I shall perhaps not a little gratify my own vanity. Indeed, I never heard or saw the introductory words "Without vanity I may say," &c., but some vain thing immediately followed. Most people dislike vanity in others, whatever share they have of it themselves; but I give it fair quarter, wherever I meet with it, being persuaded that it is often productive of good to the possessor, and to others who are within his sphere of action: and therefore, in many cases, it would not be altogether absurd if a man were to thank God for his vanity among the other comforts of life.

And now I speak of thanking God, I desire with all humility to acknowledge that I attribute the mentioned happiness of my past life to his divine providence, which led me to the means I used and gave the success. My belief of this induces me to hope, though I must not presume, that the same goodness will still be exercised towards me, in continuing that happiness or enabling me to bear a fatal[Pg 15] reverse, which I may experience as others have done; the complexion of my future fortune being known to him only, in whose power it is to bless us, even in our afflictions.

Some notes, one of my uncles (who had the same curiosity in collecting family anecdotes) once put into my hands, furnished me with several particulars relative to our ancestors. From these notes I learned that they lived in the same village, Ecton, in Northamptonshire, on a freehold of about thirty acres, for at least three hundred years, and how much longer could not be ascertained.[2]

This small estate would not have sufficed for their[Pg 16] maintenance without the business of a smith, which had continued in the family down to my uncle's time, the eldest son being always brought up to that employment; a custom which he and my father followed with regard to their eldest sons. When I searched the registers at Ecton, I found an account of their marriages and burials from the year 1555 only, as the registers kept did not commence previous thereto. I however learned from it that I was the youngest son of the youngest son for five generations back. My grandfather Thomas, who was born 1598, lived at Ecton till he was too old to continue his business, when he retired to Banbury in Oxfordshire, to the house of his son John, with whom my father served an apprenticeship. There my uncle died and lies buried. We saw his gravestone in 1758. His eldest son Thomas lived in the house at Ecton, and left it with the land to his only daughter, who, with her husband, one Fisher, of Wellingborough, sold it to Mr. Isted, now lord of the manor there. My grandfather had four sons, who grew up: viz., Thomas, John, Benjamin, and Josiah. Being at a distance from my papers, I will give you what account I can of them from memory: and if my papers are not lost in my absence, you will find among them many more particulars.[3][Pg 17]

Thomas, my eldest uncle, was bred a smith under his father; but, being ingenious, and encouraged in learning (as all my brothers were) by an Esquire[Pg 18] Palmer, then the principal inhabitant of that parish, he qualified himself for the bar, and became a considerable man in the county; was chief mover of all public-spirited enterprises for the county or town of Northampton, as well as of his own village, of which many instances were related of him: and he was much taken notice of, and patronised by Lord Halifax. He died in 1702, the 6th of January; four years to a day before I was born. The recital which some elderly persons made to us of his character, I remember, struck you as something extraordinary, from its similarity with what you knew of me. "Had he died," said you, "four years later, on the same day, one might have supposed a transmigration." John, my next uncle, was bred a dyer, I believe of wool. Benjamin was bred a silk dyer, serving an apprenticeship in London. He was an ingenious man. I remember, when I was a boy, he came to my father's in Boston, and resided in the house with us for several years. There was always a particular affection between my father and him, and I was his godson. He lived to a great age. He left behind him two quarto volumes of manuscript, of his own poetry, consisting of fugitive pieces addressed to his friends. He had invented a shorthand of his own, which he taught me, but, not having practised it, I have now forgotten it. He was very pious, and an assiduous attendant at the sermons of the best preachers, which he reduced to writing according to his method, and had thus collected several volumes of them. He was also a good deal of a politician; too much so, perhaps, for his station. There fell lately into my hands in London, a collection he made of all the principal political pamphlets relating to public affairs, from the year 1641 to 1717; many of the volumes[Pg 19] are wanting, as appears by their numbering, but there still remain eight volumes in folio, and twenty in quarto and in octavo. A dealer in old books had met with them, and knowing me by name, having bought books of him, he brought them to me. It would appear that my uncle must have left them here when he went to America, which was about fifty years ago. I found several of his notes in the margins. His grandson, Samuel Franklin, is still living in Boston.

Our humble family early embraced the reformed religion. Our forefathers continued Protestants through the reign of Mary, when they were sometimes in danger of persecution on account of their zeal against popery. They had an English Bible, and to conceal it, and place it in safety, it was fastened open with tapes under and within the cover of a joint-stool. When my great-grandfather wished to read it to his family, he placed the joint-stool on his knees, and then turned over the leaves under the tapes. One of the children stood at the door to give notice if he saw the apparitor coming, who was an officer of the spiritual court. In that case the stool was turned down again upon its feet, when the Bible remained concealed under it as before. This anecdote I had from uncle Benjamin. The family continued all of the Church of England till about the end of Charles the Second's reign, when some of the ministers that had been outed for their nonconformity holding conventicles in Northamptonshire, my uncle Benjamin and father Josiah adhered to them, and so continued all their lives: the rest of the family remained with the Episcopal church.

My father married young, and carried his wife with three children to New-England, about 1682. The conventicles being at that time forbidden by law, and frequently disturbed in their meetings, some considerable men of his acquaintance determined to go to that country, and he was prevailed with to[Pg 20] accompany them thither, where they expected to enjoy the exercise of their religion with freedom. By the same wife my father had four children more born there, and by a second wife ten others, in all seventeen; of which I remember to have seen thirteen sitting together at his table, who all grew up to years of maturity, and were married; I was the youngest son, and the youngest of all except two daughters. I was born in Boston, in New-England. My mother, the second wife of my father, was Abiah Folger, daughter of Peter Folger, one of the first settlers of New-England, of whom honourable mention is made by Cotton Mather, in his ecclesiastical history of the country, entitled Magnalia Christi Americana, as "a goodly and learned Englishman," if I remember the words rightly. I was informed he wrote several small occasional works, but only one of them was printed, which I remember to have seen several years since. It was written in 1675. It was in familiar verse, according to the taste of the times and people, and addressed to the government there. It asserts the liberty of conscience, in behalf of the Anabaptists, the Quakers, and other sectarians that had been persecuted. He attributes to this persecution the Indian wars, and other calamities that had befallen the country; regarding them as so many judgments of God, to punish so heinous an offence, so contrary to charity. This piece appeared to me as written with manly freedom and a pleasing simplicity. The last six lines I remember, but have forgotten the preceding ones of the stanza; the purpose of them was, that his censures proceeded from good-will, and, therefore, he would be known to be the author.

"Because to be a libeller (said he)

I hate it with my heart;

From Sherburne[4] town, where now I dwell,

My name I do put here;[Pg 21]

Without offence your real friend,

It is Peter Folgier."

My elder brothers were all put apprentices to different trades. I was put to the grammar-school at eight years of age; my father intended to devote me, as the tithe of his sons, to the service of the church. My early readiness in learning to read (which must have been very early, and I do not remember when I could not read), and the opinion of all my friends, that I should certainly make a good scholar, encouraged him in this purpose of his. My uncle Benjamin, too, approved of it, and proposed to give me his shorthand volumes of sermons to set up with, if I would learn shorthand.

I continued, however, at the grammar-school rather less than a year, though in that time I had risen gradually from the middle of the class of that year to be at the head of the same class, and was removed into the next class, whence I was to be placed in the third at the end of the year. But my father, burdened with a numerous family, was unable, without inconvenience, to support the expense of a college education; considering, moreover, as he said to one of his friends in my presence, the little encouragement that line of life afforded to those educated for it, he gave up his first intentions, took me from the grammar-school, and sent me to a school for writing and arithmetic, kept by a then famous man, Mr. George Brownwell. He was a skilful master, and successful in his profession, employing the mildest and most encouraging methods. Under him I learned to write a good hand pretty soon, but failed entirely in arithmetic. At ten years old I was taken to help my father in his business of a tallow-chandler and soap-boiler, a business to which he was not bred, but had assumed on his arrival in New-England, because he found that his dying trade, being in little request, would not maintain his family. Accordingly, I was employed in[Pg 22] cutting the wick for the candles, filling the moulds for cast candles, attending the shop, going of errands, &c.

I disliked the trade, and had a strong inclination to go to sea, but my father declared against it; but, residing near the water, I was much in it and on it. I learned to swim well, and to manage boats; and when embarked with other boys, I was commonly allowed to govern, especially in any case of difficulty; and upon other occasions I was generally the leader among the boys, and sometimes led them into scrapes, of which I will mention an instance, as it shows an early projecting public spirit, though not then justly conducted.

There was a salt-marsh which bounded part of the millpond, on the edge of which, at high water, we used to stand to fish for minnows; by much trampling, we had made it a mere quagmire. My proposal was to build a wharf there for us to stand upon, and I showed my comrades a large heap of stones, which were intended for a new house near the marsh, and which would very well suit our purpose. Accordingly, in the evening, when the workmen were gone home, I assembled a number of my playfellows, and we worked diligently like so many emmets, sometimes two or three to a stone, till we had brought them all to make our little wharf. The next morning the workmen were surprised on missing the stones which formed our wharf; inquiry was made after the authors of this transfer; we were discovered, complained of, and corrected by our fathers; and though I demonstrated the utility of our work, mine convinced me that that which was not truly honest could not be truly useful.

I suppose you may like to know what kind of a man my father was. He had an excellent constitution, was of a middle stature, well set, and very strong: he could draw prettily, was a little skilled in music; his voice was sonorous and agreeable, so[Pg 23] that when he played on his violin and sung withal, as he was accustomed to do after the business of the day was over, it was extremely agreeable to hear. He had some knowledge of mechanics, and, on occasion, was very handy with other tradesmen's tools; but his great excellence was his sound understanding and solid judgment in prudential matters, both in private and public affairs. It is true, he was never employed in the latter, the numerous family he had to educate and the strictness of his circumstances keeping him close to his trade: but I remember well his being frequently visited by leading men, who consulted him for his opinion in public affairs, and those of the church he belonged to, and who showed great respect for his judgment and advice: he was also much consulted by private persons about their affairs when any difficulty occurred, and frequently chosen an arbitrator between contending parties. At his table he liked to have, as often as he could, some sensible friend or neighbour to converse with, and always took care to start some ingenious or useful topic for discourse, which might tend to improve the minds of his children. By this means he turned our attention to what was good, just, and prudent in the conduct of life; and little or no notice was ever taken of what related to the victuals on the table, whether it was well or ill dressed, in or out of season, of good or bad flavour, preferable or inferior to this or that other thing of the kind, so that I was brought up in such a perfect inattention to those matters as to be quite indifferent as to what kind of food was set before me. Indeed, I am so unobservant of it, that to this day I can scarce tell a few hours after dinner of what dishes it consisted. This has been a great convenience to me in travelling, where my companions have been sometimes very unhappy for want of a suitable gratification of their more delicate, because better instructed, tastes and appetites.[Pg 24]

My mother had likewise an excellent constitution: she suckled all her ten children. I never knew either my father or mother to have any sickness but that of which they died, he at 89, and she at 85 years of age. They lie buried together at Boston, where I some years since placed a marble over their grave with this inscription:

Josiah Franklin,

and

Abiah, his wife,

lie here interred.

v

FRANKLIN

They lived lovingly together in wedlock

fifty-five years.

And without an estate, or any gainful employment,

By constant labour and honest industry,

maintained a large family comfortably,

and brought up thirteen children and seven grandchildren

respectably.

From this instance, reader,

Be encouraged to diligence in thy calling,

And distrust not Providence.

He was a pious and prudent man;

She a discreet and virtuous woman.

Their youngest son,

In filial regard to their memory,

Places this stone.

J. F. born 1655, died 1744, Ætas 89.

A. F. ——— 1667, ——— 1752, ——— 85.

By my rambling digressions, I perceive myself to be grown old. I used to write more methodically. But one does not dress for private company as for a public ball. Perhaps it is only negligence.

To return: I continued thus employed in my father's business for two years, that is, till I was twelve years old; and my brother John, who was bred to that business, having left my father, married and set up for himself at Rhode Island, there was every appearance that I was destined to supply his place, and become a tallow-chandler. But my dislike to the trade continuing, my father had apprehensions that if he did not put me to one more agreeable, I should break loose and go to sea, as my brother[Pg 25] Josiah had done to his great vexation. In consequence, he took me to walk with him, and see joiners, bricklayers, turners, braziers, &c., at their work, that he might observe my inclination, and endeavour to fix it on some trade or profession that would keep me on land. It has ever since been a pleasure to me to see good workmen handle their tools; and it has been often useful to me to have learned so much by it as to be able to do some trifling jobs in the house when a workman was not at hand, and to construct little machines for my experiments, at the moment when the intention of making them was warm in my mind. My father determined at last for the cutlers' trade, and placed me for some days on trial with Samuel, son to my uncle Benjamin, who was bred to that trade in London, and had just established himself in Boston. But the sum he exacted as a fee for my apprenticeship displeased my father, and I was taken home again. From my infancy I was passionately fond of reading, and all the money that came into my hands was laid out in the purchasing of books. I was very fond of voyages. My first acquisition was Bunyan's works in separate little volumes. I afterward sold them to enable me to buy R. Burton's Historical Collections; they were small chapmen's books, and cheap, 40 volumes in all. My father's little library consisted chiefly of books in polemic divinity, most of which I read. I have often

vi

regretted that, at a time when I had such a thirst for knowledge, more proper books had not fallen into my way, since it was resolved I should not be bred to divinity; there was among them Plutarch's Lives, which I read abundantly, and I still think that time spent to great advantage. There was also a book of De Foe's, called an Essay on Projects, and another of Dr. Mather's, called an Essay to do good, which perhaps gave me a turn of thinking that had an influence[Pg 26] on some of the principal future events of my life.

This bookish inclination at length determined my father to make me a printer, though he had already one son (James) of that profession. In 1717 my brother James returned from England with a press and letters to set up his business in Boston. I liked it much better than that of my father, but still had a hankering for the sea. To prevent the apprehended effect of such an inclination, my father was impatient to have me bound to my brother. I stood out some time, but at last was persuaded, and signed the indentures when I was yet but twelve years old. I was to serve as an apprentice till I was twenty-one years of age, only I was to be allowed journeyman's wages during the last year. In a little time I made a great progress in the business, and became a useful hand to my brother. I had now access to better books. An acquaintance with the apprentices of booksellers enabled me sometimes to borrow a small one, which I was careful to return soon and clean. Often I sat up in my chamber the greatest part of the night, when the book was borrowed in the evening to be returned in the morning, lest it should be found missing. After some time a merchant, an ingenious, sensible man, Mr. Matthew Adams, who had a pretty collection of books, frequented our printing-office, took notice of me, and invited me to see his library, and very kindly proposed to lend me such books as I chose to read. I now took a strong inclination for poetry, and wrote some little pieces; my brother, supposing it might turn to account, encouraged me, and induced me to compose two occasional ballads. One was called the Lighthouse Tragedy, and contained an account of the shipwreck of Captain Worthilake, with his two daughters: the other was a sailor's song, on the taking of the famous Teach (or Blackbeard) the pirate. They were wretched stuff, in street-ballad[Pg 27] style; and when they were printed, my brother sent me about the town to sell them. The first sold prodigiously, the event being recent, and having made a great noise. This success flattered my vanity; but my father discouraged me, by criticising my performances, and telling me verse-makers were generally beggars. Thus I escaped being a poet, and probably a very bad one: but as prose writing has been of great use to me in the course of my life, and was a principal means of my advancement, I shall tell you how, in such a situation, I acquired what little ability I may be supposed to have in that way.

There was another bookish lad in the town, John Collins by name, with whom I was intimately acquainted. We sometimes disputed, and very fond we were of argument, and very desirous of confuting one another, which disputatious turn, by-the-way, is apt to become a very bad habit, making people often extremely disagreeable in company, by the contradiction that is necessary to bring it into practice; and thence, besides souring and spoiling the conversation, it is productive of disgusts and, perhaps, enmities with those who may have occasion for friendship. I had caught this by reading my father's books of disputes on religion. Persons of good sense, I have since observed, seldom fall into it, except lawyers, university men, and, generally, men of all sorts who have been bred at Edinburgh. A question was once some how or other started, between Collins and me, on the propriety of educating the female sex in learning, and their abilities for study. He was of opinion that it was improper, and that they were naturally unequal to it. I took the contrary side, perhaps for dispute' sake. He was naturally more eloquent, having a greater plenty of words; and sometimes, as I thought, I was vanquished more by his fluency than by the strength of his reasons. As we parted without settling the[Pg 28] point, and were not to see one another again for some time, I sat down to put my arguments in writing, which I copied fair and sent to him. He answered, and I replied. Three or four letters on a side had passed, when my father happened to find my papers and read them. Without entering into the subject in dispute, he took occasion to talk to me about my manner of writing; observed that, though I had the advantage of my antagonist in correct spelling and pointing (which he attributed to the printing-house), I fell far short in elegance of expression, in method, and perspicuity, of which he convinced me by several instances. I saw the justice of his remarks, and thence grew more attentive to my manner of writing, and determined to endeavour to improve my style.

About this time I met with an odd volume of the Spectator. I had never before seen any of them. I bought it, read it over and over, and was much delighted with it. I thought the writing excellent, and wished, if possible, to imitate it. With that view I took some of the papers, and, making short hints of the sentiments in each sentence, laid them by a few days, and then, without looking at the book, tried to complete the papers again, by expressing each hinted sentiment at length and as fully as it had been expressed before in any suitable words that should occur to me. Then I compared my Spectator with an original, discovered some of my faults, and corrected them. But I found I wanted a stock of words, or a readiness in recollecting and using them, which I thought I should have acquired before that time if I had gone on making verses; since the continual search for words of the same import, but of different lengths, to suit the measure, or of different sounds for the rhyme, would have laid me under a constant necessity of searching for variety, and also have tended to fix that variety in my mind, and make me master of it. Therefore I[Pg 29] took some of the tales in the Spectator, and turned them into verse: and after a time, when I had pretty well forgotten the prose, turned them back again. I also sometimes jumbled my collection of hints into confusion, and after some weeks endeavoured to reduce them into the best order, before I began to form the full sentences and complete the subject. This was to teach me method in the arrangement of the thoughts. By comparing my work with the original, I discovered many faults and corrected them; but I sometimes had the pleasure to fancy that, in particulars of small consequence, I had been fortunate enough to improve the method or the language, and this encouraged me to think that I might in time come to be a tolerable English writer, of which I was extremely ambitious. The time I allotted for writing exercises and for reading was at night, or before work began in the morning, or on Sunday, when I contrived to be in the printing-house, avoiding as much as I could the constant attendance at public worship which my father used to exact from me when I was under his care, and which I still continued to consider as a duty, though I could not afford time to practise it.

When about sixteen years of age I happened to meet with another book, written by one Tryon, recommending a vegetable diet. I determined to go into it. My brother, being yet unmarried, did not keep house, but boarded himself and his apprentices in another family. My refusing to eat flesh occasioned an inconvenience, and I was frequently chid for my singularity. I made myself acquainted with Tryon's manner of preparing some of his dishes, such as boiling potatoes or rice, making hasty pudding, and a few others, and then proposed to my brother if he would give me, weekly, half the money he paid for my board, I would board myself. He instantly agreed to it, and I presently found that I could save half what he paid me.[Pg 30]

This was an additional fund for buying of books. But I had another advantage in it. My brother and the rest going from the printing-office to their meals, I remained there alone; and despatching presently my light repast, which was often no more than a biscuit, or a slice of bread and a handful of raisins, a tart from the pastry-cook's, and a glass of water, I had the rest of the time till their return for study, in which I made the greater progress, from that clearness of head and quick apprehension which generally attends temperance in eating and drinking.

Now it was that, being on some occasion made ashamed of my ignorance in figures, which I had twice failed learning when at school, I took Cocker's book on arithmetic, and went through the whole by myself with the greatest ease. I also read Sellers and Sturny's book on navigation, which made me acquainted with the little geometry it contained; but I never proceeded far in that science. I read about this time Locke on the Human Understanding, and the Art of Thinking, by Messrs. du Port Royal.

While I was intent on improving my language, I met with an English grammar (I think it was Greenwood's) having at the end of it two little sketches on the arts of rhetoric and logic, the latter finishing with a dispute in the Socratic method; and soon after I procured Xenophon's Memorable Things of Socrates, wherein there are many examples of the same method. I was charmed by it, adopted it, dropped my abrupt contradiction and positive argumentation, and put on the humble inquirer; and being then, from reading Shaftesbury and Collins, made a doubter, as I already was in many points of our religious doctrines, I found this method the safest for myself and very embarrassing to those against whom I used it; therefore I took delight in it, practised it continually, and grew very artful and expert in drawing people, even of superior knowledge,[Pg 31] into concessions, the consequences of which they did not foresee; entangling them in difficulties, out of which they could not extricate themselves, and so obtaining victories that neither myself nor my cause always deserved. I continued this method some few years, but gradually left it, retaining only the habit of expressing myself in terms of modest diffidence; never using, when I advanced anything that might possibly be disputed, the word certainly, undoubtedly, or any other that gave the air of positiveness to an opinion; but rather said, I conceive or apprehend a thing to be so and so; it appears to me, or I should not think it is so, for such and such reasons; or I imagine it to be so; or it is so, if I am not mistaken. This habit, I believe, has been of great advantage to me when I have had occasion to inculcate my opinions, and persuade men into measures that I have been from time to time engaged in promoting; and, as the chief ends of conversation are to inform or to be informed, to please or to persuade, I wish well-meaning and sensible men would not lessen their power of doing good by a positive, assuming manner, that seldom fails to disgust, tends to create opposition, and to defeat most of those purposes for which speech was given to us.

In fact, if you wish to instruct others, a positive and dogmatical manner in advancing your sentiments may occasion opposition and prevent a candid attention. If you desire improvement from others, you should not, at the same time, express yourself fixed in your present opinions; modest and sensible men, who do not love disputations, will leave you undisturbed in the possession of your errors. In adopting such a manner, you can seldom expect to please your hearers, or obtain the concurrence you desire. Pope judiciously observes,

"Men must be taught as if you taught them not,

And things unknown proposed as things forgot."

[Pg 32]

He also recommends it to us,

"To speak, though sure, with seeming diffidence."

And he might have joined with this line that which he has coupled with another, I think, less properly.

"For want of modesty is want of sense."

If you ask why less properly, I must repeat the lines,

"Immodest words admit of no defence,

For want of modesty is want of sense."

Now is not the want of sense (where a man is so unfortunate as to want it) some apology for his want of modesty? and would not the lines stand more justly thus?

"Immodest words admit but this defence,

That want of modesty is want of sense."

This, however, I should submit to better judgments.

My brother had, in 1720 or 21, began to print a newspaper. It was the second that appeared in America, and was called the New-England Courant. The only one before it was the Boston News-Letter. I remember his being dissuaded by some of his friends from the undertaking, as not likely to succeed, one newspaper being, in their judgment, enough for America. At this time (1771) there are not less than five-and-twenty.[5] He went on, however, with the undertaking; I was employed to carry the papers to the customers, after having worked in composing the types and printing off the sheets. He had some ingenious men among his friends, who amused themselves by writing little pieces for his paper, which gained it credit and made it more in demand, and these gentlemen often visited us.

Hearing their conversations and their accounts of the approbation their papers were received with,[Pg 33] I was excited to try my hand among them; but being still a boy, and suspecting that my brother would object to printing anything of mine in his paper if he knew it to be mine, I contrived to disguise my hand, and, writing an anonymous paper, I put it at night under the door of the printing-house. It was found in the morning, and committed to his writing friends when they called in as usual. They read it, commented on it in my hearing, and I had the exquisite pleasure of finding it had met with their approbation, and that, in their different guesses at the author, none were named but men of some character among us for learning and ingenuity. I suppose that I was rather lucky in my judges, and they were not really so very good as I then believed them to be.

Encouraged, however, by this attempt, I wrote and sent in the same way to the press several other pieces that were equally approved; and I kept my secret till all my fund of sense for such performances was exhausted, and then discovered it, when I began to be considered with a little more attention by my brother's acquaintance. However, that did not quite please him, as he thought it tended to make me too vain. This might be one occasion of the differences we began to have about this time. Though a brother, he considered himself as my master, and me as his apprentice, and, accordingly, expected the same services from me as he would from another, while I thought he degraded me too much in some he required of me, who from a brother required more indulgence. Our disputes were often brought before our father, and I fancy I was either generally in the right, or else a better pleader, because the judgment was generally in my favour. But my brother was passionate, and had often beaten me, which I took extremely amiss; and thinking my apprenticeship very tedious, I was continually wishing for some opportunity of shortening[Pg 34] it, which at length offered in a manner unexpected.

Perhaps the harsh and tyrannical treatment of me might be a means of impressing me with the aversion to arbitrary power that has stuck to me through my whole life.

One of the pieces in our newspaper on some political point, which I have now forgotten, gave offence to the Assembly. He was taken up, censured, and imprisoned for a month, by the speaker's warrant, I suppose, because he would not discover the author. I, too, was taken up and examined before the council: but though I did not give them any satisfaction, they contented themselves with admonishing me, and dismissed me, considering me, perhaps, as an apprentice, who was bound to keep his master's secrets.

During my brother's confinement, which I resented a good deal notwithstanding our differences, I had the management of the paper; and I made bold to give our rulers some rubs in it, which my brother took very kindly, while others began to consider me in an unfavourable light, as a youth that had a turn for libelling and satire. My brother's discharge was accompanied with an order (and a very odd one), that "James Franklin should no longer print the newspaper called the New-England Courant."

On a consultation held in our printing-office among his friends, what he should do in this conjuncture, it was proposed to elude the order by changing the name of the paper; but my brother, seeing inconveniences in this, came to a conclusion, as a better way, to let the paper in future be printed in the name of Benjamin Franklin: and in order to avoid the censure of the Assembly, that might fall on him as still printing it by his apprentice, he contrived and consented that my old indenture should be returned to me, with a discharge on the back of it, to show[Pg 35] in case of necessity; and, in order to secure to him the benefit of my service, I should sign new indentures for the remainder of my time, which was to be kept private. A very flimsy scheme it was; however, it was immediately executed, and the paper was printed, accordingly, under my name for several months. At length, a fresh difference arising between my brother and me, I took upon me to assert my freedom, presuming that he would not venture to produce the new indentures. It was not fair in me to take this advantage, and this I therefore reckon as one of the first errata of my life; but the unfairness of it weighed little with me, when under the impression of resentment for the blows his passion too often urged him to bestow upon me; though he was otherwise not an ill-natured man: perhaps I was too saucy and provoking.

When he found I would leave him, he took care to prevent my getting employment in any other printing-house in town, by going round and speaking to every master, who accordingly refused to give me work. I then thought of going to New-York, as the nearest place where there was a printer; and I was rather inclined to leave Boston, when I reflected that I had already made myself a little obnoxious to the governing party, and, from the arbitrary proceedings of the Assembly in my brother's case, it was likely I might, if I stayed, soon bring myself into scrapes; and farther, that my indiscreet disputations about religion began to make me pointed at with horror by good people, as an infidel or atheist. I concluded, therefore, to remove to New-York; but my father now siding with my brother, I was sensible, that if I attempted to go openly, means would be used to prevent me. My friend Collins, therefore, undertook to manage my flight. He agreed with the captain of a New-York sloop to take me. I sold my books to raise a little money, was taken on board the sloop privately, had a fair[Pg 36] wind, and in three days found myself at New-York, near three hundred miles from my home, at the age of seventeen, without the least recommendation or knowledge of any person in the place, and very little money in my pocket.

The inclination I had felt for the sea was by this time done away, or I might now have gratified it. But having another profession, and conceiving myself a pretty good workman, I offered my services to a printer of the place, old Mr W. Bradford, who had been the first printer in Pennsylvania, but had removed thence, in consequence of a quarrel with the governor, General Keith. He could give me no employment, having little to do, and hands enough already. But he said, "My son, at Philadelphia, has lately lost his principal hand, Aquilla Rose, by death; if you go thither, I believe he may employ you." Philadelphia was one hundred miles farther; I set out, however, in a boat for Amboy, leaving my chest and things to follow me round by sea. In crossing the bay we met with a squall that tore our rotten sails to pieces, prevented our getting into the kill, and drove us upon Long Island. In our way, a drunken Dutchman, who was a passenger too, fell overboard; when he was sinking, I reached through the water to his shock pate, and drew him up, so that we got him in again. His ducking sobered him a little, and he went to sleep, taking first out of his pocket a book which he desired I would dry for him. It proved to be my old favourite author, Bunyan's Pilgrim's Progress, in Dutch, finely printed on good paper, copper cuts, a dress better than I had ever seen it wear in its own language. I have since found that it has been translated into most of the languages of Europe, and suppose it has been more generally read than any other book, except perhaps the Bible. Honest John was the first that I know of who mixed narration and dialogue; a method of writing very engaging to the reader, who, in the[Pg 37] most interesting parts, finds himself, as it were, admitted into the company and present at the conversation. De Foe has imitated him successfully in his Robinson Crusoe, in his Moll Flanders, and other pieces; and Richardson has done the same in his Pamela, &c.

On approaching the island, we found it was in a place where there could be no landing, there being a great surf on the stony beach. So we dropped anchor, and swung out our cable towards the shore. Some people came down to the shore and hallooed to us, as we did to them, but the wind was so high and the surf so loud that we could not understand each other. There were some small boats near the shore, and we made signs, and called to them to fetch us; but they either did not comprehend us, or it was impracticable, so they went off. Night approaching, we had no remedy but to have patience till the wind abated, and, in the mean time, the boatmen and myself concluded to sleep if we could; and so we crowded into the hatches, where we joined the Dutchman, who was still wet, and the spray breaking over the head of our boat, leaked through to us, so that we were soon almost as wet as he. In this manner we lay all night with very little rest; but the wind abating the next day, we made a shift to reach Amboy before night, having been thirty hours on the water, without victuals, or any drink but a bottle of filthy rum, the water we sailed on being salt.

In the evening I found myself very feverish, and went to bed; but having read somewhere that cold water drank plentifully was good for a fever, I followed the prescription, and sweat plentifully most of the night: my fever left me, and in the morning crossing the ferry, I proceeded on my journey on foot, having fifty miles to Burlington, where I was told I should find boats that would carry me the rest of the way to Philadelphia.[Pg 38]

It rained very hard all the day; I was thoroughly soaked, and by noon a good deal tired, so I stopped at a poor inn, where I stayed all night, beginning now to wish I had never left home. I made so miserable a figure too, that I found, by the questions asked me, I was suspected to be some runaway indentured servant, and in danger of being taken up on that suspicion. However, I proceeded next day, and got in the evening to an inn within eight or ten miles of Burlington, kept by one Dr. Brown. He entered into conversation with me while I took some refreshment, and, finding I had read a little, became very obliging and friendly. Our acquaintance continued all the rest of his life. He had been, I imagine, an ambulatory quack doctor, for there was no town in England, or any country in Europe, of which he could not give a very particular account. He had some letters, and was ingenious; but he was an infidel, and wickedly undertook, some years after, to turn the Bible into doggerel verse, as Cotton had formerly done with Virgil. By this means he set many facts in a ridiculous light, and might have done mischief with weak minds if his work had been published; but it never was. At his house I lay that night, and arrived the next morning at Burlington, but had the mortification to find that the regular boats had gone a little before, and no other expected to go before Tuesday, this being Saturday. Wherefore I returned to an old woman in the town, of whom I had bought some gingerbread to eat on the water, and asked her advice; she proposed to lodge me till a passage by some other boat occurred. I accepted her offer, being much fatigued by travelling on foot. Understanding I was a printer, she would have had me remain in that town and follow my business, being ignorant what stock was necessary to begin with. She was very hospitable, gave me a dinner of ox-cheek with a great good-will, accepting only of a pot of[Pg 39] ale in return; and I thought myself fixed till Tuesday should come. However, walking in the evening by the side of the river, a boat came by which I found was going towards Philadelphia, with several people in her. They took me in, and as there was no wind, we rowed all the way; and about midnight, not having yet seen the city, some of the company were confident we must have passed it, and would row no farther: the others knew not where we were, so we put towards the shore, got into a creek, landed near an old fence, with the rails of which we made a fire, the night being cold, in October, and there we remained till daylight. Then one of the company knew the place to be Cooper's Creek, a little above Philadelphia, which we saw as soon as we got out of the creek, and arrived there about eight or nine o'clock, on the Sunday morning, and landed at Market-street wharf.

I have been the more particular in this description of my journey, and shall be so of my first entry into that city, that you may in your mind compare such unlikely beginnings with the figure I have since made there. I was in my working dress, my best clothes coming round by sea. I was dirty, from my being so long in the boat; my pockets were stuffed out with shirts and stockings, and I knew no one, nor where to look for lodging. Fatigued with walking, rowing, and the want of sleep, I was very hungry; and my whole stock of cash consisted in a single dollar, and about a shilling in copper coin, which I gave to the boatmen for my passage. At first they refused it on account of my having rowed, but I insisted on their taking it. Man is sometimes more generous when he has little money than when he has plenty; perhaps to prevent his being thought to have but little. I walked towards the top of the street, gazing about, still in Market-street, where I met a boy with bread. I had often made a meal of dry bread, and inquiring[Pg 40] where he had bought it, I went immediately to the baker's he directed me to. I asked for biscuits, meaning such as we had at Boston: that sort, it seems, was not made in Philadelphia. I then asked for a threepenny loaf, and was told they had none. Not knowing the different prices, nor the names of the different sorts of bread, I told him to give me threepenny worth of any sort. He gave me, accordingly, three great puffy rolls. I was surprised at the quantity, but took it, and having no room in my pockets, walked off with a roll under each arm, and eating the other. Thus I went up Market-street as far as Fourth-street, passing by the door of Mr. Read, my future wife's father; when she, standing at the door, saw me, and thought I made, as I certainly did, a most awkward, ridiculous appearance. Then I turned and went down Chestnut-street and part of Walnut-street, eating my roll all the way, and, coming round, found myself again at Market-street wharf, near the boat I came in, to which I went for a draught of the river water; and, being filled with one of my rolls, gave the other two to a woman and her child that came down the river in the boat with us, and were waiting to go farther. Thus refreshed, I walked again up the street, which by this time had many clean-dressed people in it, who were all walking the same way: I joined them, and thereby was led into the great meeting-house of the Quakers near the market. I sat down among them, and after looking round awhile, and hearing nothing said, being very drowsy, through labour and want of rest the preceding night, I fell fast asleep, and continued so till the meeting broke up, when some one was kind enough to rouse me. This, therefore, was the first house I was in, or slept in, in Philadelphia.

I then walked down towards the river, and looking in the faces of every one, I met a young Quaker man whose countenance pleased me, and, accosting[Pg 41] him, requested he would tell me where a stranger could get a lodging. We were then near the sign of the Three Mariners. "Here," said he, "is a house where they receive strangers, but it is not a reputable one; if thou wilt walk with me, I'll show thee a better one;" and he conducted me to the Crooked Billet in Water-street. There I got a dinner; and, while I was eating, several questions were asked me, as from my youth and appearance I was suspected of being a runaway. After dinner, my host having shown me to a bed, I lay myself on it, without undressing, and slept till six in the evening, when I was called to supper. I went to bed again very early, and slept very soundly till next morning. Then I dressed myself as neat as I could, and went to Andrew Bradford, the printer's. I found in the shop the old man, his father, whom I had seen at New-York, and who, travelling on horseback, had got to Philadelphia before me. He introduced me to his son, who received me civilly, gave me a breakfast, and told me he did not at present want a hand, being lately supplied with one: but there was another printer in town lately set up, one Keimer, who perhaps might employ me; if not, I should be welcome to lodge at his house, and he would give me a little work to do now and then, till fuller business should offer.

The old gentleman said he would go with me to the new printer; and when we found him, "Neighbour," said Bradford, "I have brought to see you a young man of your business; perhaps you may want such a one." He asked me a few questions, put a composing stick in my hand to see how I worked, and then said he would employ me soon, though he had just then nothing for me to do; and taking old Bradford, whom he had never seen before, to be one of the town's people that had a good will for him, entered into conversation on his present undertaking and prospects; while Bradford (not discovering[Pg 42] that he was the other printer's father), on Keimer's saying he expected soon to get the greatest part of the business into his own hands, drew him on by artful questions, and starting little doubts, to explain all his views, what influence he relied on, and in what manner he intended to proceed. I, who stood by and heard all, saw immediately that one was a crafty old sophister, and the other a true novice. Bradford left me with Keimer, who was greatly surprised when I told him who the old man was.

The printing-house, I found, consisted of an old damaged press, and a small worn-out fount of English types which he was using himself, composing an elegy on Aquilla Rose, before mentioned; an ingenious young man, of excellent character, much respected in the town, secretary to the Assembly, and a pretty poet. Keimer made verses too, but very indifferently. He could not be said to write them, for his method was to compose them in the types directly out of his head; there being no copy, but one pair of cases, and the elegy probably requiring all the letter, no one could help him. I endeavoured to put his press (which he had not yet used, and of which he understood nothing) into order to be worked with; and, promising to come and print off his elegy as soon as he should have got it ready, I returned to Bradford's, who gave me a little job to do for the present, and there I lodged and dieted. A few days after Keimer sent for me to print off the elegy. And now he had got another pair of cases, and a pamphlet to reprint, on which he set me to work.

These two printers I found poorly qualified for their business. Bradford had been bred to it, and was very illiterate; and Keimer, though something of a scholar, was a mere compositor, knowing nothing of presswork. He had been one of the French prophets, and could act their enthusiastic agitations. At this time he did not profess any particular religion,[Pg 43] but something of all on occasion; was very ignorant of the world, and had, as I afterward found, a good deal of the knave in his composition. He did not like my lodging at Bradford's while I worked with him. He had a house, indeed, but without furniture, so he could not lodge me; but he got me a lodging at Mr. Read's, before mentioned, who was the owner of his house; and my chest of clothes being come by this time, I made rather a more respectable appearance in the eyes of Miss Read than I had done when she first happened to see me eating my roll in the street.

I began now to have some acquaintance among the young people of the town that were lovers of reading, with whom I spent my evenings very pleasantly, and gained money by my industry and frugality. I lived very contented, and forgot Boston as much as I could, and did not wish it should be known where I resided, except to my friend Collins, who was in the secret, and kept it faithfully. At length, however, an incident happened that occasioned my return home much sooner than I had intended. I had a brother-in-law, Robert Holmes, master of a sloop that traded between Boston and Delaware. He being at Newcastle, forty miles below Philadelphia, and hearing of me, wrote me a letter, mentioning the grief of my relations and friends in Boston at my abrupt departure, assuring me of their good-will towards me, and that everything would be accommodated to my mind if I would return, to which he entreated me earnestly. I wrote an answer to his letter, thanking him for his advice, but stated my reasons for quitting Boston so fully, and in such a light, as to convince him that I was not so much in the wrong as he had apprehended.

Sir William Keith, governor of the province, was then at Newcastle, and Captain Holmes happening to be in company with him when my letter came to[Pg 44] hand, spoke to him of me, and showed him the letter. The governor read it, and seemed surprised when he was told my age. He said I appeared a young man of promising parts, and, therefore, should be encouraged: the printers at Philadelphia were wretched ones, and if I would set up there, he made no doubt I should succeed; for his part, he would procure me the public business, and do me every other service in his power. This my brother-in-law Holmes afterward told me in Boston, but I knew as yet nothing of it; when one day, Keimer and I being at work together near the window, we saw the governor and another gentleman (who proved to be Colonel French, of Newcastle, in the province of Delaware), finely dressed, come directly across the street to our house, and heard them at the door. Keimer ran down immediately, thinking it a visit to him; but the governor inquired for me, came up, and, with a condescension and politeness I had been quite unused to, made me many compliments, desired to be acquainted with me, blamed me kindly for not having made myself known to him when I first came to the place, and would have me away with him to the tavern, where he was going with Colonel French to taste, as he said, some excellent Madeira. I was not a little surprised, and Keimer stared with astonishment. I went, however, with the governor and Colonel French to a tavern at the corner of Third-street, and over the Madeira he proposed my setting up my business. He stated the probabilities of my success, and both he and Colonel French assured me I should have their interest and influence to obtain for me the public business of both governments. And as I expressed doubts that my father would assist me in it, Sir William said he would give me a letter to him, in which he would set forth the advantages, and he did not doubt he should determine him to comply. So it was concluded I should return to Boston by the[Pg 45] first vessel, with the governor's letter to my father. In the mean time it was to be kept a secret, and I went on working with Keimer as usual. The governor sent for me now and then to dine with him, which I considered a great honour, more particularly as he conversed with me in the most affable, familiar, and friendly manner.

About the end of April, 1724, a little vessel offered for Boston. I took leave of Keimer as going to see my friends. The governor gave me an ample letter, saying many flattering things of me to my father, and strongly recommending the project of my setting up at Philadelphia, as a thing that would make my fortune. We struck on a shoal in going down the bay, and sprung a leak; we had a blustering time at sea, and were obliged to pump almost continually, at which I took my turn. We arrived safe, however, at Boston, in about a fortnight. I had been absent seven months, and my friends had heard nothing of me; for my brother Holmes was not yet returned, and had not written about me. My unexpected appearance surprised the family; all were, however, very glad to see me, and made me welcome, except my brother: I went to see him at his printing-house. I was better dressed than ever while in his service, having a genteel new suit from head to foot, a watch, and my pockets lined with near five pounds sterling in silver. He received me not very frankly, looked me all over, and turned to his work again. The journeymen were inquisitive where I had been, what sort of a country it was, and how I liked it. I praised it much, and the happy life I led in it, expressing strongly my intention of returning to it; and one of them asking what kind of money we had there, I produced a handful of silver and spread it before them, which was a kind of raree-show they had not been used to, paper being the money of Boston. Then I took an opportunity of letting them see my watch; and,[Pg 46] lastly (my brother still grum and sullen), gave them a dollar to drink and took my leave. This visit of mine offended him extremely. For when my mother some time after spoke to him of a reconciliation, and of her wish to see us on good terms together, and that we might live for the future as brothers, he said I had insulted him in such a manner before his people, that he could never forget or forgive it. In this, however, he was mistaken.

My father received the governor's letter with some surprise, but said little of it to me for some time. Captain Holmes returning, he showed it to him, and asked him if he knew Sir William Keith, and what kind of a man he was; adding, that he must be of small discretion to think of setting a youth up in business who wanted three years to arrive at man's estate. Holmes said what he could in favour of the project, but my father was decidedly against it, and at last gave a flat denial. He wrote a civil letter to Sir William, thanking him for the patronage he had so kindly offered me, and declining to assist me as yet in setting up, I being, in his opinion, too young to be trusted with the management of an undertaking so important, and for which the preparation required a considerable expenditure.

My old companion, Collins, who was a clerk in the postoffice, pleased with the account I gave him of my new country, determined to go thither also; and while I waited for my father's determination, he set out before me by land to Rhode Island, leaving his books, which were a pretty collection of mathematics and natural philosophy, to come with mine and me to New-York, where he proposed to wait for me.

My father, though he did not approve Sir William's proposition, was yet pleased that I had been able to obtain so advantageous a character from a person of such note where I had resided, and that I had been so industrious and careful as to equip[Pg 47] myself so handsomely in so short a time; therefore, seeing no prospect of an accommodation between my brother and me, he gave his consent to my returning again to Philadelphia, advised me to behave respectfully to the people there, endeavour to obtain the general esteem, and avoid lampooning and libelling, to which he thought I had too much inclination: telling me, that by steady industry and prudent parsimony, I might save enough by the time I was one-and-twenty to set me up; and that, if I came near the matter, he would help me out with the rest. This was all I could obtain, except some small gifts, as tokens of his and my mother's love, when I embarked again for New-York, now with their approbation and their blessing. The sloop putting in at Newport, Rhode Island, I visited my brother John, who had been married and settled there some years. He received me very affectionately, for he always loved me. A friend of his, one Vernon, having some money due him in Pennsylvania (about thirty-five pounds currency), desired I would recover it for him, and keep it till I had his directions what to employ it in. Accordingly, he gave me an order to receive it. This business afterward occasioned me a good deal of uneasiness.

At Newport we took in a number of passengers, among which were two young women travelling together, and a sensible, matron-like Quaker lady, with her servants. I had shown an obliging disposition to render her some little services, which probably impressed her with sentiments of good-will towards me; for, when she witnessed the daily growing familiarity between the young women and myself, which they appeared to encourage, she took me aside and said, "Young man, I am concerned for thee, as thou hast no friend with thee, and seemest not to know much of the world, or of the snares youth is exposed to: depend upon it, these are very bad women. I can see it by all their actions;[Pg 48] and if thou art not upon thy guard, they will draw thee into some danger: they are strangers to thee, and I advise thee, in a friendly concern for thy welfare, to have no acquaintance with them." As I seemed at first not to think so ill of them as she did, she mentioned some things she had observed and heard that had escaped my notice, but now convinced me she was right. I thanked her for her kind advice, and promised to follow it. When we arrived at New-York, they told me where they lived, and invited me to come and see them, but I avoided it, and it was well I did; for the next day the captain missed a silver spoon, and some other things that had been taken out of his cabin; and knowing that these were women of bad character, he got a warrant to search their lodgings, found the stolen goods, and had the thieves punished. So, though we had escaped a sunken rock, which we scraped upon in the passage, I thought this escape of rather more importance to me.

At New-York I found my friend Collins, who had arrived there some time before me. We had been intimate from children, and had read the same books together: but he had the advantage of more time for reading and studying, and a wonderful genius for mathematical learning, in which he far outstripped me. While I lived in Boston, most of my hours of leisure for conversation were spent with him, and he continued a sober as well as industrious lad; was much respected for his learning by several of the clergy and other gentlemen, and seemed to promise making a good figure in life. But during my absence he had acquired a habit of drinking brandy, and I found by his own account, as well as that of others, that he had been drunk every day since his arrival at New-York, and behaved himself in a very extravagant manner. He had gamed too, and lost his money, so that I was obliged to discharge his lodgings, and defray his expenses on the[Pg 49] road and at Philadelphia, which proved a great burden to me. The then governor of New-York, Burnet (son of Bishop Burnet), hearing from the captain that one of the passengers had a great many books on board, desired him to bring me to see him. I waited on him, and should have taken Collins with me had he been sober. The governor received me with great civility, showed me his library, which was a considerable one, and we had a good deal of conversation relative to books and authors. This was the second governor who had done me the honour to take notice of me; and, for a poor boy like me, was very pleasing. We proceeded to Philadelphia. I received on the way Vernon's money, without which we could hardly have finished our journey. Collins wished to be employed in some counting-house; but whether they discovered his dram-drinking by his breath or by his behaviour, though he had some recommendations, he met with no success in any application, and continued lodging and boarding at the same house with me and at my expense. Knowing that I had that money of Vernon's, he was continually borrowing of me, still promising repayment as soon as he should be in business. At length he had got so much of it that I was distressed to think what I should do in case of being called on to remit it. His drinking continued, about which we sometimes quarrelled; for, when a little intoxicated, he was very irritable. Once, in a boat on the Delaware, with some other young men, he refused to row in his turn: "I will be rowed home," said he. "We will not row you," said I. "You must," said he, "or stay all night on the water, just as you please." The others said, "Let us row, what signifies it?" But my mind being soured with his other conduct, I continued to refuse. So he swore he would make me row, or throw me overboard; and coming along, stepping on the thwarts towards me, when he came up and struck[Pg 50] at me, I clapped my hand under his thighs, and rising, pitched him head foremost into the river. I knew he was a good swimmer, and so was under little concern about him; but, before he could get round to lay hold of the boat, we had, with a few strokes, pulled her out of his reach; and whenever he drew near the boat, we asked him if he would row, striking a few strokes to slide her away from him. He was ready to stifle with vexation, and obstinately would not promise to row. Finding him at last beginning to tire, we drew him into the boat, and brought him home dripping wet. We hardly exchanged a civil word after this adventure. At length a West India captain, who had a commission to procure a preceptor for the sons of a gentleman at Barbadoes, met with him, and proposed to carry him thither to fill that situation. He accepted, and promised to remit me what he owed me out of the first money he should receive; but I never heard of him after. The violation of my trust respecting Vernon's money was one of the first great errata of my life; and this showed that my father was not much out in his judgment when he considered me as too young to manage business. But Sir William, on reading his letter, said he was too prudent; that there was a great difference in persons; and discretion did hot always accompany years, nor was youth always without it. "But, since he will not set you up, I will do it myself. Give me an inventory of the things necessary to be had from England, and I will send for them. You shall repay me when you are able; I am resolved to have a good printer here, and I am sure you must succeed." This was spoken with such an appearance of cordiality, that I had not the least doubt of his meaning what he said. I had hitherto kept the proposition of my setting up a secret in Philadelphia, and I still kept it. Had it been known that I depended on the governor, probably some friend that knew him better would have[Pg 51] advised me not to rely on him; as I afterward heard it as his known character, to be liberal of promises which he never meant to keep; yet, unsolicited as he was by me, how could I think his generous offers insincere? I believed him one of the best men in the world.

I presented him an inventory of a little printing-house, amounting by my computation to about one hundred pounds sterling. He liked it, but asked me if my being on the spot in England to choose the types, and see that everything was good of the kind, might not be of some advantage; "then," said he, "when there, you may make acquaintance, and establish correspondences in the bookselling and stationary way." I agreed that this might be advantageous. "Then," said he, "get yourself ready to go with the Annis;" which was the annual ship, and the only one at that time usually passing between London and Philadelphia. But as it would be some months before the Annis sailed, I continued working with Keimer, fretting extremely about the money Collins had got from me, and in great apprehensions of being called upon for it by Vernon; this, however, did not happen for some years after.

I believe I have omitted mentioning that, in my first voyage from Boston to Philadelphia, being becalmed off Block Island, our crew employed themselves in catching cod, and hauled up a great number. Till then I had stuck to my resolution to eat nothing that had had life; and on this occasion I considered, according to my master Tryon, the taking every fish as a kind of unprovoked murder, since none of them had nor could do us any injury that might justify this massacre. All this seemed very reasonable. But I had been formerly a great lover of fish, and when it came out of the frying-pan it smelled admirably well. I balanced some time between principle and inclination, till, recollecting that when fish were opened I saw smaller[Pg 52] fish taken out of their stomachs; then, thought I, "if you eat one another, I don't see why we may not eat you." So I dined upon cod very heartily, and have since continued to eat as other people; returning only now and then occasionally to a vegetable diet. So convenient a thing it is to be a reasonable creature, since it enables one to find or make a reason for everything one has a mind to do.

Keimer and I lived on a pretty good, familiar footing, and agreed tolerably well; for he suspected nothing of my setting up. He retained a great deal of his old enthusiasm, and loved argumentation. We therefore had many disputations. I used to work him so with my Socratic method, and had trepanned him so often by questions apparently so distant from any point we had in hand, yet by degrees leading to the point, and bringing him into difficulties and contradictions, that at last he grew ridiculously cautious, and would hardly answer me the most common questions, without asking first "What do you intend to infer from that?" However, it gave him so high an opinion of my abilities in the confuting way, that he seriously proposed my being his colleague in a project he had of setting up a new sect. He was to preach the doctrines, and I was to confound all opponents. When he came to explain with me upon the doctrines, I found several conundrums which I objected to, unless I might have my way a little too, and introduce some of mine. Keimer wore his beard at full length, because somewhere in the Mosaic law it is said, "Thou shalt not mar the corners of thy beard." He likewise kept the seventh-day Sabbath; and these two points were essential with him. I disliked both; but agreed to them on condition of his adopting the doctrine of not using animal food. I doubt, said he, my constitution will not bear it. I assured him it would, and that he would be the better for it. He was usually a great eater, and I wished to give[Pg 53] myself some diversion in half starving him. He consented to try the practice if I would keep him company: I did so, and we held it for three months. Our provisions were purchased, cooked, and brought to us regularly by a woman in the neighbourhood, who had from me a list of forty dishes, which she prepared for us at different times, in which there entered neither fish, flesh, nor fowl. This whim suited me the better at this time, from the cheapness of it, not costing us above eighteen pence sterling each per week. I have since kept several Lents most strictly, leaving the common diet for that, and that for the common, abruptly, without the least inconvenience. So that I think there is little in the advice of making those changes by easy gradations. I went on pleasantly, but poor Keimer suffered grievously, grew tired of the project, longed for the fleshpots of Egypt, and ordered a roast pig. He invited me and two women friends to dine with him; but it being brought too soon upon table, he could not resist the temptation, and ate the whole before we came.

I had made some courtship during this time to Miss Read; I had a great respect and affection for her, and had some reasons to believe she had the same for me; but as I was about to take a long voyage, and we were both very young (only a little above eighteen), it was thought most prudent by her mother to prevent our going too far at present; as a marriage, if it was to take place, would be more convenient after my return, when I should be, as I hoped, set up in my business. Perhaps, too, she thought my expectations not so well founded as I imagined them to be.

My chief acquaintances at this time were Charles Osborne, Joseph Watson, and James Ralph; all lovers of reading. The first two were clerks to an eminent scrivener or conveyancer in the town (Charles Brockden), the other was a clerk to a merchant.[Pg 54] Watson was a pious, sensible young man of great integrity: the others rather more lax in their principles of religion, particularly Ralph, who, as well as Collins, had been unsettled by me, for which they both made me suffer. Osborne was sensible, candid, frank, sincere, and affectionate to his friends; but in literary matters too fond of criticism. Ralph was ingenuous, genteel in his manners, and extremely eloquent; I think I never knew a prettier talker. Both were great admirers of poetry, and began to try their hands in little pieces. Many pleasant walks we have had together on Sundays in the woods on the banks of the Schuylkill, where we read to one another, and conferred on what we had read. Ralph was inclined to give himself up entirely to poetry, not doubting but he might make great proficiency in it, and even make his fortune by it. He pretended that the greatest poets must, when they first began to write, have committed as many faults as he did. Osborne endeavoured to dissuade him, assured him he had no genius for poetry, and advised him to think of nothing beyond the business he was bred to; "that in the mercantile way, though he had no stock, he might, by his diligence and punctuality, recommend himself to employment as a factor, and in time acquire wherewith to trade on his own account." I approved, for my part, the amusing one's self with poetry now and then, so far as to improve one's language, but no farther. On this it was proposed that we should each of us, at our next meeting, produce a piece of our own composing, in order to improve by our mutual observations, criticisms, and corrections. As language and expression was what we had in view, we excluded all considerations of invention, by agreeing that the task should be a version of the eighteenth Psalm, which describes the descent of a deity. When the time of our meeting drew nigh, Ralph called on me first,[Pg 55] and let me know his piece was ready: I told him I had been busy, and, having little inclination, had done nothing. He then showed me his piece for my opinion, and I much approved it, as it appeared to me to have great merit. "Now," said he, "Osborne never will allow the least merit in anything of mine, but makes a thousand criticisms out of mere envy: he is not so jealous of you; I wish, therefore, you would take this piece and produce it as yours: I will pretend not to have had time, and so produce nothing; we shall then hear what he will say to it." It was agreed, and I immediately transcribed it, that it might appear in my own hand. We met: Watson's performance was read; there were some beauties in it, but many defects. Osborne's was read; it was much better. Ralph did it justice, remarked some faults, but applauded the beauties. He himself had nothing to produce. I was backward, seemed desirous of being excused, had not had sufficient time to correct, &c., but no excuse could be admitted; produce I must. It was read and repeated: Watson and Osborne gave up the contest, and joined in applauding it. Ralph only made some criticisms and proposed some amendments; but I defended my text. Osborne was severe against Ralph, and told me he was no better able to criticise than to compose verses. As these two were returning home, Osborne expressed himself still more strongly in favour of what he thought my production; having before refrained, as he said, lest I should think he meant to flatter me. "But who would have imagined," said he, "that Franklin was capable of such a performance; such painting, such force, such fire! He has even improved on the original. In common conversation he seems to have no choice of words; he hesitates and blunders; and yet, good God, how he writes!" When we next met, Ralph discovered the trick we had played, and Osborne was laughed at. This[Pg 56] transaction fixed Ralph in his resolution of becoming a poet. I did all I could to dissuade him from it, but he continued scribbling verses till Pope cured him.[6] He became, however, a pretty good prose writer. More of him hereafter. But as I may not have occasion to mention the other two, I shall just remark here that Watson died in my arms a few years after, much lamented, being the best of our set. Osborne went to the West Indies, where he became an eminent lawyer, and made money. He and I had made a serious agreement, that the one who happened first to die should, if possible, make a friendly visit to the other, and acquaint him how he found things in that separate state. But he never fulfilled his promise.

The governor, seeming to like my company, had me frequently at his house, and his setting me up was always mentioned as a fixed thing. I was to take with me letters recommendatory to a number of his friends, besides the letter of credit to furnish me with the necessary money for purchasing the press, types, paper, &c. For these letters I was appointed to call at different times, when they were to be ready, but a future time was still named. Thus we went on till the ship (whose departure, too, had been several times postponed) was on the point of sailing. Then, when I called to take my leave and receive the letters, his secretary, Dr. Baird, came out to me and said the governor was extremely busy in writing, but would be down at Newcastle before the ship, and then the letters would be delivered to me.

Ralph, though married, and having one child, had determined to accompany me in this voyage. It was thought he intended to establish a correspondence and obtain goods to sell on commission; but I[Pg 57] found after, that, having some cause of discontent with his wife's relations, he proposed to leave her on their hands and never return to America. Having taken leave of my friends and exchanged promises with Miss Read, I quitted Philadelphia in the ship, which anchored at Newcastle. The governor was there, but when I went to his lodging, his secretary came to me from him with expressions of the greatest regret that he could not then see me, being engaged in business of importance; but that he would send the letters to me on board, wishing me heartily a good voyage and a speedy return, &c. I returned on board a little puzzled, but still not doubting.

Mr. Andrew Hamilton, a celebrated lawyer of Philadelphia, had taken his passage in the same ship for himself and son, with Mr. Denham, a Quaker merchant, and Messrs. Oniam and Russel (masters of an iron work in Maryland), who had engaged the great cabin; so that Ralph and I were forced to take up with a birth in the steerage, and, none on board knowing us, were considered as ordinary persons. But Mr. Hamilton and his son (it was James, since governor) returned from Newcastle to Philadelphia, the father being recalled by a great fee to plead for a seized ship. And just before we sailed, Colonel French coming on board, and showing me great respect, I was more taken notice of; and, with my friend Ralph, invited by the other gentlemen to come into the cabin, there being now room; accordingly, we removed thither.

Understanding that Colonel French had brought on board the governor's despatches, I asked the captain for those letters that were to be under my care; he said all were put into the bag together, and he could not then come at them, but before we landed in England I should have an opportunity of picking them out; so I was satisfied for the present, and we proceeded on our voyage. We had a sociable[Pg 58] company in the cabin, and lived uncommonly well, having the addition of all Mr. Hamilton's stores, who had laid in plentifully. In this passage Mr. Denham contracted a friendship for me, that continued during his life. The voyage was otherwise not a pleasant one, as we had a great deal of bad weather.

When we came into the Channel, the captain kept his word with me, and gave me an opportunity of examining the bag for the governor's letters; I found some upon which my name was put, as under my care: I picked out six or seven, that by the handwriting I thought might be the promised letters, especially as one of them was addressed to Basket, the king's printer, and another to some stationer. We arrived in London the 24th December, 1724. I waited upon the stationer, who came first in my way, delivering the letter as from Governor Keith. "I don't know such a person," said he: but opening the letter, "Oh! this is from Riddlesden. I have lately found him to be a complete rascal, and I will have nothing to do with him, nor receive any letters from him." So, putting the letter into my hand, he turned on his heel and left me to serve some customer. I was surprised to find these were not the governor's letters; and, after recollecting and comparing circumstances, I began to doubt his sincerity. I found my friend Denham, and opened the whole affair to him. He let me into Keith's character; told me there was not the least probability that he had written any letters for me; that no one who knew him had the smallest dependance on him; and he laughed at the idea of the governor's giving me a letter of credit, having, as he said, no credit to give. On my expressing some concern about what I should do, he advised me to endeavour to get some employment in the way of my business. Among the printers here, said he, you will improve yourself, and when you return to America you will set up to greater advantage.[Pg 59]

We both of us happened to know, as well as the stationer, that Riddlesden, the attorney, was a very knave; he had half ruined Miss Read's father, by persuading him to be bound for him. By his letter it appeared there was a secret scheme on foot to the prejudice of Mr. Hamilton (supposed to be then coming over with us); that Keith was concerned in it, with Riddlesden. Denham, who was a friend of Hamilton's, thought he ought to be acquainted with it; so, when he arrived in England, which was soon after, partly from resentment and ill will to Keith and Riddlesden, and partly from good will to him, I waited on him and gave him the letter. He thanked me cordially, the information being of importance to him; and from that time he became my friend, greatly to my advantage afterward on many occasions.

But what shall we think of a governor playing such pitiful tricks, and imposing so grossly upon a poor ignorant boy! It was a habit he had acquired; he wished to please everybody, and having little to give, he gave expectations. He was otherwise an ingenious, sensible man, a pretty good writer, and a good governor for the people, though not for his constituents the proprietaries, whose instructions he sometimes disregarded: several of our best laws were of his planning, and passed during his administration.

Ralph and I were inseparable companions. We took lodgings together in Little Britain, at 3s. 6d. per week; as much as we could then afford. He found some relations, but they were poor, and unable to assist him. He now let me know his intentions of remaining in London, and that he never meant to return to Philadelphia. He had brought no money with him, the whole he could muster having been expended in paying his passage. I had fifteen pistoles; so he borrowed occasionally of me to subsist, while he was looking out for business. He first endeavoured to get into the playhouse, believing[Pg 60] himself qualified for an actor; but Wilkes to whom he applied, advised him candidly not to think of that employment, as it was impossible he should succeed in it. Then he proposed to Roberts, a publisher in Paternoster Row, to write for him a weekly paper like the Spectator, on certain conditions; which Roberts did not approve. Then he endeavoured to get employment as a hackney-writer, to copy for the stationers and lawyers about the Temple; but could not find a vacancy.

For myself, I immediately got into work at Palmer's, a famous printing-house in Bartholomew Close, where I continued near a year. I was pretty diligent, but I spent with Ralph a good deal of my earnings, at plays and public amusements; we had nearly consumed all my pistoles, and now just rubbed on from hand to mouth. He seemed quite to have forgotten his wife and child; and I, by degrees, my engagements with Miss Read, to whom I never wrote more than one letter, and that was to let her know I was not likely soon to return. This was another of the great errata of my life which I could wish to correct if I were to live it over again In fact, by our expenses I was constantly kept unable to pay my passage.

At Palmer's I was employed in composing for the second edition of Woollaston's Religion of Nature. Some of his reasonings not appearing to me well-founded, I wrote a little metaphysical piece, in which I made remarks on them. It was entitled, "A Dissertation on Liberty and Necessity, Pleasure and Pain." I inscribed it to my friend Ralph; I printed a small number. It occasioned my being more considered by Mr. Palmer as a young man of some ingenuity, though he seriously expostulated with me upon the principles of my pamphlet, which to him appeared abominable. My printing this pamphlet was another erratum. While I lodged in Little Britain, I made acquaintance with one Wilcox, a bookseller,[Pg 61] whose shop was next door. He had an immense collection of second-hand books. Circulating libraries were not then in use, but we agreed that on certain reasonable terms (which I have now forgotten), I might take, read, and return any of his books; this I esteemed a great advantage, and I made as much use of it as I could.

My pamphlet by some means falling into the hands of one Lyons, a surgeon, author of a book entitled "The Infallibility of Human Judgment," it occasioned an acquaintance between us; he took great notice of me, called on me often to converse on those subjects, carried me to the Horns, a pale alehouse in —— lane, Cheapside, and introduced me to Dr. Mandeville, author of the Fable of the Bees, who had a club there, of which he was the soul, being a most facetious, entertaining companion. Lyons, too, introduced me to Dr. Pemberton,[7] at Baston's Coffee-house, who promised to give me an opportunity, some time or other, of seeing Sir Isaac Newton, of which I was extremely desirous; but this never happened.

I had brought over a few curiosities, among which the principal was a purse made of the asbestos, which purifies by fire. Sir Hans Sloane heard of it, came to see me, invited me to his house in Bloomsbury Square, showed me all his curiosities, and persuaded me to add that to the number; for which he paid me handsomely.

At my first admission into the printing-house I took to working at press, imagining I felt a want of the bodily exercise I had been used to in America, where presswork is mixed with the composing. I drank only water; the other workmen, near fifty in number, were great drinkers of beer. On occasion, I carried up and down stairs a large form of types in each hand, when others carried but one in both[Pg 62] hands; they wondered to see, from this and several instances, that the Water American, as they called me, was stronger than themselves who drank strong beer! We had an alehouse-boy, who attended always in the house to supply the workmen. My companion at the press drank every day a pint before breakfast, a pint at breakfast with his bread and cheese, a pint between breakfast and dinner, a pint at dinner; a pint in the afternoon about six o'clock, and another when he had done his day's work. I thought it a detestable custom; but it was necessary, he supposed, to drink strong beer, that he might be strong to labour. I endeavoured to convince him that the bodily strength afforded by beer could only be in proportion to the grain or flour of the barley dissolved in the water of which it was made; that there was more flour in a pennyworth of bread, and, therefore, if he could eat that with a pint of water, it would give him more strength than a quart of beer. He drank on, however, and had four or five shillings to pay out of his wages every Saturday night for that vile liquor: an expense I was free from; and thus these poor devils keep themselves always under.

Watts, after some weeks, desiring to have me in the composing-room, I left the pressmen; a new bien venu for drink (being five shillings) was demanded of me by the compositors. I thought it an imposition, as I had paid one to the pressmen; the master thought so too, and forbade my paying it. I stood out two or three weeks, was accordingly considered as an excommunicate, and had so many little pieces of private malice practised on me, by mixing my sorts, transposing and breaking my matter, &c., &c., if ever I stepped out of the room, and all ascribed to the chapel ghost, which they said ever haunted those not regularly admitted, that, notwithstanding the master's protection, I found myself obliged to comply and pay the money, convinced of the folly of being on ill terms with those one is to live[Pg 63] with continually. I was now on a fair footing with them, and soon acquired considerable influence. I proposed some reasonable alterations in their chapel[8] laws, and carried them against all opposition. From my example a great many of them left their muddling breakfast of beer, bread and cheese, finding they could with me be supplied from a neighbouring house with a large porringer of hot water-gruel, sprinkled with pepper, crumbled with bread, and a bit of butter in it, for the price of a pint of beer, viz., three halfpence. This was a more comfortable as well as a cheaper breakfast, and kept their heads clearer. Those who continued sotting with their beer all day, were often, by not paying, out of credit at the alehouse, and used to make interest with me to get beer, their light, as they phrased it, being out. I watched the pay-table on Saturday night, and collected what I stood engaged for them, having to pay sometimes near thirty shillings a week on their accounts. This, and my being esteemed a pretty good rig-ite, that is, a jocular verbal satirist, supported my consequence in the society. My constant attendance (I never making a St. Monday) recommended me to the master; and my uncommon quickness at composing occasioned my being put upon work of despatch, which was generally better paid; so I went on now very agreeably.

My lodgings in Little Britain being too remote, I found another in Duke-street, opposite to the Romish Chapel. It was up three flights of stairs backward, at an Italian warehouse. A widow lady[Pg 64] kept the house; she had a daughter, and a maidservant, and a journeyman who attended the warehouse, but lodged abroad. After sending to inquire my character at the house where I last lodged, she agreed to take me in at the same rate, 3s. 6d. per week; cheaper, as she said, from the protection she expected in having a man to lodge in the house. She was a widow, an elderly woman; had been bred a Protestant, being a clergyman's daughter, but was converted to the Catholic religion by her husband, whose memory she much revered; had lived much among people of distinction, and knew a thousand anecdotes of them, as far back as Charles the Second. She was lame in her knees with the gout, and therefore seldom stirred out of her room, so she sometimes wanted company; and hers was so highly amusing to me, that I was sure to spend an evening with her whenever she desired it. Our supper was only half an anchovy each, on a very little slice of bread and butter, and half a pint of ale between us; but the entertainment was in her conversation. My always keeping good hours, and giving little trouble in the family, made her unwilling to part with me; so that, when I talked of a lodging I had heard of nearer my business, for 2s. a week, which, intent as I was on saving money, made some difference, she bid me not think of it, for she would abate me 2s. a week for the future; so I remained with her at 1s. 6d. as long as I stayed in London.

In a garret of her house there lived a maiden lady of seventy, in the most retired manner, of whom my landlady gave me this account: that she was a Roman Catholic, had been sent abroad when young, and lodged in a nunnery with an intent of becoming a nun; but, the country not agreeing with her, she returned to England, where, there being no nunnery, she had vowed to lead the life of a nun as near as might be done in those circumstances. Accordingly, she had given all her estate to charitable[Pg 65] purposes, reserving only twelve pounds a year to live on, and out of this sum she still gave a part in charity, living herself on water-gruel only, and using no fire but to boil it. She had lived many years in that garret, being permitted to remain there gratis by successive Catholic tenants of the house below, as they deemed it a blessing to have her there. A priest visited her to confess her every day: "from this I asked her," said my landlady, "how she, as she lived, could possibly find so much employment for a confessor." "Oh," said she, "it is impossible to avoid vain thoughts." I was permitted once to visit her; she was cheerful and polite, and conversed pleasantly. The room was clean, but had no other furniture than a mattress, a table with a crucifix, and a book, a stool which she gave me to sit on, and a picture over the chimney of St. Veronica displaying her handkerchief, with the miraculous figure of Christ's bleeding face on it, which she explained to me with great seriousness. She looked pale, but was never sick, and I give it as another instance on how small an income life and health may be supported.

At Watts's printing-house I contracted an acquaintance with an ingenious man, one Wygate, who, having wealthy relations, had been better educated than most printers; was a tolerable Latinist, spoke French, and loved reading. I taught him and a friend of his to swim at twice going into the river, and they soon became good swimmers. They introduced me to some gentlemen from the country, who went to Chelsea by water, to see the college and Don Saltero's curiosities. In our return, at the request of the company, whose curiosity Wygate had excited, I stripped and leaped into the river, and swam from near Chelsea to Blackfriars; performing in the way many feats of activity both upon and under the water, that surprised and pleased those to whom they were novelties. I had from a[Pg 66] child been delighted with this exercise, had studied and practised Thevenot's motions and positions, added some of mine own, aiming at the graceful and easy as well as the useful. All these I took this occasion of exhibiting to the company, and was much flattered by their admiration; and Wygate, who was desirous of becoming a master, grew more and more attached to me on that account, as well as from the similarity of our studies. He at length proposed to me travelling all over Europe together, supporting ourselves everywhere by working at our business. I was once inclined to it; but mentioning it to my good friend Mr. Denham, with whom I often spent an hour when I had leisure, he dissuaded me from it, advising me to think only of returning to Pennsylvania, which he was now about to do.

I must record one trait of this good man's character: he had formerly been in business at Bristol, but failed in debt to a number of people, compounded and went to America; there, by a close application to business as a merchant, he acquired a plentiful fortune in a few years. Returning to England in the ship with me, he invited his old creditors to an entertainment, at which he thanked them for the easy composition they had favoured him with, and when they expected nothing but the treat, every man at the first remove found under his plate an order on a banker for the full amount of the unpaid remainder, with interest.

He now told me he was about to return to Philadelphia, and should carry over a great quantity of goods in order to open a store there. He proposed to take me over as his clerk, to keep his books (in which he would instruct me), copy his letters, and attend the store; he added, that, as soon as I should be acquainted with mercantile business, he would promote me, by sending me with a cargo of flour and bread, &c., to the West Indies, and procure me[Pg 67] commissions from others which would be profitable; and, if I managed well, would establish me handsomely. The thing pleased me, for I was grown tired of London; remembered with pleasure the happy months I had spent in Pennsylvania, and wished again to see it; therefore I immediately agreed on the terms of fifty pounds a year, Pennsylvania money; less, indeed, than my present gettings as a compositor, but affording better prospects.

I now took leave of printing, as I thought, for ever, and was daily employed in my new business: going about with Mr. Denham among the tradesmen, to purchase various articles and see them packed up, delivering messages, calling upon workmen to despatch, &c.; and, when all was on board, I had a few days' leisure. On one of these days I was, to my surprise, sent for by a great man, I knew only by name (Sir William Wyndham), and I waited upon him; he had heard, by some means or other, of my swimming from Chelsea to Blackfriars, and of my teaching Wygate and another young man to swim in a few hours: he had two sons, about to set out on their travels; he wished to have them first taught swimming, and proposed to gratify me handsomely if I would teach them. They were not yet come to town, and my stay was uncertain, so I could not undertake it; but from the incident I thought it likely, that if I were to remain in England and open a swimming school, I might get a good deal of money; and it struck me so strongly, that, had the overture been made me sooner, probably I should not so soon have returned to America. Many years after, you and I had something of more importance to do with one of those sons of Sir William Wyndham, become Earl of Egremont, which I shall mention in its place.

Thus I passed about eighteen months in London, most part of the time I worked hard at my business, and spent but little upon myself, except in[Pg 68] seeing plays and in books. My friend Ralph had kept me poor; he owed me about twenty-seven pounds, which I was now never likely to receive; a great sum out of my small earnings! I loved him, notwithstanding, for he had many amiable qualities. I had improved my knowledge, however, though I had by no means improved my fortune; but I had made some very ingenious acquaintance, whose conversation was of great advantage to me, and I had read considerably.

We sailed from Gravesend on the 23d of July, 1726. For the incidents of the voyage I refer you to my journal, where you will find them all minutely related. Perhaps the most important part of that journal is the plan to be found in it, which I formed at sea, for regulating the future conduct of my life. It is the more remarkable as being formed when I was so young, and yet being pretty faithfully adhered to quite through to old age.

We landed at Philadelphia the 11th of October, where I found sundry alterations. Keith was no longer governor, being superseded by Major Gordon; I met him walking the streets as a common citizen; he seemed a little ashamed at seeing me, and passed without saying anything. I should have been as much ashamed at seeing Miss Read, had not her friends, despairing with reason of my return after the receipt of my letter, persuaded her to marry another, one Rogers, a potter, which was done in my absence. With him, however, she was never happy, and soon parted from him, refusing to cohabit with him or bear his name, it being now said he had another wife. He was a worthless fellow, though an excellent workman, which was the temptation to her friends; he got into debt, ran away in 1727 or 1728, went to the West Indies, and died there. Keimer had got a better house, a shop well supplied with stationary, plenty of new types, and a number of hands, though none good, and seemed to have a great deal of business.[Pg 69]

Mr. Denham took a store in Water-street, where we opened our goods; I attended the business diligently, studied accounts, and grew in a little time expert at selling. We lodged and boarded together; he counselled me as a father, having a sincere regard for me: I respected and loved him, and we might have gone on together very happily, but in the beginning of February, 1727, when I had just passed my twenty-first year, we both were taken ill. My distemper was a pleurisy, which very nearly carried me off; I suffered a good deal, gave up the point in my own mind, and was at the time rather disappointed when I found myself recovering; regretting in some degree that I must now, some time or other, have all that disagreeable work to go over again. I forget what Mr. Denham's distemper was; it held him a long time, and at length carried him off. He left me a small legacy in a nuncupative will, as a token of his kindness to me, and he left me once more to the wide world, for the store was taken into the care of his executors, and my employment under him ended. My brother-in-law, Holmes, being now at Philadelphia, advised my return to my business; and Keimer tempted me with an offer of large wages by the year, to come and take the management of his printing-house, that he might better attend to his stationer's shop. I had heard a bad character of him in London from his wife and her friends, and was not for having any more to do with him. I wished for employment as a merchant's clerk, but not meeting with any, I closed again with Keimer. I found in his house these hands: Hugh Meredith, a Welsh Pennsylvanian, thirty years of age, bred to country work; he was honest, sensible, a man of experience, and fond of reading, but addicted to drinking. Stephen Potts, a young countryman of full age, bred to the same, of uncommon natural parts, and great wit and humour, but a little idle. These he had[Pg 70] agreed with at extreme low wages per week, to be raised a shilling every three months as they should deserve by improving in their business; and the expectation of these high wages to come on hereafter was what he had drawn them in with. Meredith was to work at press, Potts at bookbinding, which he, by agreement, was to teach them, though he knew neither one nor the other. John Savage, an Irishman, brought up to no business, whose service for four years Keimer had purchased from the captain of a ship; he too was to be made a pressman. George Webb, an Oxford scholar, whose time for four years he had likewise bought, intending him for a compositor (of whom more presently), and David Harry, a country boy, whom he had taken apprentice.

I soon perceived that the intention of engaging me, at wages so much higher than he had been used to give, was to have these raw, cheap hands formed through me; and, as soon as I had instructed them (they being all articled to him), he should be able to do without me. I went, however, very cheerfully, put his printing-house in order, which had been in great confusion, and brought his hands by degrees to mind their business, and to do it better.

It was an odd thing to find an Oxford scholar in the situation of a bought servant; he was not more than eighteen years of age; he gave me this account of himself: that he was born in Gloucester, educated at a grammar-school, and had been distinguished among the scholars for some apparent superiority in performing his part when they exhibited plays; belonged to the Wit's club there, and had written some pieces in prose and verse, which were printed in the Gloucester newspapers; thence was sent to Oxford; there he continued about a year, but not well satisfied, wishing of all things to see London and become a player. At length, receiving his quarterly allowance of fifteen guineas[Pg 71] instead of discharging his debts he went out of town, hid his gown in a furz bush, and walked to London, where, having no friend to advise him, he fell into bad company, soon spent his guineas, found no means of being introduced among the players, grew necessitous, pawned his clothes, and wanted bread. Walking the street, very hungry, and not knowing what to do with himself, a crimp's bill was put into his hand, offering immediate entertainment and encouragement to such as would bind themselves to serve in America; he went directly, signed the indentures, was put into the ship, and came over, never writing a line to his friends to acquaint them what was become of him. He was lively, witty, good-natured, and a pleasant companion; but idle, thoughtless, and imprudent to the last degree.

John, the Irishman, soon ran away; with the rest I began to live very agreeably, for they all respected me the more, as they found Keimer incapable of instructing them, and that from me they learned something daily.

My acquaintance with ingenious people in the town increased. We never worked on Saturday, that being Keimer's Sabbath, so that I had two days for reading. Keimer himself treated me with great civility and apparent regard, and nothing now made me uneasy but my debt to Vernon, which I was yet unable to pay, being hitherto but a poor economist; he, however, kindly made no demand of it.

Our printing-house often wanted sorts, and there was no letter foundry in America. I had seen types cast at James's in London, but without much attention to the manner; however, I now contrived a mould, and made use of the letters we had as puncheons, struck the matrices in lead, and thus supplied, in a pretty tolerable way, all deficiencies. I also engraved several things on occasion; made the ink; I was warehouse-man, and, in short, quite a factotum.[Pg 72]

But, however serviceable I might be, I found that my services became every day of less importance, as the other hands improved in their business; and when Keimer paid me a second quarter's wages, he let me know that he felt them too heavy, and thought I should make an abatement. He grew by degrees less civil, put on more the airs of master, frequently found fault, was captious, and seemed ready for an outbreaking. I went on, nevertheless, with a good deal of patience, thinking that his encumbered circumstances were partly the cause. At length a trifle snapped our connexion; for a great noise happening near the courthouse, I put my head out of the window to see what was the matter. Keimer, being in the street, looked up and saw me; called out to me in a loud voice and an angry tone, to mind my business; adding some reproachful words, that nettled me the more for their publicity; all the neighbours, who were looking out on the same occasion, being witnesses how I was treated. He came up immediately into the printing-house; continued the quarrel; high words passed on both sides; he gave me the quarter's warning we had stipulated, expressing a wish that he had not been obliged to so long a warning. I told him his wish was unnecessary, for I would leave him that instant; and so, taking my hat, walked out of doors, desiring Meredith, whom I saw below, to take care of some things I left and bring them to my lodgings.

Meredith came accordingly in the evening, when we talked my affair over. He had conceived a great regard for me, and was very unwilling that I should leave the house while he remained in it. He dissuaded me from returning to my native country, which I began to think of; he reminded me that Keimer was in debt for all he possessed; that his creditors began to be uneasy; that he kept his shop miserably, sold often without a profit for ready money, and often trusted without keeping accounts[Pg 73] that he must therefore fail, which would make a vacancy I might profit of. I objected my want of money. He then let me know that his father had a high opinion of me, and, from some discourse that had passed between them, he was sure he would advance money to set me up, if I would enter into partnership with him. My time, said he, will be out with Keimer in the spring; by that time we may have our press and types in from London. I am sensible I am no workman: if you like it, your skill in the business shall be set against the stock I furnish, and we will share the profits equally. The proposal was agreeable to me, and I consented; his father was in town and approved of it; the more, he said, as I had great influence with his son; had prevailed on him to abstain long from dram-drinking, and he hoped might break him of that wretched habit entirely when we came to be so closely connected. I gave an inventory to the father, who carried it to a merchant: the things were sent for, the secret was to be kept till they should arrive, and in the mean time I was to get work, if I could, at the other printing-house. But I found no vacancy there, and so remained idle a few days, when Keimer, on a prospect of being employed to print some paper money in New-Jersey, which would require cuts and various types that I only could supply, and apprehending Bradford might engage me and get the job from him, sent me a very civil message, that old friends should not part for a few words, the effect of sudden passion, and wishing me to return. Meredith persuaded me to comply, as it would give more opportunity for his improvement under my daily instructions; so I returned, and we went on more smoothly than for some time before. The New-Jersey job was obtained; I contrived a copperplate press for it, the first that had been seen in the country; I cut several ornaments and checks for the bills. We went together to Burlington, where I executed[Pg 74] the whole to satisfaction; and he received so large a sum for the work as to be enabled thereby to keep himself longer from ruin.

At Burlington I made an acquaintance with many principal people of the province. Several of them had been appointed by the Assembly a committee to attend the press, and take care that no more bills were printed than the law directed. They were, therefore, by turns, constantly with us, and generally he who attended brought with him a friend or two for company. My mind having been much more improved by reading than Keimer's, I suppose it was for that reason my conversation seemed to be more valued. They had me to their houses, introduced me to their friends, and showed me much civility; while he, though the master, was a little neglected. In truth, he was an odd creature; ignorant of common life, fond of rudely opposing received opinions; slovenly to extreme dirtiness; enthusiastic in some points of religion, and a little knavish withal. We continued there near three months, and by that time I could reckon among my acquired friends Judge Allen, Samuel Bustill, the secretary of the province, Isaac Pearson, Joseph Cooper, and several of the Smiths, members of Assembly, and Isaac Decow, the surveyor-general. The latter was a shrewd, sagacious old man, who told me that he began for himself, when young, by wheeling clay for the brickmakers, learned to write after he was of age, carried the chain for surveyors, who taught him surveying, and he had now, by his industry, acquired a good estate; and, said he, I foresee you will soon work this man out of his business, and make a fortune in it at Philadelphia. He had then not the least intimation of my intention to set up there or anywhere. These friends were afterward of great use to me, as I occasionally was to some of them. They all continued their regard for me as long as they lived.[Pg 75]

Before I enter upon my public appearance in business, it may be well to let you know the then state of my mind with regard to my principles and morals, that you may see how far those influenced the future events of my life. My parents had early given me religious impressions, and brought me through my childhood piously in the dissenting way. But I was scarce fifteen, when, after doubting by turns several points, as I found them disputed in the different books I read, I began to doubt of the revelation itself. Some books against Deism fell into my hands; they were said to be the substance of the sermons which had been preached at Boyle's Lectures. It happened that they wrought an effect on me quite contrary to what was intended by them; for the arguments of the Deists, which were quoted to be refuted, appeared to me much stronger than the refutation; in short, I soon became a thorough Deist. My arguments perverted some others, particularly Collins and Ralph: but each of these having wronged me greatly without the least compunction; and recollecting Keith's conduct towards me (who was another freethinker), and my own towards Vernon and Miss Read, which at times gave me great trouble, I began to suspect that this doctrine, though it might be true, was not very useful. My London pamphlet (printed in 1725)—which had for its motto these lines of Dryden:

"Whatever is, is right. Though purblind man

Sees but a part o' the chain, the nearest link,

His eye not carrying to that equal beam

That poises all above—"

and which, from the attributes of God, his infinite wisdom, goodness, and power, concluded that nothing could possibly be wrong in the world; and that vice and virtue were empty distinctions, no such things existing—appeared now not so clever a performance as I once thought it; and I doubted[Pg 76] whether some error had not insinuated itself unperceived into my argument, so as to infect all that followed, as is common in metaphysical reasonings. I grew convinced that truth, sincerity, and integrity, in dealings between man and man, were of the utmost importance to the felicity of life; and I formed written resolutions (which still remain in my journal-book) to practise them ever while I lived. Revelation had indeed no weight with me as such; but I entertained an opinion that, though certain actions might not be bad because they were forbidden by it, or good because it commanded them, yet probably those actions might be forbidden because they were bad for us, or commanded because they were beneficial to us, in their own natures, all the circumstances of things considered. And this persuasion, with the kind hand of Providence, or some guardian angel, or accidental favourable circumstances and situations, or all together, preserved me through the dangerous time of youth and the hazardous situations I was sometimes in among strangers, remote from the eye and advice of my father, free from any wilful gross immorality or injustice that might have been expected from my want of religion; I say wilful, because the instances I have mentioned had something of necessity in them, from my youth, inexperience, and the knavery of others: I had, therefore, a tolerable character to begin the world with; I valued it properly, and determined to preserve it.

We had not been long returned to Philadelphia before the new types arrived from London. We settled with Keimer, and left him by his consent before he heard of it. We found a house to hire near the market, and took it. To lessen the rent (which was then but twenty-four pounds a year, though I have since known it to let for seventy), we took in Thomas Godfrey, a glazier, and his family, who were to pay a considerable part of it to us,[Pg 77] and we to board with them. We had scarce opened our letters and put our press in order, before George House, an acquaintance of mine, brought a countryman to us, whom he had met in the street inquiring for a printer. All our cash was now expended in the variety of particulars we had been obliged to procure, and this countryman's five shillings, being our first fruits, and coming so seasonably, gave me more pleasure than any crown I have since earned; and, from the gratitude I felt towards House, has made me often more ready than perhaps I otherwise should have been, to assist young beginners.

There are croakers in every country always boding its ruin. Such a one there lived in Philadelphia, a person of note, an elderly man, with a wise look and a very grave manner of speaking; his name was Samuel Mickle. This gentleman, a stranger to me, stopped me one day at my door, and asked me if I was the young man who had lately opened a new printing-house. Being answered in the affirmative, he said he was sorry for me, because it was an expensive undertaking, and the expense would be lost, for Philadelphia was a sinking place; the people already half bankrupts, or near being so; all the appearances of the country, such as new buildings and the rise of rents, being to his certain knowledge fallacious; for they were, in fact, among the things that would ruin us. Then he gave me such a detail of misfortunes now existing, or that were soon to exist, that he left me half melancholy. Had I known him before I engaged in this business, probably I never should have done it. This person continued to live in this decaying place, and to declaim in the same strain, refusing for many years to buy a house there, because all was going to destruction; and at last I had the pleasure of seeing him give five times as much for[Pg 78] one as he might have bought it for when he first began croaking.

I should have mentioned before, that in the autumn of the preceding year I had formed most of my ingenious acquaintance into a club for mutual improvement, which we called the Junto; we met on Friday evenings. The rules that I drew up required that every member in his turn should produce one or more queries on any point of morals, politics, or natural philosophy, to be discussed by the company; and once in three months produce and read an essay of his own writing, on any subject he pleased. Our debates were to be under the direction of a president, and to be conducted in the sincere spirit of inquiry after truth, without fondness for dispute or desire of victory; and to prevent warmth, all expressions of positiveness in opinions or direct contradiction were after some time made contraband, and prohibited under small pecuniary penalties.

The first members were Joseph Brientnal, a copier of deeds for the scriveners; a good-natured, friendly, middle-aged man, a great lover of poetry, reading all he could meet with, and writing some that was tolerable; very ingenious in making little knickknackeries, and of sensible conversation.

Thomas Godfrey, a self-taught mathematician, great in his way, and afterward inventor of what is now called Hadley's Quadrant. But he knew little out of his way, and was not a pleasing companion; as, like most great mathematicians I have met with, he expected universal precision in everything said, or was for ever denying or distinguishing upon trifles, to the disturbance of all conversation; he soon left us.

Nicholas Scull, a surveyor, afterward surveyor-general, who loved books, and sometimes made a few verses.

William Parsons, bred a shoemaker, but loving[Pg 79] reading, had acquired a considerable share of mathematics, which he first studied with a view to astrology, and afterward laughed at it; he also became surveyor-general.

William Maugridge, joiner, but a most exquisite mechanic, and a solid, sensible man.

Hugh Meredith, Stephen Potts, and George Webb, I have characterized before.

Robert Grace, a young gentleman of some fortune, generous, lively, and witty; a lover of punning and of his friends.

Lastly, William Coleman, then a merchant's clerk, about my age, who had the coolest, clearest head, the best heart, and the exactest morals of almost any man I ever met with. He became afterward a merchant of great note, and one of our provincial judges. Our friendship continued without interruption to his death, upward of forty years; and the club continued almost as long, and was the best school of philosophy, morality, and politics that then existed in the province; for our queries (which were read the week preceding their discussion) put us upon reading with attention on the several subjects, that we might speak more to the purpose: and here, too, we acquired better habits of conversation, everything being studied in our rules which might prevent our disgusting each other; hence the long continuance of the club, which I shall have frequent occasion to speak farther of hereafter. But my giving this account of it here is to show something of the interest I had, every one of these exerting themselves in recommending business to us. Brientnal particularly procured us from the Quakers the printing of forty sheets of their history, the rest being to be done by Keimer; and upon these we worked exceeding hard, for the price was low. It was a folio, pro patria size, in pica, with long-primer notes. I composed a sheet a day, and Meredith worked it off at press; it was often[Pg 80] eleven at night, and sometimes later, before I had finished my distribution for the next day's work, for the little jobs sent in by our other friends now and then put us back. But so determined I was to continue doing a sheet a day of the folio, that one night, when, having imposed my forms, I thought my day's work over, one of them by accident was broken, and two pages reduced to pi, I immediately distributed and composed it over again before I went to bed; and this industry, visible to our neighbours, began to give us character and credit; particularly, I was told, that mention being made of the new printing-office at the merchants' every-night club, the general opinion was that it must fail, there being already two printers in the place, Keimer and Bradford; but Dr. Baird (whom you and I saw many years after at his native place, St. Andrew's in Scotland), gave a contrary opinion: "For the industry of that Franklin," said he, "is superior to anything I ever saw of the kind; I see him still at work when I go home from the club, and he is at work again before his neighbours are out of bed." This struck the rest, and we soon after had offers from one of them to supply us with stationary; but, as yet, we did not choose to engage in shop business.

I mention this industry the more particularly and the more freely, though it seems to be talking in my own praise, that those of my posterity who shall read it may know the use of that virtue, when they see its effects in my favour throughout this relation.

George Webb, who had found a female friend that lent him wherewith to purchase his time of Keimer, now came to offer himself as a journeyman to us. We could not then employ him; but I foolishly let him know, as a secret, that I soon intended to begin a newspaper, and might then have work for him. My hopes of success, as I told him, were founded on this, that the then only newspaper[Pg 81] printed by Bradford, was a paltry thing, wretchedly managed, no way entertaining, and yet was profitable to him; I therefore freely thought a good paper would scarcely fail of good encouragement. I requested Webb not to mention it, but he told it to Keimer, who immediately, to be beforehand with me, published proposals for one himself, on which Webb was to be employed. I was vexed at this, and to counteract them, not being able to commence our paper, I wrote several amusing pieces for Bradford's paper, under the title of the Busybody, which Brientnal continued some months. By this means the attention of the public was fixed on that paper, and Keimer's proposals, which we burlesqued and ridiculed, were disregarded. He began his paper, however, and before carrying it on three quarters of a year, with at most only ninety subscribers, he offered it me for a trifle; and I having been ready some time to go on with it, took it in hand directly, and it proved in a few years extremely profitable to me.

I perceive that I am apt to speak in the singular number, though our partnership still continued; it may be that, in fact, the whole management of the business lay upon me. Meredith was no compositor, a poor pressman, and seldom sober. My friends lamented my connexion with him, but I was to make the best of it.

Our first papers made quite a different appearance from any before printed in the province; a better type, and better printed; but some remarks of my writing on the dispute then going on between Governor Burnet and the Massachusetts Assembly, struck the principal people, occasioned the paper and the manager of it to be much talked of, and in a few weeks brought them all to be our subscribers.

Their example was followed by many, and our number went on growing continually. This was one of the first good effects of my having learned[Pg 82] a little to scribble; another was, that the leading men, seeing a newspaper now in the hands of those who could also handle a pen, thought it convenient to oblige and encourage me. Bradford still printed the votes, and laws, and other public business. He had printed an address of the house to the governor in a coarse, blundering manner; we reprinted it elegantly and correctly, and sent one to every member. They were sensible of the difference; it strengthened the hands of our friends in the house; and they voted us their printers for the year ensuing.

Among my friends in the house I must not forget Mr. Hamilton, before mentioned, who was then returned from England, and had a seat in it. He interested himself for me strongly in that instance, as he did in many others afterward, continuing his patronage till his death.[9]

Mr. Vernon, about this time, put me in mind of the debt I owed him, but did not press me. I wrote him an ingenuous letter of acknowledgment, craving his forbearance a little longer, which he allowed me; as soon as I was able, I paid the principal with the interest, and many thanks: so that erratum was in some degree corrected.

But now another difficulty came upon me which I had never the least reason to expect. Mr. Meredith's father, who was to have paid for our printing-house, according to the expectations given me, was able to advance only one hundred pounds currency, which had been paid; and a hundred more was due to the merchant, who grew impatient, and sued us all. We gave bail, but saw that, if the money could not be raised in time, the suit must soon come to a judgment and execution, and our hopeful prospects must with us be ruined, as the press and letters must be sold for payment, perhaps at half price.[Pg 83] In this distress two true friends, whose kindness I have never forgotten, nor ever shall forget while I can remember anything, came to me separately, unknown to each other, and without any application from me, offered each of them to advance me all the money that should be necessary to enable me to take the whole business upon myself, if that should be practicable; but they did not like my continuing the partnership with Meredith, who, as they said, was often seen drunk in the street, playing at low games in alehouses much to our discredit; these two friends were William Coleman and Robert Grace. I told them I could not propose a separation while any prospect remained of the Merediths fulfilling their part of our agreement, because I thought my self under great obligations to them for what they had done and would do if they could: but if they finally failed in their performance, and our partnership must be dissolved, I should then think myself at liberty to accept the assistance of my friends: thus the matter rested for some time; when I said to my partner, perhaps your father is dissatisfied at the part you have undertaken in this affair of ours, and is unwilling to advance for you and me what he would for you? If that is the case, tell me, and I will resign the whole to you, and go about my business. No, said he, my father has really been disappointed, and is really unable; and I am unwilling to distress him farther. I see this is a business I am not fit for. I was bred a farmer, and it was a folly in me to come to town and put myself, at thirty years of age, an apprentice to learn a new trade. Many of our Welsh people are going to settle in North Carolina, where land is cheap. I am inclined to go with them, and follow my old employment: you may find friends to assist you: if you will take the debts of the company upon you, return to my father the hundred pounds he has advanced, pay my little personal debts, and give me[Pg 84] thirty pounds and a new saddle, I will relinquish the partnership, and leave the whole in your hands. I agreed to this proposal; it was drawn up in writing, signed and sealed immediately. I gave him what he demanded, and he went soon after to Carolina; whence he sent me, next year, two long letters, containing the best account that had been given of that country, the climate, the soil, husbandry, &c., for in those matters he was very judicious: I printed them in the papers, and they gave great satisfaction to the public.

As soon as he was gone I recurred to my two friends; and because I would not give an unkind preference to either, I took half what each had offered, and I wanted, of one, and half of the other; paid off the company's debts, and went on with the business in my own name, advertising that the partnership was dissolved. I think this was in or about the year 1729.

About this time there was a cry among the people for more paper money; only fifteen thousand pounds being extant in the province, and that soon to be sunk. The wealthy inhabitants opposed any addition, being against all currency, from the apprehension that it would depreciate, as it had done in New-England, to the injury of all creditors. We had discussed this point in our junto, where I was on the side of an addition; being persuaded that the first small sum, struck in 1723, had done much good by increasing the trade, employment, and number of inhabitants in the province; since I now saw all the old houses inhabited, and many new ones building; whereas I remembered well, when I first walked about the streets of Philadelphia (eating my roll), I saw many of the houses in Walnut-street, between Second and Front streets, with bills on their doors "to be let;" and many, likewise, in Chestnut-street and other streets which made me think the inhabitants of the city[Pg 85] were one after another deserting it. Our debates possessed me so fully of the subject, that I wrote and printed an anonymous pamphlet on it, entitled, "The Nature and Necessity of a Paper Currency." It was well received by the common people in general, but the rich men disliked it, for it increased and strengthened the clamour for more money; and they happening to have no writers among them that were able to answer it, their opposition slackened, and the point was carried by a majority in the house. My friends there, who considered I had been of some service, thought fit to reward me by employing me in printing the money; a very profitable job, and a great help to me; this was another advantage gained by my being able to write.

The utility of this currency became by time and experience so evident, that the principles upon which it was founded were never afterward much disputed; so that it grew soon to fifty-five thousand pounds; and in 1739, to eighty thousand pounds, trade, building, and inhabitants all the while increasing: though I now think there are limits beyond which the quantity may be hurtful.

I soon after obtained, through my friend Hamilton, the printing of the Newcastle paper money, another profitable job, as I then thought it, small things appearing great to those in small circumstances: and these to me were really great advantages, as they were great encouragements. Mr. Hamilton procured me also the printing of the laws and votes of that government, which continued in my hands as long as I followed the business.

I now opened a small stationer's shop: I had in it blanks of all kinds, the correctest that ever appeared among us. I was assisted in that by my friend Breintnal: I had also paper, parchment, chapmen's books, &c. One Whitemash, a compositor I had known in London, an excellent workman, now came to me, and worked with me constantly and[Pg 86] diligently; and I took an apprentice, the son of Aquilla Rose.

I began now gradually to pay off the debt I was under for the printing-house. In order to secure my credit and character as a tradesman, I took care not only to be in reality industrious and frugal, but to avoid the appearances to the contrary. I dressed plain, and was seen at no places of idle diversion: I never went out a fishing or shooting: a book, indeed, sometimes debauched me from my work, but that was seldom, was private, and gave no scandal: and to show that I was not above my business, I sometimes brought home the paper I purchased at the stores through the streets on a wheelbarrow. Thus, being esteemed an industrious, thriving young man, and paying duly for what I bought, the merchants who imported stationary solicited my custom; others proposed supplying me with books, and I went on prosperously. In the mean time Keimer's credit and business declining daily, he was at last forced to sell his printing-house to satisfy his creditors. He went to Barbadoes, and there lived some years in very poor circumstances.

His apprentice, David Harry, whom I had instructed while I worked with him, set up in his place at Philadelphia, having bought his materials. I was at first apprehensive of a powerful rival in Harry, as his friends were very able, and had a good deal of interest: I therefore proposed a partnership to him, which he, fortunately for me, rejected with scorn. He was very proud, dressed like a gentleman, lived expensively, took much diversion and pleasure abroad, ran in debt, and neglected his business; upon which, all business left him; and, finding nothing to do, he followed Keimer to Barbadoes, taking the printing-house with him. There this apprentice employed his former master as a journeyman; they quarrelled often, and Harry went continually behindhand, and at length was obliged to sell[Pg 87] his types and return to country-work in Pennsylvania. The person who bought them employed Keimer to use them, but a few years after he died.

There remained now no other printer in Philadelphia but the old Bradford; but he was rich and easy, did a little in the business by straggling hands, but was not anxious about it: however, as he held the postoffice, it was imagined he had better opportunities of obtaining news, his paper was thought a better distributor of advertisements than mine, and therefore had many more; which was a profitable thing to him, and a disadvantage to me. For though I did indeed receive and send papers by the post, yet the public opinion was otherwise; for what I did send was by bribing the riders, who took them privately; Bradford being unkind enough to forbid it, which occasioned some resentment on my part, and I thought so meanly of the practice, that, when I afterward came into his situation, I took care never to imitate it.

I had hitherto continued to board with Godfrey, who lived in part of my house with his wife and children, and had one side of the shop for his glazier's business, though he worked little, being always absorbed in his mathematics. Mrs. Godfrey projected a match for me with a relation's daughter, took opportunities of bringing us often together, till a serious courtship on my part ensued, the girl being in herself very deserving. The old folks encouraged me by continual invitations to supper, and by leaving us together, till at length it was time to explain. Mrs. Godfrey managed our little treaty. I let her know that I expected as much money with their daughter as would pay off my remaining debt for the printing-house; which I believe was not then above a hundred pounds. She brought me word they had no such sum to spare: I said they might mortgage their house in the loan office. The answer to this after some days was, that they did not approve the[Pg 88] match; that, on inquiry of Bradford, they had been informed the printing business was not a profitable one; the types would soon be worn out, and more wanted; that Keimer and David Harry had failed one after the other, and I should probably soon follow them; and, therefore, I was forbidden the house, and the daughter shut up. Whether this was a real change of sentiment, or only artifice on a supposition of our being too far engaged in affection to retract, and therefore that we should steal a marriage, which would leave them at liberty to give or withhold what they pleased, I know not. But I suspected the motive, resented it, and went no more. Mrs. Godfrey brought me afterward some more favourable accounts of their disposition, and would have drawn me on again; but I declared absolutely my resolution to have nothing more to do with that family. This was resented by the Godfreys; we differed, and they removed, leaving me the whole house, and I resolved to take no more inmates. But this affair having turned my thoughts to marriage, I looked round me and made overtures of acquaintance in other places; but soon found that the business of a printer being generally thought a poor one, I was not to expect money with a wife, unless with such a one as I should not otherwise think agreeable.

A friendly correspondence, as neighbours, had continued between me and Miss Read's family, who all had a regard for me from the time of my first lodging in their house. I was often invited there, and consulted in their affairs, wherein I sometimes was of service. I pitied poor Miss Read's unfortunate situation, who was generally dejected, seldom cheerful, and avoided company: I considered my giddiness and inconstancy when in London, as in a great degree the cause of her unhappiness, though the mother was good enough to think the fault more her own than mine, as she had prevented our marrying[Pg 89] before I went thither, and persuaded the other match in my absence. Our mutual affection was revived, but there was now great objections to our union; that match was indeed looked upon as invalid, a preceding wife being said to be living in England; but this could not easily be proved, because of the distance, &c., and though there was a report of his death, it was not certain. Then, though it should be true, he had left many debts which his successor might be called upon to pay: we ventured, however, over all these difficulties, and I took her to wife, Sept. 1, 1730. None of the inconveniences happened that we had apprehended; she proved a good and faithful helpmate, assisted me much by attending to the shop; we throve together, and ever mutually endeavoured to make each other happy. Thus I corrected that great erratum as well as I could.

About this time our club, meeting, not at a tavern, but in a little room of Mr. Grace's set apart for that purpose, a proposition was made by me, that, since our books were often referred to in our disquisitions upon the queries, it might be convenient to us to have them all together when we met, that, upon occasion, they might be consulted; and by thus clubbing our books to a common library, we should, while we liked to keep them together, have each of us the advantage of using the books of all the other members, which would be nearly as beneficial as if each owned the whole. It was liked and agreed to, and we filled one end of the room with such books as we could best spare. The number was not so great as we expected; and though they had been of great use, yet some inconveniences occurring for want of due care of them, the collection, after about a year, was separated, and each took his books home again.

And now I set on foot my first project of a public nature, that for a subscription library; I drew up[Pg 90] the proposals, got them put into form by our great scrivener, Brockden, and, by the help of my friends in the junto, procured fifty subscribers of forty shillings each to begin with, and ten shillings a year for fifty years, the term our company was to continue. We afterward obtained a charter, the company being increased to one hundred; this was the mother of all the North American subscription libraries, now so numerous. It is become a great thing itself, and continually goes on increasing: these libraries have improved the general conversation of the Americans, made the common tradesmen and farmers as intelligent as most gentlemen from other countries, and perhaps have contributed in some degree to the stand so generally made throughout the colonies in defence of their privileges.

[Thus far was written with the intention expressed in the beginning; and, getting abroad, it excited great interest on account of its simplicity and candour; and induced many applications for a continuance. What follows was written many years after, in compliance with the advice contained in the letters that follow, and has, therefore, less of a family picture and more of a public character. The American revolution occasioned the interruption.]

FOOTNOTES:

[1] Dr. Shipley.

[2] Perhaps from the time when the name of Franklin, which before was the name of an order of people, was assumed by them for a surname, when others took surnames all over the kingdom.

As a proof that Franklin was anciently the common name of an order or rank in England, see Judge Fortescue, De laudibus Legum Angliæ, written about the year 1412, in which is the following passage, to show that good juries might easily be formed in any part of England:

"Regio etiam illa, ita respersa refertaque est possessoribus terrarum et agrorum, quod in ea, villula tam parva reperiri non poterit, in qua non est miles, armiger, vel pater-familias, qualis ibidem Frankleri vulgariter nuncupatur, magnis ditatus possessionibus, nec non libere tenentes et alii valecti plurimi, suis patrimoniis sufficientes, ad faciendum juratam, in forma prænotata.

"Moreover, the same country is so filled and replenished with landed menne, that therein so small a thorpe cannot be found wherein dweleth not a knight, an esquire, or such a householder as is there commonly called a Franklin, enriched with great possessions; and also other freeholders and many yeomen, able for their livelihoodes to make a jury in form aforementioned."—Old Translation.

Chaucer, too, calls his country-gentleman a Franklin; and after describing his good housekeeping, thus characterizes him:

"This worthy Franklin bore a purse of silk

Fix'd to his girdle, white as morning milk;

Knight of the shire, first justice at th' assize,

To help the poor, the doubtful to advise.

In all employments, generous, just he proved,

Renown'd for courtesy, by all beloved."

[3]

Copy of an original letter, found among Dr. Franklin's papers, from Josiah to B. Franklin.

Boston, May 26, 1739.

Loving Son,—As to the original of our name there is various opinions; some say that it came from a sort of title of which a book, that you bought when here, gives a lively account. Some think we are of a French extract, which was formerly called Franks; some of a free line; a line free from that vassalage which was common to subjects in days of old; some from a bird of long red legs. Your uncle Benjamin made inquiry of one skilled in heraldry, who told him there is two coats of armour, one belonging to the Franklins of the north, and one to the Franklins of the west. However, our circumstances have been such as that it hath hardly been worth while to concern ourselves much about these things, any farther than to tickle the fancy a little.

The first that I can give account of is my great grandfather, as it was a custom in those days among young men too many times to goe to seek their fortune, and in his travels he went upon liking to a taylor; but he kept such a stingy house, that he left him and travelled farther, and came to a smith's house, and coming on a fasting day, being in popish times, he did not like there the first day; the next morning the servant was called up at five in the morning, but after a little time came a good toast and good beer, and he found good housekeeping there; he served and learned the trade of a smith.

In Queen Mary's days, either his wife, or my grandmother by father's side, informed my father that they kept their Bible fastened under the top of a joint-stool that they might turn up the book and read in the Bible; that, when anybody came to the dore, they turned up the stool for fear of the apparitor; for if it was discovered they would be in hazard of their lives. My grandfather was a smith also, and settled at Ecton, in Northamptonshire, and he was imprisoned a year and a day on suspicion of his being the author of some poetry that touched the character of some great man. He had only one son and one daughter; my grandfather's name was Henry, my father's name was Thomas, my mother's name was Jane. My father was born at Ecton or Eton, Northamptonshire, on the 18th of October, 1598; married to Miss Jane White, niece to Coll White, of Banbury, and died in the 84th year of his age. There was nine children of us who were happy in our parents, who took great care by their instructions and pious example to breed us up in a religious way. My eldest brother had but one child, which was married to one Mr. Fisher, at Wallingborough, in Northamptonshire. The town was lately burned down, and whether she was a sufferer or not I cannot tell, or whether she be living or not. Her father died worth fifteen hundred pounds, but what her circumstances are now I know not. She hath no child. If you by the freedom of your office, makes it more likely to convey a letter to her, it would be acceptable to me. There is also children of brother John and sister Morris, but I hear no thing from them, and they write not to me, so that I know not where to find them. I have been again to about seeing ... but have missed of being informed. We received yours, and are glad to hear poor Jammy is recovered so well. Son John received the letter, but is so busy just now that he cannot write you an answer, but will do the best he can. Now with hearty love to, and prayer for you all, I rest your affectionate father,

JOSIAH FRANKLIN.

[4] Sherburne, in the island of Nantucket.

[5] The number in 1817 exceeds 400

[6]

"Silence, ye wolves, while Ralph to Cynthia howls,

And makes night hideous: answer him, ye owls!"

Pope's Dunciad, b. iii., v. 165.

[7] F. R. S., author of "A View of Sir Isaac Newton's Philosophy," and "A Treatise on Chymistry;" died in 1771.

[8] A printing-house is always called a chapel by the workmen, because printing was first carried on in England in an ancient chapel, and the title has been preserved by tradition. The bien venu among the printers, answers to the terms entrance and footing among mechanics; thus a journeyman, on entering a printing-house, was accustomed to pay one or more gallons of beer for the good of the chapel; this custom was falling into disuse thirty years ago; it is very properly rejected entirely in the United States.

[9] I afterward obtained for his son five hundred pounds.

[Pg 91]

PART II.

From Mr. Abel James (received in Paris).

"My dear and honoured Friend,

"I have often been desirous of writing to thee, but could not be reconciled to the thought that the letter might fall into the hands of the British, lest some printer or busybody should publish some part of the contents, and give our friend pain and myself censure.

"Some time since there fell into my hands, to my great joy, about twenty-three sheets in thy own handwriting, containing an account of the parentage and life of thyself, directed to thy son, ending in the year 1730, with which there were notes, likewise in thy writing; a copy of which I enclose, in hopes it may be a means, if thou continued it up to a later period, that the first and latter part may be put together; and if it is not yet continued, I hope thee will not delay it. Life is uncertain, as the preacher tells us; and what will the world say, if kind, humane, and benevolent Ben Franklin should leave his friends and the world deprived of so pleasing and profitable a work; a work which would be useful and entertaining not only to a few, but to millions? The influence writings under that class have on the minds of youth is very great, and has nowhere appeared to me so plain as in our public friend's journals. It almost insensibly leads the youth into the resolution of endeavouring to become as good and eminent as the journalist. Should thine, for instance, when published (and I think they could not fail of it), lead the youth to equal the industry and temperance of thy early youth, what a blessing[Pg 92] with that class would such a work be! I know of no character living, nor many of them put together, who has so much in his power as thyself to promote a greater spirit of industry and early attention to business, frugality, and temperance, with the American youth. Not that I think the work would have no other merit and use in the world; far from it: but the first is of such vast importance, that I know nothing that can equal it."

The foregoing letter, and the minutes accompanying it, being shown to a friend, I received from him the following:

From Mr. Benjamin Vaughan.

"Paris, January 31, 1783.

"My dearest Sir,

"When I had read over your sheets of minutes of the principal incidents of your life, recovered for you by your Quaker acquaintance, I told you I would send you a letter expressing my reasons why I thought it would be useful to complete and publish it as he desired. Various concerns have, for some time past, prevented this letter being written, and I do not know whether it was worth any expectation; happening to be at leisure, however, at present, I shall, by writing, at least interest and instruct myself; but as the terms I am inclined to use may tend to offend a person of your manners, I shall only tell you how I would address any other person who was as good and as great as yourself, but less diffident. I would say to him, sir, I solicit the history of your life, from the following motives:

"Your history is so remarkable, that, if you do not give it, somebody else will most certainly give it; and perhaps so as nearly to do as much harm as your own management of the thing might do good.

"It will, morever, present a table of the internal circumstances of your country, which will very much tend to invite to it settlers of virtuous and manly[Pg 93] minds. And, considering the eagerness with which such information is sought by them, and the extent of your reputation, I do not know of a more efficacious advertisement than your biography would give.

"All that has happened to you is also connected with the detail of the manners and situation of a rising people; and in this respect I do not think that the writings of Cæsar and Tacitus can be more interesting to a true judge of human nature and society.

"But these, sir, are small reasons, in my opinion, compared with the chance which your life will give for the forming of future great men; and, in conjunction with your Art of Virtue (which you design to publish), of improving the features of private character, and, consequently, of aiding all happiness, both public and domestic.

"The two works I allude to, sir, will, in particular, give a noble rule and example of self-education. School and other education constantly proceed upon false principles, and show a clumsy apparatus pointed at a false mark; but your apparatus is simple, and the mark a true one; and while parents and young persons are left destitute of other just means of estimating and becoming prepared for a reasonable course in life, your discovery, that the thing is in many a man's private power, will be invaluable!

"Influence upon the private character, late in life, is not only an influence late in life, but a weak influence. It is in youth that we plant our chief habits and prejudices; it is in youth that we take our party as to profession, pursuits, and matrimony. In youth, therefore, the turn is given; in youth the education even of the next generation is given; in youth the private and public character is determined; and the term of life extending but from youth to age, life ought to begin well from youth; and more especially before we take our party as to our principal objects.[Pg 94]

"But your biography will not merely teach self-education, but the education of a wise man; and the wisest man will receive lights and improve his progress by seeing detailed the conduct of another wise man. And why are weaker men to be deprived of such helps, when we see our race has been blundering on in the dark, almost without a guide in this particular, from the farthest trace of time? Show then, sir, how much is to be done, both to sons and fathers; and invite all wise men to become like yourself, and other men to become wise.

"When we see how cruel statesmen and warriors can be to the human race, and how absurd distinguished men can be to their acquaintance, it will be instructive to observe the instances multiply of pacific, acquiescing manners; and to find how compatible it is to be great and domestic; enviable and yet good-humoured.

"The little private incidents which you will also have to relate, will have considerable use, as we want, above all things, rules of prudence in ordinary affairs; and it will be curious to see how you have acted in these. It will be so far a sort of key to life, and explain many things that all men ought to have once explained to them, to give them a chance of becoming wise by foresight.

"The nearest thing to having experience of one's own, is to have other people's affairs brought before us in a shape that is interesting; this is sure to happen from your pen. Your affairs and management will have an air of simplicity or importance that will not fail to strike; and I am convinced you have conducted them with as much originality as if you had been conducting discussions in politics or philosophy; and what more worthy of experiments and system (its importance and its errors considered) than human life!

"Some men have been virtuous blindly, others have speculated fantastically, and others have been[Pg 95] shrewd to bad purposes; but you, sir, I am sure, will give, under your hand, nothing but what is at the same moment wise, practical, and good.

"Your account of yourself (for I suppose the parallel I am drawing for Dr. Franklin will hold not only in point of character, but of private history) will show that you are ashamed of no origin; a thing the more important as you prove how little necessary all origin is to happiness, virtue, or greatness.

"As no end, likewise, happens without a means, so we shall find, sir, that even you yourself framed a plan by which you became considerable; but, at the same time, we may see that, though the event is flattering, the means are as simple as wisdom could make them; that is, depending upon nature, virtue, thought, and habit.

"Another thing demonstrated will be the propriety of every man's waiting for his time for appearing upon the stage of the world. Our sensations being very much fixed to the moment, we are apt to forget that more moments are to follow the first, and, consequently, that man should arrange his conduct so as to suit the whole of a life. Your attribution appears to have been applied to your life, and the passing moments of it have been enlivened with content and enjoyment, instead of being tormented with foolish impatience or regrets. Such a conduct is easy for those who make virtue and themselves their standard, and who try to keep themselves in countenance by examples of other truly great men, of whom patience is so often the characteristic.

"Your Quaker correspondent, sir (for here again I will suppose the subject of my letter to resemble Dr. Franklin), praised your frugality, diligence, and temperance, which he considered as a pattern for all youth: but it is singular that he should have forgotten your modesty and your disinterestedness, without which you never could have waited for your[Pg 96] advancement, or found your situation in the mean time comfortable; which is a strong lesson to show the poverty of glory, and the importance of regulating our minds.

"If this correspondent had known the nature of your reputation as well as I do, he would have said, your former writings and measures would secure attention to your Biography and Art of Virtue; and your Biography and Art of Virtue, in return, would secure attention to them. This is an advantage attendant upon a various character, and which brings all that belongs to it into greater play; and it is the more useful, as, perhaps, more persons are at a loss for the means of improving their minds and characters than they are for the time or the inclination to do it.

"But there is one concluding reflection, sir, that will show the use of your life as a mere piece of biography. This style of writing seems a little gone out of vogue, and yet it is a very useful one; and your specimen of it may be particularly serviceable, as it will make a subject of comparison with the lives of various public cutthroats and intriguers, and with absurd monastic self-tormentors or vain literary triflers. If it encourages more writings of the same kind with your own, and induces more men to spend lives fit to be written, it will be worth all Plutarch's Lives put together.

"But being tired of figuring to myself a character of which every figure suits only one man in the world, without giving him the praise of it, I shall end my letter, my dear Dr. Franklin, with a personal application to your proper self.

"I am earnestly desirous, then, my dear sir, that you should let the world into the traits of your genuine character, as civil broils may otherwise tend to disguise or traduce it. Considering your great age, the caution of your character, and your peculiar style of thinking, it is not likely that any one besides[Pg 97] yourself can be sufficiently master of the facts of your life or the intentions of your mind.

"Besides all this, the immense revolution of the present period will necessarily turn our attention towards the author of it; and when virtuous principles have been pretended in it, it will be highly important to show that such have really influenced; and, as your own character will be the principal one to receive a scrutiny, it is proper (even for its effects upon your vast and rising country, as well as upon England and upon Europe) that it should stand respectable and eternal. For the furtherance of human happiness, I have always maintained that it is necessary to prove that man is not even at present a vicious and detestable animal; and still more to prove that good management may greatly amend him; and it is for much the same reason that I am anxious to see the opinion established, that there are fair characters among the individuals of the race; for the moment that all men, without exception, shall be conceived abandoned, good people will cease efforts deemed to be hopeless, and, perhaps, think of taking their share in the scramble of life, or, at least, of making it comfortable principally for themselves.

"Take then, my dear sir, this work most speedily into hand: show yourself good as you are good; temperate as you are temperate; and, above all things, prove yourself as one who, from your infancy, have loved justice, liberty, and concord, in a way that has made it natural and consistent for you to act as we have seen you act in the last seventeen years of your life. Let Englishmen be made not only to respect, but even to love you. When they think well of individuals in your native country, they will go nearer to thinking well of your country; and when your countrymen see themselves thought well of by Englishmen, they will go nearer to thinking well of England. Extend[Pg 98] your views even farther; do not stop at those who speak the English tongue, but, after having settled so many points in nature and politics, think of bettering the whole race of men.

"As I have not read any part of the life in question, but know only the character that lived it, I write somewhat at hazard. I am sure, however, that the life, and the treatise I allude to (on the Art of Virtue), will necessarily fulfil the chief of my expectations; and still more so if you take up the measure of suiting these performances to the several views above stated. Should they even prove unsuccessful in all that a sanguine admirer of yours hopes from them, you will at least have framed pieces to interest the human mind; and whoever gives a feeling of pleasure that is innocent to man, has added so much to the fair side of a life otherwise too much darkened by anxiety and too much injured by pain.

"In the hope, therefore, that you will listen to the prayer addressed to you in this letter, I beg to subscribe myself, my dear sir, &c., &c.,

Benj. Vaughan."

CONTINUATION,

Begun at Passy, near Paris, 1784.

It is some time since I received the above letters, but I have been too busy till now to think of complying with the request they contain. It might, too, be much better done if I were at home among my papers, which would aid my memory, and help to ascertain dates; but my return being uncertain, and having just now a little leisure, I will endeavour to recollect and write what I can: if I live to get home, it may there be corrected and improved.

Not having any copy here of what is already written, I know not whether an account is given of the[Pg 99] means I used to establish the Philadelphia public library, which, from a small beginning, is now become so considerable, though I remember to have come down near the time of that transaction (1730). I will, therefore, begin here with an account of it, which may be struck out if found to have been already given.

At the time I established myself in Pennsylvania, there was not a good bookseller's shop in any of the colonies to the southward of Boston. In New-York and Philadelphia the printers were, indeed, stationers, but they sold only paper, &c., almanacs, ballads, and a few common schoolbooks. Those who loved reading were obliged to send for their books from England: the members of the Junto had each a few. We had left the alehouse where we first met, and hired a room to hold our club in. I proposed that we should all of us bring our books to that room, where they would not only be ready to consult in our conferences, but become a common benefit, each of us being at liberty to borrow such as he wished to read at home. This was accordingly done, and for some time contented us: finding the advantage of this little collection, I proposed to render the benefit from the books more common, by commencing a public subscription library. I drew a sketch of the plan and rules that would be necessary, and got a skilful conveyancer, Mr. Charles Brockden, to put the whole in form of articles of agreement to be subscribed; by which each subscriber engaged to pay a certain sum down for the first purchase of the books, and an annual contribution for increasing them. So few were the readers at that time in Philadelphia, and the majority of us so poor, that I was not able, with great industry, to find more than fifty persons (mostly young tradesmen) willing to pay down for this purpose forty shillings each, and ten shillings per annum; with this little fund we began. The books were imported; the library was[Pg 100] open one day in the week for lending them to subscribers, on their promissory notes to pay double the value if not duly returned. The institution soon manifested its utility; was imitated by other towns and in other provinces. The libraries were augmented by donations; reading became fashionable; and our people, having no public amusements to divert their attention from study, became better acquainted with books, and in a few years were observed by strangers to be better instructed and more intelligent than people of the same rank generally are in other countries.

When we were about to sign the above-mentioned articles, which were to be binding on us, our heirs, &c., for fifty years, Mr. Brockden, the scrivener, said to us: "You are young men, but it is scarce probable that any of you will live to see the expiration of the term fixed in the instrument." A number of us, however, are yet living; but the instrument was, after a few years, rendered null by a charter that incorporated and gave perpetuity to the company.

The objections and reluctances I met with in soliciting the subscriptions, made me soon feel the impropriety of presenting one's self as the proposer of any useful project that might be supposed to raise one's reputation in the smallest degree above that of one's neighbours, when one has need of their assistance to accomplish that project. I therefore put myself as much as I could out of sight, and stated it as a scheme of a number of friends, who had requested me to go about and propose it to such as they thought lovers of reading. In this way my affairs went on more smoothly, and I ever after practised it on such occasions, and from my frequent successes can heartily recommend it. The present little sacrifice of your vanity will afterward be amply repaid. If it remains a while uncertain to whom the merit belongs, some one more vain than yourself will be encouraged to claim it, and then even[Pg 101] envy will be disposed to do you justice, by plucking those assumed feathers and restoring them to their right owner.

This library afforded me the means of improvement by constant study, for which I set apart an hour or two each day; and thus I repaired, in some degree, the loss of the learned education my father once intended for me. Reading was the only amusement I allowed myself. I spent no time in taverns, games, or frolics of any kind, and my industry in my business continued as indefatigable as it was necessary. I was indebted for my printing-house, I had a young family coming on to be educated, and I had two competitors to contend with for business who were established in the place before me. My circumstances, however, grew daily easier. My original habits of frugality continuing, and my father having, among his instructions to me when a boy, frequently repeated a Proverb of Solomon, "seest thou a man diligent in his calling, he shall stand before kings, he shall not stand before mean men," I thence considered industry as a means of obtaining wealth and distinction, which encouraged me; though I did not think that I should ever literally stand before kings, which, however, has since happened; for I have stood before five, and even had the honour of sitting down with one (the king of Denmark) to dinner.

We have an English proverb that says,

"He that would thrive

Must ask his wife."

It was lucky for me that I had one as much disposed to industry and frugality as myself. She assisted me cheerfully in my business, folding and stitching pamphlets, tending shop, purchasing old linen rags for the paper-makers, &c. We kept no idle servants; our table was plain and simple, our furniture of the cheapest. For instance, my breakfast was,[Pg 102] for a long time, bread and milk (no tea), and I ate it out of a twopenny earthen porringer, with a pewter spoon: but mark how luxury will enter families, and make a progress in spite of principle; being called one morning to breakfast, I found it in a china bowl, with a spoon of silver. They had been bought for me without my knowledge by my wife, and had cost her the enormous sum of three-and-twenty shillings; for which she had no other excuse or apology to make, but that she thought her husband deserved a silver spoon and china bowl as well as any of his neighbours. This was the first appearance of plate and china in our house, which afterward, in a course of years, as our wealth increased, augmented gradually to several hundred pounds in value.

I had been religiously educated as a Presbyterian; but though some of the dogmas of that persuasion appeared unintelligible, and I early absented myself from their public assemblies (Sunday being my studying day), I never was without some religious principles: I never doubted, for instance, the existence of a Deity; that he made the world, and governed it by his providence; that the most acceptable service of God was the doing good to man; that our souls are immortal; and that all crimes will be punished, and virtue rewarded, either here or hereafter. These I esteemed the essentials of every religion; and being to be found in all the religions we had in our country, I respected them all, though with different degrees of respect, as I found them more or less mixed with other articles, which, without any tendency to inspire, promote, or confirm morality, served principally to divide us, and make us unfriendly to one another. This respect to all, with an opinion that the worst had some effects, induced me to avoid all discourse that might tend to lessen the good opinion another might have of his own religion; and as our province increased in people,[Pg 103] and new places of worship were continually wanted and generally erected by voluntary contribution, my mite for such purpose, whatever might be the sect, was never refused.

Though I seldom attended any public worship, I had still an opinion of its propriety and of its utility when rightly conducted, and I regularly paid my annual subscription for the support of the only Presbyterian minister or meeting we had in Philadelphia. He used to visit me sometimes as a friend, and admonish me to attend his administrations; and I was now and then prevailed on to do so; once for five Sundays successively. Had he been in my opinion a good preacher, perhaps I might have continued, notwithstanding the occasion I had for the Sunday's leisure in my course of study: but his discourses were chiefly either polemic arguments, or explications of the peculiar doctrines of our sect, and were all to me very dry, uninteresting, and unedifying, since not a single moral principle was inculcated or enforced. I had some years before composed a little liturgy or form of prayer for my own private use (viz., in 1728), entitled Articles of Belief and Acts of Religion. I returned to the use of this, and went no more to the public assemblies. My conduct might be blameable, but I leave it without attempting farther to excuse it; my present purpose being to relate facts, and not to make apologies for them.

xli

It was about this time I conceived the bold and arduous project of arriving at moral perfection; I wished to live without committing any fault at any time, and to conquer all that either natural inclination, custom, or company might lead me into. As I knew, or thought I knew, what was right and wrong, I did not see why I might not always do the one and avoid the other. But I soon found I had undertaken a task of more difficulty than I had imagined: while my attention was taken up, and[Pg 104] care employed in guarding against one fault, I was often surprised by another; habit took the advantage of inattention; inclination was sometimes too strong for reason. I concluded, at length, that the mere speculative conviction, that it was our interest to be completely virtuous, was not sufficient to prevent our slipping; and that the contrary habits must be broken, and good ones acquired and established, before we can have any dependance on a steady, uniform rectitude of conduct. For this purpose I therefore tried the following method.

In the various enumerations of the moral virtues I had met with in my reading, I found the catalogue more or less numerous, as different writers included more or fewer ideas under the same name. Temperance, for example, was by some confined to eating and drinking; while by others it was extended to mean the moderating of every other pleasure, appetite, inclination, or passion, bodily or mental, even to our avarice and ambition. I proposed to myself, for the sake of clearness, to use rather more names, with fewer ideas annexed to each, than a few names with more ideas; and I included, under thirteen names of virtues, all that at that time occurred to me as necessary or desirable, and annexed to each a short precept, which fully expressed the extent I gave to its meaning.

These names of virtues, with their precepts, were,

1. Temperance.—Eat not to dulness: drink not to elevation.

2. Silence.—Speak not but what may benefit others or yourself: avoid trifling conversation.

3. Order.—Let all your things have their places: let each part of your business have its time.

4. Resolution.—Resolve to perform what you ought: perform without fail what you resolve.

5. Frugality.—Make no expense but to do good to others or yourself: i.e., waste nothing.[Pg 105]

6. Industry.—Lose no time: be always employed in something useful: cut off all unnecessary actions.

7. Sincerity.—Use no hurtful deceit: think innocently and justly: and, if you speak, speak accordingly.

8. Justice.—Wrong none by doing injuries, or omitting the benefits that are your duty.

9. Moderation.—Avoid extremes: forbear resenting injuries so much as you think they deserve.

10. Cleanliness.—Tolerate no uncleanliness in body, clothes, or habitation.

11. Tranquillity.—Be not disturbed at trifles, nor at accidents common or unavoidable.

12. Chastity.

13. Humility.

My intention being to acquire the habitude of all these virtues, I judged it would be well not to distract my attention by attempting the whole at once, but to fix it on one of them at a time; and when I should be master of that, then to proceed to another; and so on till I should have gone through the thirteen: and as the previous acquisition of some might facilitate the acquisition of certain others, I arranged them with that view as they stand above. Temperance first, as it tends to promote that coolness and clearness of head which is so necessary where constant vigilance was to be kept up, and a guard maintained against the unremitting attraction of ancient habits and the force of perpetual temptations. This being acquired and established, Silence would be more easy; and my desire being to gain knowledge at the same time that I improved in virtue; and considering that in conversation it was obtained rather by the use of the ear than of the tongue, and, therefore, wishing to break a habit I was getting into of prattling, punning, and jesting (which only made me acceptable to trifling company),[Pg 106] I gave Silence the second place. This and the next, Order, I expected would allow me more time for attending to my project and my studies Resolution, once become habitual, would keep me firm in my endeavours to obtain all the subsequent virtues. Frugality and Industry, relieving me from my restraining debt, and producing affluence and independence, would make more easy the practice of Sincerity and Justice, &c., &c. Conceiving then, that, agreeably to the advice of Pythagoras in his Golden Verses, daily examination would be necessary, I contrived the following method for conducting that examination.

I made a little book, in which I allotted a page for each of the virtues. I ruled each page with red ink, so as to have seven columns, one for each day of the week, marking each column with a letter for the day. I crossed these columns with thirteen red lines, marking the beginning of each line with the first letter of one of the virtues; on which line, and in its proper column, I might mark, by a little black spot, every fault I found upon examination to have been committed respecting that virtue upon that day.[10][Pg 107]

Form of the pages.

TEMPERANCE.

Eat not to dulness: drink not to elevation.

	Sun.	M.	T.	W.	Th.	F.	S.
Tem.							
Sil.	*	*		*		*	
Ord.	*	*	*		*	*	*
Res.		*				*	
Fru.		*				*	
Ind.			*				
Sinc.							
Jus.							
Mod.							
Clea.							
Tran.							
Chas.							
Hum.							

I determined to give a week's strict attention to each of the virtues successively. Thus, in the first week, my great guard was to every the least offence against Temperance; leaving the other virtues to their ordinary chance, only marking every evening the faults of the day. Thus, if in the first week I could keep my first line marked T. clear of spots, I supposed the habit of that virtue so much strengthened, and its opposite weakened, that I might venture extending my attention to include the next, and for the following week keep both lines clear of spots. Proceeding thus to the last, I could get through a course complete in thirteen weeks, and four courses in a year. And like him who, having a garden to weed, does not attempt to eradicate all the bad herbs at once (which would exceed his reach and his strength), but works on one of the beds at a time, and having accomplished the first, proceeds to a second, so I should have (I hoped)[Pg 108] the encouraging pleasure of seeing on my pages the progress made in virtue, by clearing successively my lines of their spots, till, in the end, by a number of courses, I should be happy in viewing a clean book, after a thirteen week's daily examination.

This my little book had for its motto these lines from Addison's Cato:

"Here will I hold; if there's a power above us

(And that there is, all nature cries aloud

Through all her works), he must delight in virtue;

And that which he delights in must be happy."

Another from Cicero:

O vitæ philosophia dux! O virtutum indagatrix et expultrixque vitiorum! Unus dies bene, et ex præceptis tuis actus, peccanti immortalitati est anteponendus."

"Oh Philosophy, guide of life! Diligent inquirer after virtue, and banisher of vice! A single day well spent, and as thy precepts direct, is to be preferred to an eternity of sin."

Another from the Proverbs of Solomon, speaking of wisdom or virtue:

"Length of days is in her right hand, and in her left hand riches and honour. Her ways are ways of pleasantness, and all her paths are peace."

And conceiving God to be the fountain of wisdom, I thought it right and necessary to solicit his assistance for obtaining it; to this end I formed the following little prayer, which was prefixed to my tables of examination, for daily use.

"O powerful Goodness! bountiful Father! merciful Guide! Increase me in that wisdom which discovers my truest interest: Strengthen my resolution to perform what that wisdom dictates! Accept my kind offices to thy other children as the only return in my power for thy continual favours to me."

I used also, sometimes, a little prayer which I took from Thomson's Poems, viz.,[Pg 109]

"Father of light and life, thou God supreme!

Oh teach me what is good; teach me thyself!

Save me from folly, vanity, and vice,

From every low pursuit; and fill my soul

With knowledge, conscious peace, and virtue pure;

Sacred, substantial, never-fading bliss!"

The precept of Order, requiring that every part of my business should have its allotted time, one page in my little book contained the following scheme of employment for the twenty-four hours of a natural day.

SCHEME.

Hours.

Morning.

xlv

FRANKLIN

The Question

What good shall

I do this day?

{

5

6

7

}

Rise, wash, and address Powerful

Goodness! Contrive day's business, and

take the resolution of the day; prosecute

the present study, and breakfast.

8

9

10

11

}

Work.

Noon. {

12

1

}

Read, or look over my accounts, and

dine.

Afternoon. {

2

3

4

5

}

Work.

Evening.

The Question,

What good have

I done to-day?

{

6

7

8

9

}

Put things in their places. Supper,

music, or diversion, or conversation.

Examination of the day.

Night. {

10

11

12

1

2

3

4

}

Sleep.

    I entered upon the execution of this plan for self-examination, and continued it, with occasional intermissions, for some time. I was surprised to find myself so much fuller of faults than I had[Pg 110] imagined; but I had the satisfaction of seeing them diminish. To avoid the trouble of renewing now and then my little book, which, by scraping out the marks on the paper of old faults to make room for new ones in a new course, became full of holes, I transferred my tables and precepts to the ivory leaves of a memorandum book, on which the lines were drawn with red ink, that made a durable stain; and on those lines I marked my faults with a black lead pencil; which marks I could easily wipe out with a wet sponge. After a while I went through one course only in a year; and afterward only one in several years; till at length I omitted them entirely, being employed in voyages and business abroad, with a multiplicity of affairs that interfered; but I always carried my little book with me. My scheme of Order gave me the most trouble; and I found that though it might be practicable where a man's business was such as to leave him the disposition of his time, that of a journeyman-printer, for instance, it was not possible to be exactly observed by a master, who must mix with the world, and often receive people of business at their own hours. Order, too, with regard to places for things, papers, &c., I found it extremely difficult to acquire. I had not been early accustomed to method, and having an exceeding good memory, I was not so sensible of the inconvenience attending want of method. This article, therefore, cost me much painful attention, and my faults in it vexed me so much, and I made so little progress in amendment, and had such frequent relapses, that I was almost ready to give up the attempt, and content myself with a faulty character in that respect. Like the man who, in buying an axe of a smith my neighbour, desired to have the whole of its surface as bright as the edge, the smith consented to grind it bright for him if he would turn the wheel: he turned while the smith pressed the broad face of the axe hard and heavily[Pg 111] on the stone, which made the turning of it very fatiguing. The man came every now and then from the wheel to see how the work went on; and at length would take his axe as it was, without farther grinding. "No," said the smith, "turn on, we shall have it bright by-and-by; as yet 'tis only speckled." "Yes," said the man, "but I think I like a speckled axe best." And I believe this may have been the case with many, who having, for the want of some such means as I employed, found the difficulty of obtaining good and breaking bad habits in other points of vice and virtue, have given up the struggle, and concluded that "a speckled axe was best." For something that pretended to be reason was every now and then suggesting to me, that such extreme nicety as I exacted of myself, might be a kind of foppery in morals, which, if it were known, would make me ridiculous; that a perfect character might be attended with the inconvenience of being envied and hated; and that a benevolent man should allow a few faults in himself, to keep his friends in countenance. In truth, I found myself incorrigible with respect to Order; and, now I am grown old and my memory bad, I feel very sensibly the want of it. But, on the whole, though I never arrived at the perfection I had been so ambitious of obtaining, but fell far short of it, yet I was, by the endeavour, a better and a happier man than I otherwise should have been if I had not attempted it; as those who aim at perfect writing by imitating the engraved copies, though they may never reach the wished-for excellence of those copies, their hand is mended by the endeavour, and is tolerable while it continues fair and legible.

It may be well my posterity should be informed, that to this little artifice, with the blessing of God, their ancestor owed the constant felicity of his life down to the 79th year, in which this is written. What reverses may attend the remainder is in the[Pg 112] hand of Providence: but if they arrive, the reflection on past happiness enjoyed ought to help his bearing them with more resignation. To temperance he ascribes his long-continued health, and what is still left to him of a good constitution. To industry and frugality, the early easiness of his circumstances and acquisition of his fortune, with all that knowledge that enabled him to be a useful citizen and obtained for him some degree of reputation among the learned. To sincerity and justice, the confidence of his country, and the honourable employs it conferred upon him: and to the joint influence of the whole mass of the virtues, even in the imperfect state he was able to acquire them, all that evenness of temper and that cheerfulness in conversation which makes his company still sought for, and agreeable even to his young acquaintance: I hope, therefore, that some of my descendants may follow the example and reap the benefit.

It will be remarked that, though my scheme was not wholly without religion, there was in it no mark of any of the distinguishing tenets of any particular sect; I had purposely avoided them; for being fully persuaded of the utility and excellence of my method, and that it might be serviceable to people in all religions, and intending some time or other to publish it, I would not have anything in it that would prejudice any one of any sect against it. I proposed writing a little comment on each virtue, in which I would have shown the advantages of possessing it, and the mischiefs attending its opposite vice; I should have called my book The Art of Virtue, because it would have shown the means and manner of obtaining virtue, which would have distinguished it from the mere exhortation to be good, that does not instruct and indicate the means; but is like the apostle's man of verbal charity, who, without showing to the naked and hungry how or where they might get clothes or victuals, only exhorted[Pg 113] them to be fed and clothed James ii., 15, 16.

But it so happened that my intention of writing and publishing this comment was never fulfilled. I had, indeed, from time to time, put down short hints of the sentiments, reasonings, &c., to be made use of in it, some of which I have still by me: but the necessary close attention to private business in the earlier part of life, and public business since, have occasioned my postponing it. For it being connected in my mind with a great and extensive project, that required the whole man to execute, and which an unforeseen succession of employs prevented my attending to, it has hitherto remained unfinished.

In this piece it was my design to explain and enforce this doctrine, that vicious actions are not hurtful because they are forbidden, but forbidden because they are hurtful; the nature of man alone considered: that it was, therefore, every one's interest to be virtuous, who wished to be happy even in this world: and I should, from this circumstance (there being always in the world a number of rich merchants, nobility, states, and princes who have need of honest instruments for the management of their affairs, and such being so rare), have endeavoured to convince young persons, that no qualities are so likely to make a poor man's fortune as those of probity and integrity.

My list of virtues contained at first but twelve: but a Quaker friend having kindly informed me that I was generally thought proud; that my pride showed itself frequently in conversation; that I was not content with being in the right when discussing any point, but was overbearing, and rather insolent (of which he convinced me by mentioning several instances), I determined to endeavour to cure myself, if I could, of this vice or folly among the rest; and I added humility to my list, giving an extensive[Pg 114] meaning to the word. I cannot boast of much success in acquiring the reality of this virtue, but I had a good deal with regard to the appearance of it. I made it a rule to forbear all direct contradiction to the sentiments of others, and all positive assertion of mine own. I even forbid myself, agreeably to the old laws of our junto, the use of every word or expression in the language that imported a fixed opinion; such as certainly, undoubtedly, &c., and I adopted, instead of them, I conceive, I apprehend, or I imagine a thing to be so or so; or it so appears to me at present.

When another asserted something that I thought an error, I denied myself the pleasure of contradicting him abruptly, and of showing immediately some absurdity in his proposition; and in answering I began by observing that in certain cases or circumstances his opinion would be right, but in the present case there appeared, or seemed to me, some difference, &c. I soon found the advantage of this change in my manners; the conversations I engaged in went on more pleasantly. The modest way in which I proposed my opinions procured them a readier reception and less contradiction; I had less mortification when I was found to be in the wrong, and I more easily prevailed with others to give up their mistakes and join with me when I happened to be in the right. And this mode, which I at first put on with some violence to natural inclination, became at length easy, and so habitual to me, that perhaps for the fifty years past no one has ever heard a dogmatical expression escape me. And to this habit (after my character of integrity) I think it principally owing that I had early so much weight with my fellow-citizens when I proposed new institutions or alterations in the old, and so much influence in public councils when I became a member: for I was but a bad speaker, never eloquent, subject to much hesitation in my choice of words, hardly correct in language, and yet I generally carried my point.[Pg 115]

In reality, there is, perhaps, no one of our natural passions so hard to subdue as pride; disguise it, struggle with it, stifle it, mortify it as much as you please, it is still alive, and will every now and then peep out and show itself; you will see it perhaps often in this history. For even if I could conceive that I had completely overcome it, I should probably be proud of my humility.

[Here concludes what was written at Passy, near Paris.]

MEMORANDUM.

I am now about to write at home (Philadelphia), August, 1788, but cannot have the help expected from my papers, many of them being lost in the war. I have, however, found the following:

Having mentioned a great and extensive project which I had conceived, it seems proper that some account should be here given of that project and its object. Its first rise in my mind appears in the above-mentioned little paper, accidentally preserved, viz.:

Observations on my reading history, in library, May 9, 1731.

"That the great affairs of the world, the wars, revolutions, &c., are carried on and effected by parties.

"That the view of these parties is their present general interest; or what they take to be such.

"That the different views of these different parties occasion all confusion.

1

"That while a party is carrying on a general design, each man has his particular private interest in view.

"That, as soon as a party has gained its general point, each member becomes intent upon his particular[Pg 116] interest, which, thwarting others, breaks that party into divisions and occasions more confusion.

"That few in public affairs act from a mere view of the good of their country, whatever they may pretend; and though their actings bring real good to their country, yet men primarily considered that their own and their country's interest were united, and so did not act from a principle of benevolence.

"That fewer still, in public affairs, act with a view to the good of mankind.

"There seems to me at present to be great occasion for raising a United Party for Virtue, by forming the virtuous and good men of all nations into a regular body, to be governed by suitable good and wise rules, which good and wise men may probably be more unanimous in their obedience to than common people are to common laws.

"I at present think, that whoever attempts this aright, and is well qualified, cannot fail of pleasing God and of meeting with success.

B. F."

Revolving this project in my mind as to be undertaken hereafter, when my circumstances should afford me the necessary leisure, I put down from time to time, on pieces of paper, such thoughts as occurred to me respecting it. Most of these are lost, but I find one purporting to be the substance of an intended creed, containing, as I thought, the essentials of every known religion, and being free of everything that might shock the professors of any religion. It is expressed in these words: viz.,

"That there is one God, who made all things.

"That he governs the world by his providence.

"That he ought to be worshipped by adoration, prayer, and thanksgiving.

"But that the most acceptable service to God is doing good to man.

"That the soul is immortal.

"And that God will certainly reward virtue and punish vice, either here or hereafter."[Pg 117]

My ideas at that time were, that the sect should be begun and spread at first among young and single men only; that each person to be initiated should not only declare his assent to such creed, but should have exercised himself with the thirteen weeks' examination and practice of the virtues, as in the before-mentioned model; that the existence of such a society should be kept a secret till it was become considerable, to prevent solicitations for the admission of improper persons; but that the members should, each of them, search among his acquaintance for ingenious, well-disposed youths, to whom, with prudent caution, the scheme should be gradually communicated. That the members should engage to afford their advice, assistance, and support to each other in promoting one another's interest, business, and advancement in life: that, for distinction, we should be called The Society of the Free and Easy. Free, as being, by the general practice and habits of the virtues, free from the dominion of vice; and particularly by the practice of industry and frugality, free from debt, which exposes a man to constraint, and a species of slavery to his creditors.

This is as much as I can now recollect of the project, except that I communicated it in part to two young men, who adopted it with enthusiasm: but my then narrow circumstances, and the necessity I was under of sticking close to my business, occasioned my postponing the farther prosecution of it at that time, and my multifarious occupations, public and private, induced me to continue postponing, so that it has been omitted, till I have no longer strength or activity left sufficient for such an enterprise. Though I am still of opinion it was a practicable scheme, and might have been very useful, by forming a great number of good citizens: and I was not discouraged by the seeming magnitude of the undertaking, as I have always thought that one[Pg 118] man of tolerable abilities may work great changes and accomplish great affairs among mankind, if he first forms a good plan; and, cutting off all amusements or other employments that would divert his attention, makes the connexion of that same plan his sole study and business.

In 1732 I first published my Almanac under the name of Richard Saunders; it was continued by me about twenty-five years, and commonly called Poor Richard's Almanac. I endeavoured to make it both entertaining and useful, and it accordingly came to be in such demand that I reaped considerable profit from it, vending annually near ten thousand. And observing that it was generally read (scarce any neighbourhood in the province being without it), I considered it as a proper vehicle for conveying instruction among the common people, who bought scarcely any other books. I therefore filled all the little spaces that occurred between the remarkable days in the calendar with proverbial sentences, chiefly such as inculcated industry and frugality as the means of procuring wealth, and thereby securing virtue; it being more difficult for a man in want to act always honestly, as (to use here one of those proverbs) "it is hard for an empty sack to stand upright." These proverbs, which contained the wisdom of many ages and nations, I assembled and formed into a connected discourse, prefixed to the Almanac of 1757 as the harangue of a wise old man to the people attending an auction: the bringing all these scattered counsels thus into a focus, enabled them to make greater impression. The piece, being universally approved, was copied in all the newspapers of the American Continent; reprinted in Britain on a large sheet of paper, to be stuck up in houses; two translations were made of it in French, and great numbers bought by the clergy and gentry to distribute gratis among their poor parishioners and tenants. In Pennsylvania, as it[Pg 119] discouraged useless expense in foreign superfluities, some thought it had its share of influence in producing that growing plenty of money which was observable for several years after its publication.

I considered my newspaper also another means of communicating instruction, and in that view frequently reprinted in it extracts from the Spectator and other moral writers; and sometimes published little pieces of mine own, which had been first composed for reading in our Junto. Of these are a Socratic dialogue, tending to prove that, whatever might be his parts and abilities, a vicious man could not properly be called a man of sense; and a discourse on self-denial, showing that virtue was not secure till its practice became a habitude, and was free from the opposition of contrary inclinations: these may be found in the papers about the beginning of 1735. In the conduct of my newspaper I carefully excluded all libelling and personal abuse, which is of late years become so disgraceful to our country. Whenever I was solicited to insert anything of that kind, and the writers pleaded (as they generally did) the liberty of the press, and that a newspaper was like a stagecoach, in which any one who would pay had a right to a place, my answer was, that I would print the piece separately if desired, and the author might have as many copies as he pleased to distribute himself, but that I would not take upon me to spread his detraction; and that, having contracted with my subscribers to furnish them with what might be either useful or entertaining, I could not fill their papers with private altercation, in which they had no concern, without doing them manifest injustice. Now, many of our printers make no scruple of gratifying the malice of individuals by false accusations of the fairest characters among ourselves, augmenting animosity even to the producing of duels; and are, moreover, so indiscreet as to print scurrilous reflections on the[Pg 120] government of neighbouring states, and even on the conduct of our best national allies, which may be attended with the most pernicious consequences. These things I mention as a caution to young printers, and that they may be encouraged not to pollute the presses and disgrace their profession by such infamous practices, but refuse steadily, as they may see by my example that such a course of conduct will not, on the whole, be injurious to their interests.

In 1733 I sent one of my journeymen to Charleston, South Carolina, where a printer was wanting. I furnished him with a press and letters, on an agreement of partnership, by which I was to receive one third of the profits of the business, paying one third of the expense. He was a man of learning, but ignorant in matters of account; and, though he sometimes made me remittances, I could get no account from him, nor any satisfactory state of our partnership while he lived. On his decease the business was continued by his widow, who, being born and bred in Holland, where (as I have been informed) the knowledge of accounts makes a part of female education, she not only sent me as clear a statement as she could find of the transactions past, but continued to account with the greatest regularity and exactness every quarter afterward; and managed the business with such success, that she not only reputably brought up a family of children, but, at the expiration of the term, was able to purchase of me the printing-house and establish her son in it. I mention this affair chiefly for the sake of recommending that branch of education for our young women, as likely to be of more use to them and their children in case of widowhood than either music or dancing; by preserving them from losses by imposition of crafty men, and enabling them to continue, perhaps, a profitable mercantile house, with established correspondence, till a son is grown[Pg 121] up fit to undertake and go on with it, to the lasting advantage and enriching of the family.

I had begun in 1733 to study languages; I soon made myself so much master of the French as to be able to read the books in that language with ease. I then undertook the Italian: an acquaintance, who was also learning it, used often to tempt me to play chess with him: finding this took up too much of the time I had to spare for study, I at length refused to play any more, unless on this condition, that the victor in every game should have a right to impose a task, either of parts of the grammar to be got by heart, or in translations, &c., which tasks the vanquished was to perform upon honour before our next meeting: as we played pretty equally, we thus beat one another into that language. I afterward, with a little painstaking, acquired as much of the Spanish as to read their books also. I have already mentioned that I had only one year's instruction in a Latin school, and that when very young, after which I neglected that language entirely. But when I had attained an acquaintance with the French, Italian, and Spanish, I was surprised to find, on looking over a Latin Testament, that I understood more of that language than I had imagined, which encouraged me to apply myself again to the study of it; and I met with the more success, as those preceding languages had greatly smoothed my way. From these circumstances, I have thought there was some inconsistency in our common mode of teaching languages. We are told that it is proper to begin first with the Latin, and, having acquired that, it will be more easy to attain those modern languages which are derived from it; and yet we do not begin with the Greek in order more easily to acquire the Latin. It is true, that if we can clamber and get to the top of a staircase without using the steps, we shall more easily gain them in descending; but certainly, if we begin with[Pg 122] the lowest, we shall with more ease ascend to the top; and I would therefore offer it to the consideration of those who superintend the education of our youth, whether—since many of those who begin with the Latin, quit the same after spending some years without having made any great proficiency and what they have learned becomes almost useless, so that their time has been lost—it would not have been better to have begun with the French, proceeding to the Italian and Latin. For though, after spending the same time, they should quit the study of languages and never arrive at the Latin, they would, however, have acquired another tongue or two, that, being in modern use, might be serviceable to them in common life.

After ten years' absence from Boston, and having become easy in my circumstances, I made a journey thither to visit my relations, which I could not sooner afford. In returning, I called at Newport to see my brother James, then settled there with his printing-house: our former differences were forgotten, and our meeting was very cordial and affectionate: he was fast declining in health, and requested of me that, in case of his death, which he apprehended not far distant, I would take home his son, then but ten years of age, and bring him up to the printing business. This I accordingly performed, sending him a few years to school before I took him into the office. His mother carried on the business till he was grown up, when I assisted him with an assortment of new types, those of his father being in a manner worn out. Thus it was that I made my brother ample amends for the service I had deprived him of by leaving him so early.

In 1736 I lost one of my sons, a fine boy of four years old, by the smallpox, taken in the common way. I long regretted him bitterly, and still regret that I had not given it to him by inoculation. This I mention for the sake of parents who omit that[Pg 123] operation, on the supposition that they should never forgive themselves if a child died under it; my example showing that the regret may be the same either way, and, therefore, that the safer should be chosen.

Our club, the Junto, was found so useful, and afforded such satisfaction to the members, that some were desirous of introducing their friends, which could not well be done without exceeding what we had settled as a convenient number, viz., twelve. We had, from the beginning, made it a rule to keep our institution a secret, which was pretty well observed; the intention was to avoid applications of improper persons for admittance, some of whom, perhaps, we might find it difficult to refuse. I was one of those who were against any addition to our number; but, instead of it, made in writing a proposal, that every member, separately, should endeavour to form a subordinate club, with the same rules respecting queries, &c., and without informing them of the connexion with the Junto. The advantages proposed were the improvement of so many more young citizens by the use of our institutions; our better acquaintance with the general sentiments of the inhabitants on any occasion, as the junto member might propose what queries we should desire, and was to report to the Junto what passed in his separate club: the promotion of our particular interests in business by more extensive recommendation, and the increase of our influence in public affairs, and our power of doing good by spreading through the several clubs the sentiments of the Junto. The project was approved, and every member undertook to form his club: but they did not all succeed. Five or six only were completed, which were called by different names, as the Vine, the Union, the Band, &c.; they were useful to themselves, and afforded us a good deal of amusement, information, and instruction, besides answering, in[Pg 124] some degree, our views of influencing the public on particular occasions; of which I shall give some instances in course of time as they happened.

My first promotion was my being chosen, in 1736, clerk of the General Assembly. The choice was made that year without opposition; but the year following, when I was again proposed (the choice, like that of the members, being annual), a new member made a long speech against me, in order to favour some other candidate. I was, however, chosen, which was the more agreeable to me, as, besides the pay for the immediate service of clerk, the place gave me a better opportunity of keeping up an interest among the members, which secured to me the business of printing the votes, laws, paper money, and other occasional jobs for the public, that, on the whole, were very profitable. I therefore did not like the opposition of this new member, who was a gentleman of fortune and education, with talents that were likely to give him, in time, great influence in the house, which, indeed, afterward happened. I did not, however, aim at gaining his favour by paying any servile respect to him, but after some time took this other method. Having heard that he had in his library a certain very scarce and curious book, I wrote a note to him, expressing my desire of perusing that book, and requesting that he would do me the favour of lending it to me for a few days. He sent it immediately; and I returned it in about a week with another note, expressing strongly my sense of the favour. When we next met in the house, he spoke to me (which he had never done before), and with great civility; and he ever after manifested a readiness to serve me on all occasions, so that we became great friends, and our friendship continued to his death. This is another instance of the truth of an old maxim I had learned, which says, "He that has once done you a kindness will be more ready to do you another than he whom you yourself[Pg 125] have obliged." And it shows how much more profitable it is prudently to remove, than to resent, return, and continue inimical proceedings.

In 1737, Colonel Spotswood, late governor of Virginia, and then postmaster-general, being dissatisfied with his deputy at Philadelphia respecting some negligence in rendering, and want of exactness in framing, his accounts, took from him his commission and offered it to me. I accepted it readily, and found it of great advantage; for, though the salary was small, it facilitated the correspondence that improved my newspaper, increased the number demanded, as well as the advertisements to be inserted, so that it came to afford me a considerable income. My old competitor's newspaper declined proportionally, and I was satisfied, without retaliating his refusal, while postmaster, to permit my papers being carried by the riders. Thus he suffered greatly from his neglect in due accounting; and I mention it as a lesson to those young men who may be employed in managing affairs for others, that they should always render accounts and make remittances with great clearness and punctuality. The character of observing such a conduct is the most powerful of recommendations to new employments and increase of business.

I began now to turn my thoughts to public affairs, beginning, however, with small matters. The city watch was one of the first things that I conceived to want regulation. It was managed by the constables of the respective wards in turn; the constable summoned a number of housekeepers to attend him for the night. Those who chose never to attend, paid him six shillings a year to be excused, which was supposed to go to hiring substitutes, but was, in reality, more than was necessary for that purpose, and made the constableship a place of profit; and the constable, for a little drink, often got such ragamuffins about him as a watch that respectable[Pg 126] housekeepers did not choose to mix with. Walking the rounds, too, was often neglected, and most of the nights spent in tippling: I thereupon wrote a paper, to be read in Junto, representing these irregularities, but insisting more particularly on the inequality of this six-shilling tax of the constables, respecting the circumstances of those who paid it, since a poor widow housekeeper, all whose property to be guarded by the watch did not perhaps exceed the value of fifty pounds, paid as much as the wealthiest merchant who had thousands of pounds worth of goods in his stores. On the whole, I proposed, as a more effectual watch, the hiring of proper men to serve constantly in the business; and, as a more equitable way of supporting the charge, the levying of a tax that should be proportioned to the property. This idea, being approved by the Junto, was communicated to the other clubs, but as originating in each of them; and though the plan was not immediately carried into execution, yet, by preparing the minds of the people for the change, it paved the way for the law, obtained a few years after, when the members of our clubs were grown into more influence.

About this time I wrote a paper (first to be read in the Junto, but it was afterward published) on the different accidents and carelessnesses by which houses were set on fire, with cautions against them, and means proposed of avoiding them. This was spoken of as a useful piece, and gave rise to a project, which soon followed it, of forming a company for the more ready extinguishing of fires, and mutual assistance in removing and securing of goods when in danger. Associates in this scheme were presently found amounting to thirty. Our articles of agreement obliged every member to keep always in good order and fit for use a certain number of leathern buckets, with strong bags and baskets (for packing and transporting goods), which were to be[Pg 127] brought to every fire; and we agreed about once a month to spend a social evening together in discoursing and communicating such ideas as occurred to us upon the subject of fires as might be useful in our conduct on such occasions. The utility of this institution soon appeared; and many more desiring to be admitted than we thought convenient for one company, they were advised to form another, which was accordingly done; and thus went on one new company after another, till they became so numerous as to include most of the inhabitants who were men of property; and now, at the time of my writing this (though upward of fifty years since its establishment), that which I first formed, called the Union Fire Company, still subsists; though the first members are all deceased but one, who is older by a year than I am. The fines that have been paid by members for absence at the monthly meetings have been applied to the purchase of fire-engines, ladders, fire-hooks, and other useful implements for each company; so that I question whether there is a city in the world better provided with the means of putting a stop to beginning conflagrations; and, in fact, since these institutions, the city has never lost by fire more than one or two houses at a time, and the flames have often been extinguished before the house in which they began has been half consumed.

In 1739 arrived among us from Ireland the Reverend Mr. Whitefield, who had made himself remarkable there as an itinerant preacher. He was at first permitted to preach in some of our churches; but the clergy, taking a dislike to him, soon refused him their pulpits, and he was obliged to preach in the fields. The multitude of all sects and denominations that attended his sermons were enormous, and it was a matter of speculation to me (who was one of the number) to observe the extraordinary influence of his oratory on his hearers, and how much[Pg 128] they admired and respected him. It was wonderful to see the change soon made in the manners of our inhabitants. From being thoughtless or indifferent about religion, it seemed as if all the world were growing religious, so that one could not walk through the town in an evening without hearing psalms sung in different families of every street. And it being found inconvenient to assemble in the open air, subject to its inclemencies, the building of a house to meet in was no sooner proposed, and persons appointed to receive contributions, than sufficient sums were soon received to procure the ground and erect the building, which was one hundred feet long and seventy broad; and the work was carried with such spirit as to be finished in a much shorter time than could have been expected. Both house and ground were vested in trustees, expressly for the use of any preacher of any religious persuasion who might desire to say something to the people at Philadelphia. The design in building not being to accommodate any particular sect, but the inhabitants in general.

Mr. Whitefield, on leaving us, went preaching all the way through the colonies to Georgia. The settlement of that province had lately been begun; but, instead of being made with hardy, industrious husbandmen, accustomed to labour, the only people fit for such an enterprise, it was with families of broken shopkeepers and other insolvent debtors; many of indolent and idle habits, taken out of the jails, who, being set down in the woods, unqualified for clearing land, and unable to endure the hardships of a new settlement, perished in numbers, leaving many helpless children unprovided for. The sight of their miserable situation inspired the benevolent heart of Mr. Whitefield with the idea of building an orphan-house there, in which they might be supported and educated. Returning northward, he preached up this charity and made large collections, for[Pg 129] his eloquence had a wonderful power over the hearts and purses of his hearers, of which I myself was an instance. I did not disapprove of the design, but as Georgia was then destitute of materials and workmen, and it was proposed to send them from Philadelphia at a great expense, I thought it would have been better to build the house at Philadelphia, and bring the children to it. This I advised; but he was resolute in his first project, rejected my counsel, and I therefore refused to contribute. I happened soon after to attend one of his sermons, in the course of which I perceived he intended to finish with a collection, and I silently resolved he should get nothing from me: I had in my pocket a handful of copper-money, three or four silver dollars, and five pistoles in gold; as he proceeded I began to soften, and concluded to give the copper. Another stroke of his oratory made me ashamed of that, and determined me to give the silver; and he finished so admirably, that I emptied my pocket wholly into the collector's dish, gold and all! At this sermon there was also one of our club, who, being of my sentiments respecting the building in Georgia, and suspecting a collection might be intended, had, by precaution, emptied his pockets before he came from home; towards the conclusion of the discourse, however, he felt a strong inclination to give, and applied to a neighbour who stood near him to lend him some money for the purpose. The request was fortunately made to perhaps the only man in the company who had the firmness not to be affected by the preacher. His answer was, "At any other time, friend Hopkinson, I would lend to thee freely; but not now, for thee seems to me to be out of thy right senses."

Some of Mr. Whitefield's enemies affected to suppose that he would apply these collections to his own private emolument; but I, who was intimately acquainted with him (being employed in[Pg 130] printing his sermons, journals, &c.), never had the least suspicion of his integrity, but am to this day decidedly of opinion that he was in all his conduct a perfectly honest man; and methinks my testimony in his favour ought to have the more weight, as we had no religious connexion. He used, indeed, sometimes to pray for my conversion, but never had the satisfaction of believing that his prayers were heard. Ours was a mere civil friendship, sincere on both sides, and lasted to his death.

The last time I saw Mr. Whitefield was in London, when he consulted me about his orphan-house concern, and his purpose of appropriating it to the establishment of a college.

He had a loud and clear voice, and articulated his words so perfectly that he might be heard and understood at a great distance, especially as his auditors observed the most perfect silence. He preached one evening from the top of the courthouse steps, which are in the middle of Market-street, and on the west side of Second-street, which crosses it at right angles. Both streets were filled with his hearers to a considerable distance: being among the hindmost in Market-street, I had the curiosity to learn how far he could be heard, by retiring backward down the street towards the river, and I found his voice distinct till I came near Front-street, when some noise in that street obscured it. Imagining then a semicircle, of which my distance should be the radius, and that it was filled with auditors, to each of whom I allowed two square feet, I computed that he might well be heard by more than thirty thousand. This reconciled me to the newspaper accounts of his having preached to 25,000 people in the fields, and to the history of generals haranguing whole armies, of which I had sometimes doubted.

By hearing him often I came to distinguish easily between sermons newly composed and those which[Pg 131] he had often preached in the course of his travels. His delivery of the latter was so improved by frequent repetition, that every accent, every emphasis, every modulation of voice, was so perfectly well-turned and well-placed, that, without being interested in the subject, one could not help being pleased with the discourse; a pleasure of much the same kind with that received from an excellent piece of music. This is an advantage itinerant preachers have over those who are stationary, as the latter cannot well improve their delivery of a sermon by so many rehearsals. His writing and printing from time to time gave great advantage to his enemies; unguarded expressions, and even erroneous opinions delivered in preaching, might have been afterward explained or qualified, by supposing others that might have accompanied them, or they might have been denied; but litera scripta manet—what is written remains: critics attacked his writings violently, and with so much appearance of reason as to diminish the number of his votaries and prevent their increase. So that I am satisfied that if he had never written anything, he would have left behind him a much more numerous and important sect; and his reputation might in that case have been still growing, even after his death; as there being nothing of his writing on which to found a censure and give him a lower character, his proselytes would be left at liberty to attribute to him as great a variety of excellences as their enthusiastic admiration might wish him to have possessed.

My business was now constantly augmenting, and my circumstances growing daily easier, my newspaper having become very profitable, as being for a time almost the only one in this and the neighbouring provinces. I experienced, too, the truth of the observation, "that after getting the first hundred pounds it is more easy to get the second;" money itself being of a prolific nature.[Pg 132]

The partnership at Carolina having succeeded, I was encouraged to engage in others, and to promote several of my workmen who had behaved well, by establishing them with printing-houses in different colonies, on the same terms with that in Carolina. Most of them did well, being enabled at the end of our term (six years) to purchase the types of me and go on working for themselves, by which means several families were raised. Partnerships often finish in quarrels; but I was happy in this, that mine were all carried on and ended amicably; owing, I think, a good deal to the precaution of having very explicitly settled in our articles everything to be done by, or expected from, each partner, so that there was nothing to dispute, which precaution I would therefore recommend to all who enter into partnership; for whatever esteem partners may have for, and confidence in, each other at the time of the contract, little jealousies and disgusts may arise, with ideas of inequality in the care and burden, business, &c., which are attended often with breach of friendship and of the connexion; perhaps with lawsuits and other disagreeable consequences.

I had, on the whole, abundant reason to be satisfied with my being established in Pennsylvania; there were, however, some things that I regretted, there being no provision for defence nor for a complete education of youth; no militia, nor any college: I therefore, in 1743, drew up a proposal for establishing an academy; and at that time, thinking the Rev. Richard Peters, who was out of employ, a fit person to superintend such an institution, I communicated the project to him; but he, having more profitable views in the service of the proprietors, which succeeded, declined the undertaking: and not knowing another at that time suitable for such a trust, I let the scheme lie a while dormant. I succeeded better the next year, 1744, in proposing[Pg 133] and establishing a Philosophical Society. The paper I wrote for that purpose will be found among my writings, if not lost with many others.

With respect to defence, Spain having been several years at war against Great Britain, and being at length joined by France, which brought us into great danger; and the laboured and long-continued endeavour of our governor, Thomas, to prevail with our Quaker assembly to pass a militia law, and make other provisions for the security of the province, having proved abortive, I proposed to try what might be done by a voluntary subscription of the people: to promote this, I first wrote and published a pamphlet, entitled Plain Truth, in which I stated our helpless situation in strong lights, with the necessity of a union and discipline for our defence, and promised to propose in a few days an association, to be generally signed for that purpose. The pamphlet had a sudden and surprising effect. I was called upon for the instrument of association; having settled the draught of it with a few friends, I appointed a meeting of the citizens in the large building before-mentioned. The house was pretty full; I had prepared a number of printed copies, and provided pens and ink dispersed all over the room. I harangued them a little on the subject, read the paper, explained it, and then distributed the copies, which were eagerly signed, not the least objection being made. When the company separated and the papers were collected, we found above twelve hundred signatures; and other copies being dispersed in the country, the subscribers amounted at length to upward of ten thousand. These all furnished themselves, as soon as they could, with arms, formed themselves into companies and regiments, chose their own officers, and met every week to be instructed in the manual exercise and other parts of military discipline. The women, by subscriptions among themselves, provided silk collours,[Pg 134] which they presented to the companies, painted with different devices and mottoes, which I supplied. The officers of the companies composing the Philadelphia regiment, being met, chose me for their colonel; but, conceiving myself unfit, I declined that station, and recommended Mr. Lawrence, a fine person and a man of influence, who was accordingly appointed. I then proposed a lottery to defray the expense of building a battery below the town, and furnished with cannon: it filled expeditiously, and the battery was soon erected, the merlons being framed of logs and filled with earth. We bought some old cannon from Boston; but these not being sufficient, we wrote to London for more, soliciting, at the same time, our proprietaries for some assistance, though without much expectation of obtaining it. Meanwhile, Colonel Lawrence, —— Allen, Abraham Taylor, Esquires, and myself, were sent to New-York by the associators, commissioned to borrow some cannon of Governor Clinton. He at first refused us peremptorily; but at a dinner with his council, where there was great drinking of Madeira wine, as the custom of that place then was, he softened by degrees, and said he would lend us six. After a few more bumpers he advanced to ten; and at length he very good-naturedly conceded eighteen. They were fine cannon, 18 pounders, with their carriages, which were soon transported and mounted on our batteries, where the associators kept a nightly guard while the war lasted: and, among the rest, I regularly took my turn of duty there as a common soldier.

My activity in these operations was agreeable to the governor and council; they took me into confidence, and I was consulted by them in every measure where their concurrence was thought useful to the association. Calling in the aid of religion, I proposed to them the proclaiming a fast, to promote reformation and implore the blessing of Heaven on[Pg 135] our undertaking. They embraced the motion; but as it was the first fast ever thought of in the province, the secretary had no precedent from which to draw the proclamation. My education in New-England, where a fast is proclaimed every year, was here of some advantage: I drew it in the accustomed style; it was translated into German, printed in both languages, and circulated through the province. This gave the clergy of the different sects an opportunity of influencing their congregations to join in the association, and it would probably have been general among all but the Quakers if the peace had not soon intervened.

In order of time, I should have mentioned before, that having, in 1742, invented an open stove for the better warming of rooms, and, at the same time, saving fuel, as the fresh air admitted was warmed in entering, I made a present of the model to Mr. Robert Grace, one of my early friends, who, having an iron furnace, found the casting of the plates for these stoves a profitable thing, as they were growing in demand. To promote that demand, I wrote and published a pamphlet, entitled, "An Account of the new-invented Pennsylvania Fireplaces; wherein their construction and manner of operation is particularly explained, their advantages above every method of warming rooms demonstrated, and all objections that have been raised against the use of them answered and obviated," &c. This pamphlet had a good effect. Governor Thomas was so pleased with the construction of this stove, as described in it, that he offered to give me a patent for the sole vending of them for a term of years; but I declined it, from a principle which has ever weighed with me on such occasions, viz., That as we enjoy great advantages from the inventions of others, we should be glad of an opportunity to serve others by any invention of ours; and this we should do freely and generously.

An ironmonger in London, however, assuming a[Pg 136] good deal of my pamphlet, and working it up into his own, and making some small change in the machine, which rather hurt its operation, got a patent for it there, and made, as I was told, a little fortune by it. And this is not the only instance of patents taken out of my inventions by others, though not always with the same success; which I never contested, as having no desire of profiting by patents myself, and hating disputes. The use of these fireplaces in very many houses, both here in Pennsylvania and the neighbouring states, has been, and is, a great saving of wood to the inhabitants.

Peace being concluded, and the association business therefore at an end, I turned my thoughts again to the affair of establishing an academy. The first step I took was to associate in the design a number of active friends, of whom the Junto furnished a good part: the next was to write and publish a pamphlet, entitled, "Proposals relating to the Education of Youth in Pennsylvania." This I distributed among the principal inhabitants gratis: and as soon as I could suppose their minds a little prepared by the perusal of it, I set on foot a subscription for opening and supporting an academy; it was to be paid in quotas yearly for five years; by so dividing it, I judged the subscription might be larger; and I believe it was so, amounting to no less, if I remember right, than five thousand pounds.

In the introduction to these proposals, I stated their publication not as an act of mine, but of some public-spirited gentleman; avoiding as much as I could, according to my usual rule, the presenting myself to the public as the author of any scheme for their benefit.

The subscribers, to carry the project into immediate execution, chose out of their number twenty-four trustees, and appointed Mr. Francis, then attorney-general, and myself, to draw up constitutions for the government of the academy; which being[Pg 137] done and signed, a house was hired, masters engaged, and the schools opened; I think in the same year, 1749.

The scholars increasing fast, the house was soon found too small, and we were looking out for a piece of ground, properly situated, with intent to build, when accident threw into our way a large house ready built, which, with a few alterations, might well serve our purpose: this was the building before mentioned, erected by the hearers of Mr. Whitefield, and was obtained for us in the following manner.

It is to be noted, that the contributions to this building being made by people of different sects, care was taken in the nomination of trustees, in whom the building and ground were to be vested, that a predominance should not be given to any sect, lest in time that predominance might be a means of appropriating the whole to the use of such sect, contrary to the original intention; it was for this reason that one of each sect was appointed; viz., one Church of England man, one Presbyterian, one Baptist, one Moravian, &c., who, in case of vacancy by death, were to fill it by election among the contributors. The Moravian happened not to please his colleagues, and on his death they resolved to have no other of that sect; the difficulty then was, how to avoid having two of some other sect, by means of the new choice. Several persons were named, and for that reason not agreed to: at length one mentioned me, with the observation that I was merely an honest man, and of no sect at all, which prevailed with them to choose me. The enthusiasm which existed when the house was built had long since abated, and its trustees had not been able to procure fresh contributions for paying the ground rent and discharging some other debts the building had occasioned, which embarrassed them greatly. Being now a member of both boards of[Pg 138] trustees, that for the building and that for the academy, I had a good opportunity of negotiating with both and brought them finally to an agreement, by which the trustees for the building were to cede it to those of the academy; the latter undertaking to discharge the debt, to keep for ever open in the building a large hall for occasional preachers, according to the original intention, and maintain a free school for the instruction of poor children. Writings were accordingly drawn; and on paying the debts, the trustees of the academy were put in possession of the premises; and by dividing the great and lofty hall into stories, and different rooms above and below for the several schools, and purchasing some additional ground, the whole was soon made fit for our purpose, and the scholars removed into the building. The whole care and trouble of agreeing with the workmen, purchasing materials, and superintending the work, fell upon me, and I went through it the more cheerfully, as it did not then interfere with my private business, having the year before taken a very able, industrious, and honest partner, Mr. David Hall, with whose character I was well acquainted, as he had worked for me four years; he took off my hands all care of the printing-office, paying me punctually my share of the profits. This partnership continued eighteen years, successfully for us both.

The trustees of the academy, after a while, were incorporated by a charter from the governor; their funds were increased by contributions in Britain, and grants of land from the proprietors, to which the Assembly has since made considerable addition; and thus was established the present University of Philadelphia. I have been continued one of its trustees from the beginning (now near forty years), and have had the very great pleasure of seeing a number of the youth who have received their education in it distinguished by their improved abilities,[Pg 139] serviceable in public stations, and ornaments to their country.

When I was disengaged myself, as above mentioned, from private business, I flattered myself that, by the sufficient though moderate fortune I had acquired, I had found leisure during the rest of my life for philosophical studies and amusements. I purchased all Dr. Spence's apparatus, who had come from England to lecture in Philadelphia, and I proceeded in my electrical experiments with great alacrity; but the public, now considering me as a man of leisure, laid hold of me for their purposes; every part of our civil government, and almost at the same time, imposing some duty upon me. The governor put me into the commission of the peace; the corporation of the city chose me one of the common council, and soon after alderman; and the citizens at large elected me a burgess to represent them in Assembly; this latter station was the more agreeable to me, as I grew at length tired with sitting there to hear the debates, in which, as clerk, I could take no part, and which were often so uninteresting that I was induced to amuse myself with making magic squares or circles, or anything to avoid weariness; and I conceived my becoming a member would enlarge my power of doing good. I would not, however, insinuate that my ambition was not flattered by all these promotions: it certainly was; for, considering my low beginning, they were great things to me: and they were still more pleasing, as being so many spontaneous testimonies of the public good opinion, and by me entirely unsolicited.

The office of justice of the peace I tried a little, by attending a few courts and sitting on the bench to hear causes; but finding that more knowledge of the common law than I possessed was necessary to act in that station with credit, I gradually withdrew from it, excusing myself by my being obliged to[Pg 140] attend the higher duties of a legislator in the Assembly. My election to this trust was repeated every year for ten years, without my ever asking any elector for his vote, or signifying either directly or indirectly any desire of being chosen. On taking my seat in the house, my son was appointed their clerk.

The year following, a treaty being to be held with the Indians at Carlisle, the governor sent a message to the house, proposing that they should nominate some of their members, to be joined with some members of council, as commissioners for that purpose. The house named the speaker (Mr. Norris) and myself; and, being commissioned, we went to Carlisle and met the Indians accordingly. As those people are extremely apt to get drunk, and, when so, are very quarrelsome and disorderly, we strictly forbade the selling any liquor to them; and when they complained of this restriction, we told them that, if they would continue sober during the treaty, we would give them plenty of rum when the business was over. They promised this, and they kept their promise, because they could get no rum; and the treaty was conducted very orderly, and concluded to mutual satisfaction. They then claimed and received the rum; this was in the afternoon; they were near one hundred men, women, and children, and were lodged in temporary cabins, built in the form of a square, just without the town. In the evening, hearing a great noise among them, the commissioners walked to see what was the matter; we found they had made a great bonfire in the middle of the square: they were all drunk, men and women, quarrelling and fighting. Their dark-coloured bodies, half naked, seen only by the gloomy light of the bonfire, running after and beating one another with firebrands, accompanied by their horrid yellings, formed a scene the most diabolical that could well be imagined; there was no appeasing[Pg 141] the tumult, and we retired to our lodging. At midnight a number of them came thundering at our door, demanding more rum, of which we took no notice. The next day, sensible they had misbehaved in giving us that disturbance, they sent three of their old counsellors to make their apology. The orator acknowledged the fault, but laid it upon the rum; and then endeavoured to excuse the rum by saying, "The Great Spirit, who made all things, made everything for some use, and whatever use he designed anything for, that use it should always be put to: now, when he made rum, he said, 'let this be for the Indians to get drunk with;' and it must be so." And, indeed, if it be the design of Providence to extirpate these savages, in order to make room for the cultivators of the earth, it seems not impossible that rum may be the appointed means. It has already annihilated all the tribes who formerly inhabited the seacoast.

In 1751, Dr. Thomas Bond, a particular friend of mine, conceived the idea of establishing a hospital in Philadelphia (a very beneficent design, which has been ascribed to me, but was originally and truly his) for the reception and cure of poor sick persons, whether inhabitants of the province or strangers. He was zealous and active in endeavouring to procure subscriptions for it; but the proposal being a novelty in America, and, at first, not well understood, he met with but little success. At length he came to me with the compliment, that he found there was no such a thing as carrying a public-spirited project through without my being concerned in it. "For," said he, "I am often asked by those to whom I propose subscribing, Have you consulted Franklin on this business? And what does he think of it? And when I tell them that I have not (supposing it rather out of your line), they do not subscribe, but say, they will consider it." I inquired into the nature and probable utility of the scheme, and, receiving from him a very satisfactory explanation,[Pg 142] I not only subscribed to it myself, but engaged heartily in the design of procuring subscriptions from others: previous, however, to the solicitation, I endeavoured to prepare the minds of the people, by writing on the subject in the newspapers, which was my usual custom in such cases, but which Dr. Bond had omitted. The subscriptions afterward were more free and generous; but, beginning to flag, I saw they would be insufficient without assistance from the Assembly, and therefore proposed to petition for it, which was done. The country members did not at first relish the project: they objected that it could only be serviceable to the city, and, therefore, the citizens alone should be at the expense of it; and they doubted whether the citizens themselves generally approved of it. My allegation, on the contrary, that it met with such approbation as to leave no doubt of our being able to raise two thousand pounds by voluntary donations, they considered as a most extravagant supposition, and utterly impossible. On this I formed my plan; and asking leave to bring in a bill for incorporating the contributors according to the prayer of their petition, and granting them a blank sum of money, which leave was obtained chiefly on the consideration that the house could throw the bill out if they did not like it, I drew it so as to make the important clause a conditional one, viz.: "And be it enacted by the authority aforesaid, that when the said contributors shall have met and chosen their managers and treasurer, and shall have raised by their contributions a capital stock of two thousand pounds value (the yearly interest of which is to be applied to the accommodation of the sick poor in the said hospital, and of charge for diet, attendance, advice, and medicines), and shall make the same appear to the satisfaction of the Speaker of the Assembly for the time being, that then it shall and may be lawful for the said speaker, and he is hereby required to sign an order[Pg 143] on the provincial treasurer, for the payment of two thousand pounds, in two yearly payments, to the treasurer of the said hospital, to be applied to the founding, building, and finishing of the same." This condition carried the bill through; for the members who had opposed the grant, and now conceived they might have the credit of being charitable without the expense, agreed to its passage; and then, in soliciting subscriptions among the people, we urged the conditional promise of the law as an additional motive to give, since every man's donation would be doubled: thus the clause worked both ways. The subscriptions accordingly soon exceeded the requisite sum, and we claimed and received the public gift, which enabled us to carry the design into execution. A convenient and handsome building was soon erected; the institution has, by constant experience, been found useful, and flourishes to this day; and I do not remember any of my political manœuvres, the success of which, at the time, gave me more pleasure, or wherein, after thinking of it, I more easily excused myself for having made some use of cunning.

It was about this time that another projector, the Rev. Gilbert Tennent, came to me with a request that I would assist him in procuring a subscription for erecting a new meeting-house. It was to be for the use of a congregation he had gathered among the Presbyterians, who were originally disciples of Mr. Whitefield. Unwilling to make myself disagreeable to my fellow-citizens by too frequently soliciting their contributions, I absolutely refused. He then desired I would furnish him with a list of the names of persons I knew by experience to be generous and public spirited. I thought it would be unbecoming in me, after their kind compliance with my solicitation, to mark them out to be worried by other beggars, and therefore refused to give such a list. He then desired I would at least give him my[Pg 144] advice. That I will do, said I; and, in the first place, I advise you to apply to all those who you know will give something; next, to those who you are uncertain whether they will give anything or not, and show them the list of those who have given; and, lastly, do not neglect those who you are sure will give nothing, for in some of them you may be mistaken. He laughed and thanked me, and said he would take my advice. He did so, for he asked everybody, and he obtained a much larger sum than he expected, with which he erected the capacious and elegant meeting-house that stands in Arch-street.

Our city, though laid out with a beautiful regularity, the streets large, straight, and crossing each other at right angles, had the disgrace of suffering those streets to remain long unpaved, and in wet weather the wheels of heavy carriages ploughed them into a quagmire, so that it was difficult to cross them; and in dry weather the dust was offensive. I had lived near what was called the Jersey market, and saw, with pain, the inhabitants wading in mud while purchasing their provisions. A strip of ground down the middle of that market was at length paved with brick, so that, being once in the market, they had firm footing, but were often over their shoes in dirt to get there. By talking and writing on the subject, I was at length instrumental in getting the streets paved with stone between the market and the brick foot-pavement that was on the side next the houses. This for some time gave an easy access to the market dry shod; but the rest of the street not being paved, whenever a carriage came out of the mud upon this pavement, it shook off and left its dirt upon it, and it was soon covered with mire, which was not removed, the city as yet having no scavengers. After some inquiry I found a poor industrious man who was willing to undertake keeping the pavement clean, by sweeping it[Pg 145] twice a week, carrying off the dirt from before all the neighbours' doors, for the sum of sixpence per month, to be paid by each house. I then wrote and printed a paper, setting forth the advantages to the neighbourhood that might be obtained from this small expense; the greater ease in keeping our houses clean, so much dirt not being brought in by people's feet; the benefit to the shops by more custom, as buyers could more easily get at them; and by not having, in windy weather, the dust blown in upon their goods, &c. I sent one of these papers to each house, and in a day or two went round to see who would subscribe to an agreement to pay these sixpences; it was unanimously signed, and, for a time, well executed. All the inhabitants of the city were delighted with the cleanliness of the pavement that surrounded the market, it being a convenience to all, and this raised a general desire to have all the streets paved, and made the people more willing to submit to a tax for that purpose. After some time I drew a bill for paving the city and brought it into the Assembly. It was just before I went to England, in 1757, and did not pass till I was gone, and then with an alteration in the mode of assessment, which I thought not for the better; but with an additional provision for lighting as well as paving the streets, which was a great improvement. It was by a private person, the late Mr. John Clifton, giving a sample of the utility of lamps, by placing one at his door, that the people were first impressed with the idea of lighting all the city. The honour of this public benefit has also been ascribed to me, but it belongs truly to that gentleman. I did but follow his example, and have only some merit to claim respecting the form of our lamps, as differing from the globe lamps we were at first supplied with from London. They were found inconvenient in these respects: they admitted no air below; the smoke, therefore, did not readily go out[Pg 146] above, but circulated in the globe, lodged on its inside, and soon obstructed the light they were intended to afford; giving, besides, the daily trouble of wiping them clean: and an accidental stroke on one of them would demolish it, and render it totally useless. I therefore suggested the composing them of four flat panes, with a long funnel above to draw up the smoke, and crevices admitting air below to facilitate the ascent of the smoke; by this means they were kept clean, and did not grow dark in a few hours, as the London lamps do, but continued bright till morning; and an accidental stroke would generally break but a single pane, easily repaired. I have sometimes wondered that the Londoners did not, from the effect holes in the bottom of the globe-lamps used at Vauxhall have in keeping them clean, learn to have such holes in their street-lamps. But these holes being made for another purpose, viz., to communicate flame more suddenly to the wick by a little flax hanging down through them, the other use of letting in air seems not to have been thought of: and, therefore, after the lamps have been lit a few hours, the streets of London are very poorly illuminated.

The mention of these improvements puts me in mind of one I proposed, when in London, to Dr. Fothergill,[11] who was among the best men I have known, and a great promoter of useful projects. I had observed that the streets, when dry, were never swept, and the light dust carried away; but it was suffered to accumulate till wet weather reduced it to mud; and then, after lying some days so deep on the pavement that there was no crossing but in paths kept clean by poor people with brooms, it was with great labour raked together and thrown up into carts open above, the sides of which suffered some[Pg 147] of the slush at every jolt on the pavement to shake out and fall; sometimes to the annoyance of foot-passengers. The reason given for not sweeping the dusty streets was, that the dust would fly into the windows of shops and houses. An accidental occurrence had instructed me how much sweeping might be done in a little time; I found at my door in Craven-street one morning a poor woman sweeping my pavement with a birch broom; she appeared very pale and feeble, as just come out of a fit of sickness. I asked who employed her to sweep there; she said, "Nobody; but I am poor and in distress, and I sweep before gentlefolkses doors, and hopes they will give me something." I bid her sweep the whole street clean, and I would give her a shilling; this was at nine o'clock; at noon she came for the shilling. From the slowness I saw at first in her working, I could scarcely believe that the work was done so soon, and sent my servant to examine it, who reported that the whole street was swept perfectly clean, and all the dust placed in the gutter which was in the middle; and the next rain washed it quite away, so that the pavement and even the kennel were perfectly clean. I then judged that if that feeble woman could sweep such a street in three hours, a strong, active man might have done it in half the time. And here let me remark the convenience of having but one gutter in such a narrow street, running down its middle, instead of two, one on each side, near the footway. For where all the rain that falls on a street runs from the sides and meets in the middle, it forms there a current strong enough to wash away all the mud it meets with: but when divided into two channels, it is often too weak to cleanse either, and only makes the mud it finds more fluid, so that the wheels of carriages and feet of horses throw and dash it upon the foot pavement (which is thereby[Pg 148] rendered foul and slippery), and sometimes splash it upon those who are walking.

Some may think these trifling matters, not worth minding or relating; but when they consider that though dust blown into the eyes of a single person or into a single shop in a windy day is but of small importance, yet the great number of the instances in a populous city, and its frequent repetition, gives it weight and consequence, perhaps they will not censure very severely those who bestow some attention to affairs of this seemingly low nature. Human felicity is produced, not so much by great pieces of good fortune that seldom happen, as by little advantages that occur every day. Thus, if you teach a poor young man to shave himself and keep his razor in order, you may contribute more to the happiness of his life than in giving him a thousand guineas. This sum may be soon spent, the regret only remaining of having foolishly consumed it: but, in the other case, he escapes the frequent vexation of waiting for barbers, and of their sometimes dirty fingers, offensive breaths, and dull razors: he shaves when most convenient to him, and enjoys daily the pleasure of its being done with a good instrument. With these sentiments I have hazarded the few preceding pages, hoping they may afford hints which some time or other may be useful to a city I love (having lived many years in it very happily), and perhaps to some of our towns in America.

Having been some time employed by the postmaster-general of America as his comptroller in regulating the several offices and bringing the officers to account, I was, upon his death in 1753, appointed jointly with Mr. William Hu—— to succeed him, by a commission from the postmaster-general in England. The American office had hitherto never paid anything to that of Britain; we were to have £600 a year between us, if we could[Pg 149] make that sum out of the profits of the office. To do this, a variety of improvements were necessary; some of these were inevitably at first expensive; so that, in the first four years, the office became above £900 in debt to us. But it soon after began to repay us; and, before I was displaced by a freak of the ministers (of which I shall speak hereafter), we had brought it to yield three times as much clear revenue to the crown as the postoffice of Ireland. Since that imprudent transaction, they have received from it—not one farthing!

The business of the postoffice occasioned my taking a journey this year to New-England, where the college of Cambridge, of their own motion, presented me with the degree of Master of Arts. Yale College, in Connecticut, had before made me a similar compliment. Thus, without studying in any college, I am to partake of their honours. They were conferred in consideration of my improvements and discoveries in the electric branch of Natural Philosophy.

In 1754, war with France being again apprehended, a congress of commissioners from the different colonies was, by an order of the lords of trade, to be assembled at Albany, there to confer with the chiefs of the Six Nations concerning the means of defending both their country and ours. Governor Hamilton having received this order, acquainted the house with it, requesting they would furnish proper presents for the Indians, to be given on this occasion; and naming the speaker (Mr. Norris) and myself, to join Mr. John Penn and Mr. Secretary Peters, as commissioners to act for Pennsylvania. The house approved the nomination, and provided the goods for the presents, though they did not much like treating out of the province; and we met the other commissioners at Albany about the middle of June. In our way thither I projected and drew up a plan for the union of all the colonies under one government,[Pg 150] so far as might be necessary for defence and other important general purposes. As we passed through New-York, I had there shown my project to Mr. James Alexander and Mr. Kennedy, two gentlemen of great knowledge in public affairs, and being fortified by their approbation, I ventured to lay it before the Congress. It then appeared that several of the commissioners had formed plans of the same kind. A previous question was first taken, whether a union should be established, which passed in the affirmative unanimously. A committee was then appointed, one member from each colony, to consider the several plans and report. Mine happened to be preferred, and, with a few amendments, was accordingly reported. By this plan the general government was to be administered by a president-general, appointed and supported by the crown; and a grand council, to be chosen by the representatives of the people of the several colonies, met in their respective assemblies. The debates upon it in Congress went on daily, hand in hand with the Indian business. Many objections and difficulties were started, but at length they were all overcome, and the plan was unanimously agreed to, and copies ordered to be transmitted to the board of trade and to the assemblies of the several provinces. Its fate was singular: the assemblies did not adopt it, as they all thought there was too much prerogative in it, and in England it was judged to have too much of the democratic; the board of trade did not approve of it, nor recommend it for the approbation of his majesty: but another scheme was formed, supposed to answer the same purpose better, whereby the governors of the provinces, with some members of their respective councils, were to meet and order the raising of troops, building of forts, &c., and to draw on the treasury of Great Britain for the expense, which was afterward to be refunded by an act of Parliament laying a tax on[Pg 151] America. My plan, with my reasons in support of it, is to be found among my political papers that were printed. Being the winter following in Boston, I had much conversation with Governor Shirley upon both the plans. Part of what passed between us on this occasion may also be seen among those papers. The different and contrary reasons of dislike to my plan makes me suspect that it was really the true medium, and I am still of opinion it would have been happy for both sides if it had been adopted. The colonies, so united, would have been sufficiently strong to defend themselves: there would then have been no need of troops from England, of course the subsequent pretext for taxing America; and the bloody contest it occasioned would have been avoided: but such mistakes are not new: history is full of the errors of states and princes.

"Look, round the habitable world, how few

Know their own good, or, knowing it, pursue!"

Those who govern, having much business on their hands, do not generally like to take the trouble of considering and carrying into execution new projects. The best public measures are, therefore, seldom adopted from previous wisdom, but forced by the occasion.

The governor of Pennsylvania, in sending it down to the Assembly, expressed his approbation of the plan "as appearing to him to be drawn up with great clearness and strength of judgment, and therefore recommended it as well worthy their closest and most serious attention." The house, however, by the management of a certain member, took it up when I happened to be absent (which I thought not very fair), and reprobated it without paying any attention to it at all, to my no small mortification.

In my journey to Boston this year, I met at New-York with our new governor, Mr. Morris, just arrived[Pg 152] there from England, with whom I had been before intimately acquainted. He brought a commission to supersede Mr. Hamilton, who, tired with the disputes his proprietary instructions subjected him to, had resigned. Mr. Morris asked me if I thought he must expect as uncomfortable an administration. I said "No; you may, on the contrary, have a very comfortable one, if you will only take care not to enter into any dispute with the Assembly." "My dear friend," said he, pleasantly, "how can you advise my avoiding disputes? You know I love disputing; it is one of my greatest pleasures; however, to show the regard I have for your counsel, I promise you I will, if possible, avoid them." He had some reason for loving to dispute, being eloquent, an acute sophister, and, therefore, generally successful in argumentative conversation. He had been brought up to it from a boy, his father, as I have heard, accustoming his children to dispute with one another for his diversion, while sitting at table after dinner; but I think the practice was not wise; for, in the course of my observation, those disputing, contradicting, and confuting people are generally unfortunate in their affairs. They get victory sometimes, but they never get good-will, which would be of more use to them. We parted, he going to Philadelphia and I to Boston. In returning, I met at New-York with the votes of the Assembly of Pennsylvania, by which it appeared that, notwithstanding his promise to me, he and the house were already in high contention; and it was a continual battle between them as long as he retained the government. I had my share of it; for, as soon as I got back to my seat in the Assembly, I was put on every committee for answering his speeches and messages, and by the committees always desired to make the draughts. Our answers, as well as his messages, were often tart, and sometimes indecently abusive; and as he knew[Pg 153] I wrote for the Assembly, one might have imagined that, when we met, we could hardly avoid cutting throats. But he was so good-natured a man, that no personal difference between him and me was occasioned by the contest, and we often dined together. One afternoon, in the height of this public quarrel, we met in the street; "Franklin," said he, "you must go home with me and spend the evening; I am to have some company that you will like;" and, taking me by the arm, led me to his house. In gay conversation after supper, he told us jokingly that he much admired the idea of Sancho Panza, who, when it was proposed to give him a government, requested it might be a government of blacks; as then, if he could not agree with his people, he might sell them. One of his friends, who sat next to me, said, "Franklin, why do you continue to side with those Quakers? had you not better sell them? the proprietor would give you a good price." "The governor," said I, "has not yet blacked them enough." He, indeed, had laboured hard to blacken the Assembly in all his messages, but they wiped off his colouring as fast as he laid it on, and placed it in return thick upon his own face; so that, finding he was likely to be negrofied himself, he, as well as Mr. Hamilton, grew tired of the contest and quitted the government.

These public quarrels were all at bottom owing to the proprietaries our hereditary governors; who, when any expense was to be incurred for the defence of their province, with incredible meanness, instructed their deputies to pass no act for levying the necessary taxes, unless their vast estates were in the same act expressly exonerated; and they had even taken the bonds of these deputies to observe such instructions. The assemblies for three years held out against this injustice, though constrained to bend at last. At length Captain Denny, who was governor Morris's successor, ventured to disobey[Pg 154] those instructions; how that was brought about I shall show hereafter.

But I am got forward too fast with my story: there are still some transactions to be mentioned that happened during the administration of Governor Morris.

War being in a manner commenced with France, the government of Massachusetts Bay projected an attack upon Crown Point, and sent Mr. Quincy to Pennsylvania, and Mr. Pownal (afterward Governor Pownal) to New-York, to solicit assistance. As I was in the Assembly, knew its temper, and was Mr. Quincy's countryman, he applied to me for my influence and assistance: I dictated his address to them, which was well received. They voted an aid of ten thousand pounds, to be laid out in provisions. But the governor refusing his assent to their bill (which included this with other sums granted for the use of the crown) unless a clause were inserted exempting the proprietary estate from bearing any part of the tax that would be necessary, the Assembly, though very desirous of making their grant to New-England, were at a loss how to accomplish it. Mr. Quincy laboured hard with the governor to obtain his assent, but he was obstinate. I then suggested a method of doing the business without the governor, by orders on the trustees of the loan-office, which, by law, the Assembly had the right of drawing. There was, indeed, little or no money at the time in the office, and therefore I proposed that the orders should be payable in a year, and to bear an interest of five per cent.: with these orders I supposed the provisions might easily be purchased. The Assembly, with very little hesitation, adopted the proposal; the orders were immediately printed, and I was one of the committee directed to sign and dispose of them. The fund for paying them was the interest of all the paper currency then extant in the province upon loan,[Pg 155] together with the revenue arising from the excise, which, being known to be more than sufficient, they obtained credit, and were not only taken in payment for the provisions, but many moneyed people who had cash lying by them vested it in those orders, which they found advantageous, as they bore interest while upon hand, and might on any occasion be used as money; so that they were eagerly all bought up, and in a few weeks none of them were to be seen. Thus this important affair was by my means completed. Mr. Quincy returned thanks to the Assembly in a handsome memorial, went home highly pleased with the success of his embassy, and ever after bore for me the most cordial and affectionate friendship.

The British government, not choosing to permit the union of the colonies as proposed at Albany, and to trust that union with their defence, lest they should thereby grow too military and feel their own strength (suspicion and jealousies at this time being entertained of them), sent over General Braddock with two regiments of regular English troops for that purpose. He landed at Alexandria, in Virginia, and thence marched to Fredericktown, in Maryland, where he halted for carriages. Our Assembly, apprehending from some information that he had received violent prejudices against them as averse to the service, wished me to wait upon him, not as from them, but as postmaster-general, under the guise of proposing to settle with him the mode of conducting, with the greatest celerity and certainty, the despatches between him and the governors of the several provinces, with whom he must necessarily have continual correspondence, and of which they proposed to pay the expense. My son accompanied me on this journey. We found the general at Fredericktown, waiting impatiently for the return of those whom we had sent through the back parts of Maryland and Virginia to collect wagons.[Pg 156] I stayed with him several days, dined with him daily, and had full opportunities of removing his prejudices, by the information of what the Assembly had, before his arrival, actually done, and were still willing to do, to facilitate his operations. When I was about to depart, the returns of wagons to be obtained were brought in, by which it appeared that they amounted only to twenty-five, and not all of those were in serviceable condition. The general and the officers were surprised; declared the expedition was then at an end, being impossible; and exclaimed against the ministers for ignorantly sending them into a country destitute of the means of conveying their stores, baggage, &c., not less than one hundred and fifty wagons being necessary. I happened to say, I thought it was a pity they had not been landed in Pennsylvania, as in that country almost every farmer had his wagon. The general eagerly laid hold of my words, and said, "Then you, sir, who are a man of interest there, can probably procure them for us, and I beg you will undertake it." I asked what terms were to be offered the owners of the wagons; and I was desired to put on paper the terms that appeared to me necessary. This I did, and they were agreed to; and a commission and instructions accordingly prepared immediately. What those terms were will appear in the advertisement I published soon as I arrived at Lancaster; which being, from the great and sudden effect it produced, a piece of some curiosity, I shall insert it at length, as follows:

"ADVERTISEMENT.

"Lancaster, April 26th, 1753.

"Whereas, one hundred and fifty wagons, with four horses to each wagon, and fifteen hundred saddle or packhorses, are wanted for the service of his majesty's forces, now about to rendezvous at Will's Creek; and his excellency General Braddock, having[Pg 157] been pleased to empower me to contract for the hire of the same, I hereby give notice, that I shall attend for that purpose at Lancaster from this day to next Wednesday evening, and at York from next Thursday morning till Friday evening, where I shall be ready to agree for wagons and teams, or single horses, on the following terms, viz.: 1. That there shall be paid for each wagon, with four good horses and a driver, fifteen shillings per diem. And for each able horse, with a packsaddle or other saddle and furniture, two shillings per diem. And for each able horse without a saddle, eighteen pence per diem. 2. That the pay commence from the time of their joining the forces at Will's Creek (which must be on or before the 20th of May ensuing), and that a reasonable allowance be paid over and above for the time necessary for their travelling to Will's Creek and home again after their discharge. 3. Each wagon and team, and every saddle or packhorse, is to be valued by indifferent persons, chosen between me and the owner; and in case of the loss of any wagon, team, or other horse in the service, the price, according to such valuation, is to be allowed and paid. 4. Seven days' pay is to be advanced and paid in hand by me to the owner of each wagon and team, or horse, at the time of contracting, if required; and the remainder to be paid by General Braddock, or by the paymaster of the army, at the time of their discharge; or from time to time, as it shall be demanded. 5. No drivers of wagons or persons taking care of the hired horses are, on any account, to be called upon to do the duty of soldiers, or be otherwise employed than in conducting or taking care of their carriages or horses. 6. All oats, Indian corn, or other forage that wagons or horses bring to the camp, more than is necessary for the subsistence of the horses, is to be taken for the use of the army, and a reasonable price paid for the same.[Pg 158]

"Note.—My son, William Franklin, is empowered to enter into like contracts with any person in Cumberland county.

"B. Franklin."

I received of the general about eight hundred pounds, to be disbursed in advance-money to the wagon owners, &c.; but that sum being insufficient, I advanced upward of two hundred pounds more; and in two weeks, the one hundred and fifty wagons, with two hundred and fifty-nine carrying horses, were on their march for the camp. The advertisement promised payment according to the valuation, in case any wagons or horses should be lost. The owners, however, alleging they did not know General Braddock, or what dependance might be had on his promise, insisted on my bond for the performance, which I accordingly gave them.

While I was at the camp, supping one evening with the officers of Colonel Dunbar's regiment, he represented to me his concern for the subalterns, who, he said, were generally not in affluence, and could ill afford, in this dear country, to lay in the stores that might be necessary in so long a march through a wilderness where nothing was to be purchased. I commiserated their case, and resolved to endeavour procuring them some relief. I said nothing, however, to him of my intention, but wrote the next morning to the committee of Assembly, who had the disposition of some public money, warmly recommending the case of these officers to their consideration, and proposing that a present should be sent them of necessaries and refreshments. My son, who had some experience of a camp life and of its wants, drew up a list for me, which I enclosed in my letter. The committee approved, and used such diligence that, conducted by my son, the stores arrived at the camp as soon as[Pg 159] the wagons. They consisted of twenty parcels, each containing

6 lbs. Loaf Sugar,

6 do. Muscovado do.,

1 do. Green Tea,

1 do. Bohea do.,

6 do. Ground Coffee,

6 do. Chocolate,

1-2 chest best white Biscuit,

1-2 lb. Pepper,

1 quart white Vinegar,

1 Gloucester Cheese,

1 keg containing 20 lbs. good Butter,

2 doz. old Madeira Wine,

2 gallons Jamaica Spirits,

1 bottle Flour of Mustard,

2 well-cured Hams,

1-2 dozen dried Tongues,

6 lbs. Rice,

6 do. Raisins.

These parcels, well packed, were placed on as many horses, each parcel, with the horse, being intended as a present for one officer. They were very thankfully received, and the kindness acknowledged by letters to me from the colonels of both regiments, in the most grateful terms. The general, too, was highly satisfied with my conduct in procuring him the wagons, &c., &c., and readily paid my account of disbursements; thanking me repeatedly, and requesting my farther assistance in sending provisions after him. I undertook this also, and was busily employed in it till we heard of his defeat; advancing for the service, of my own money, upward of one thousand pounds sterling, of which I sent him an account. It came to his hands, luckily for me, a few days before the battle, and he returned me immediately an order on the paymaster for the round sum of one thousand pounds, leaving the remainder to the next account. I consider this[Pg 160] payment as good luck, having never been able to obtain that remainder, of which more hereafter.

This general was, I think, a brave man, and might probably have made a figure as a good officer in some European war; but he had too much self-confidence, too high an opinion of the validity of regular troops, and too mean a one of both Americans and Indians. George Croghan, our Indian interpreter, joined him on his march with one hundred of those people, who might have been of great use to his army as guides, scouts, &c., if he had treated them kindly; but he slighted and neglected them, and they gradually left him. In conversation with him one day, he was giving me some account of his intended progress. "After taking Fort Duquesne," said he, "I am to proceed to Niagara; and having taken that, to Frontenac, if the season will allow time, and I suppose it will; for Duquesne can hardly detain me above three or four days; and then I see nothing that can obstruct my march to Niagara." Having before revolved in my mind the long line his army must make in their march by a very narrow road, to be cut for them through the woods and bushes; and also what I had read of a former defeat of fifteen hundred French who invaded the Illinois country, I had conceived some doubts and some fears for the event of the campaign. But I ventured only to say, "To be sure, sir, if you arrive well before Duquesne, with the fine troops so well provided with artillery, the fort, though completely fortified, and assisted with a very strong garrison, can probably make but a short resistance. The only danger I apprehend of obstruction to your march is from the ambuscades of the Indians, who, by constant practice, are dexterous in laying and executing them: and the slender line, near four miles long, which your army must make, may expose it to be attacked by surprise in its flanks, and to be cut like a thread into several pieces, which,[Pg 161] from their distance, cannot come up in time to support each other." He smiled at my ignorance, and replied, "These savages may indeed be a formidable enemy to your raw American militia; but upon the king's regular and disciplined troops, sir, it is impossible they should make any impression." I was conscious of an impropriety in my disputing with a military man in matters of his profession, and said no more. The enemy, however, did not take the advantage of his army which I apprehend its long line of march exposed it to, but let it advance without interruption till within nine miles of the place; and then, when more in a body (for it had just passed a river, where the front had halted till all were come over), and in a more open part of the woods than any it had passed, attacked its advanced guard by a heavy fire from behind trees and bushes; which was the first intelligence the general had of an enemy's being near him. This guard being disordered, the general hurried the troops up to their assistance, which was done in great confusion, through wagons, baggage, and cattle; and presently the fire came upon their flank: the officers, being on horseback, were more easily distinguished, picked out as marks, and fell very fast; and the soldiers were crowded together in a huddle, having or hearing no orders, and standing to be shot at till two thirds of them were killed; and then, being seized with a panic, the remainder fled with precipitation. The wagoners took each a horse out of his team and scampered; their example was immediately followed by others; so that all the wagons, provisions, artillery, and stores were left to the enemy. The general, being wounded, was brought off with difficulty; his secretary, Mr. Shirley, was killed by his side; and out of eighty-six officers, sixty-three were killed or wounded, and seven hundred and fourteen men killed out of eleven hundred. These eleven hundred had been picked men[Pg 162] from the whole army; the rest had been left behind with Colonel Dunbar, who was to follow with the heavier part of the stores, provisions, and baggage. The fliers, not being pursued, arrived at Dunbar's camp, and the panic they brought with them instantly seized him and all his people. And though he had now above one thousand men, and the enemy who had beaten Braddock did not at most exceed four hundred Indians and French together, instead of proceeding and endeavouring to recover some of the lost honour, he ordered all the stores, ammunition, &c., to be destroyed, that he might have more horses to assist his flight towards the settlements, and less lumber to remove. He was there met with requests from the Governor of Virginia, Maryland, and Pennsylvania, that he would post his troops on the frontiers, so as to afford some protection to the inhabitants; but he continued his hasty march through all the country, not thinking himself safe till he arrived at Philadelphia, where the inhabitants could protect him. This whole transaction gave us Americans the first suspicion that our exalted ideas of the prowess of British regular troops had not been well founded.

In their first march, too, from their landing till they got beyond the settlements, they had plundered and stripped the inhabitants, totally ruining some poor families, besides insulting, abusing, and confining the people if they remonstrated. This was enough to put us out of conceit of such defenders, if we had really wanted any. How different was the conduct of our French friends in 1781, who, during a march through the most inhabited part of our country, from Rhode Island to Virginia, near seven hundred miles, occasioned not the smallest complaint for the loss of a pig, a chicken, or even an apple!

Captain Orme, who was one of the general's aidsdecamp, and being grievously wounded, was[Pg 163] brought off with him, and continued with him to his death, which happened in a few days, told me he was totally silent all the first day, and at night only said, "Who would have thought it?" That he was silent again the following day, saying only at last, "We shall better know how to deal with them another time;" and died in a few minutes after.

The secretary's papers, with all the general's orders, instructions, and correspondence, falling into the enemy's hands, they selected and translated into French a number of the articles, which they printed, to prove the hostile intentions of the British court before the declaration of war. Among these I saw some letters of the general to the ministry, speaking highly of the great service I had rendered the army, and recommending me to their notice. David Hume, who was some years after secretary to Lord Hertford when minister in France, and afterward to General Conway when secretary of state, told me he had seen among the papers in that office letters from Braddock highly recommending me. But the expedition having been unfortunate, my service, it seems, was not thought of much value, for those recommendations were never of any use to me. As to rewards from himself, I asked only one, which was, that he would give orders to his officers not to enlist any more of our bought servants, and that he would discharge such as had been already enlisted. This he readily granted, and several were accordingly returned to their masters on my application. Dunbar, when the command devolved on him, was not so generous. He being at Philadelphia on his retreat, or, rather, flight, I applied to him for the discharge of the servants of three poor farmers of Lancaster county that he had enlisted, reminding him of the late general's orders on that head. He promised me that, if the masters would come to him at Trenton, where he should be in a few days on his march to New-York, he would[Pg 164] there deliver their men to them. They accordingly were at the expense and trouble of going to Trenton, and there he refused to perform his promise, to their great loss and disappointment.

As soon as the loss of the wagons and horses was generally known, all the owners came upon me for the valuation which I had given bond to pay. Their demands gave me a great deal of trouble: I acquainted them that the money was ready in the paymaster's hands, but the order for paying it must first be obtained from General Shirley, and that I had applied for it; but he being at a distance, an answer could not soon be received, and they must have patience. All this, however, was not sufficient to satisfy, and some began to sue me: General Shirley at length relieved me from this terrible situation, by appointing commissioners to examine the claims, and ordering payment. They amounted to near twenty thousand pounds, which to pay would have ruined me.

Before we had the news of this defeat, the two Doctors Bond came to me with a subscription-paper for raising money to defray the expense of a grand fireworks, which it was intended to exhibit at a rejoicing on receiving the news of our taking Fort Duquesne. I looked grave, and said, "It would, I thought, be time enough to prepare the rejoicing when we knew we should have occasion to rejoice." They seemed surprised that I did not immediately comply with their proposal. "Why the d—l," said one of them, "you surely don't suppose that the fort will not be taken?" "I don't know that it will not be taken; but I know that the events of war are subject to great uncertainty." I gave them the reasons of my doubting: the subscription was dropped, and the projectors thereby missed the mortification they would have undergone if the fireworks had been prepared. Dr. Bond, on some other occasion afterward, said that he did not like Franklin's forebodings.[Pg 165]

Governor Morris, who had continually worried the Assembly with message after message, before the defeat of Braddock, to beat them into the making of acts to raise money for the defence of the province, without taxing, among others, the proprietary estates, and had rejected all their bills for not having such an exempting clause, now redoubled his attacks with more hope of success, the danger and necessity being greater. The Assembly, however, continued firm, believing they had justice on their side, and that it would be giving up an essential right if they suffered the governor to amend their money-bills. In one of the last, indeed, which was for granting fifty thousand pounds, his proposed amendment was only of a single word: the bill expressed "that all estates, real and personal, were to be taxed; those of the proprietaries not excepted." His amendment was, for not read only. A small but very material alteration! However, when the news of the disaster reached England, our friends there, whom we had taken care to furnish will all the Assembly's answers to the governor's messages, raised a clamour against the proprietaries for their meanness and injustice in giving their governor such instructions; some going so far as to say that, by obstructing the defence of their province, they forfeited their right to it. They were intimidated by this, sent orders to their receiver-general to add five thousand pounds of their money to whatever sum might be given by the Assembly for such purpose. This being testified to the house, was accepted in lieu of their share of a general tax, and a new bill was formed, with an exempting clause, which passed accordingly. By this act I was appointed one of the commissioners for disposing of the money, sixty thousand pounds. I had been active in modelling the bill and procuring its passage, and had, at the same time, drawn one for establishing and disciplining a voluntary militia, which[Pg 166] I carried through the house without much difficulty, as care was taken in it to leave the Quakers at liberty. To promote the association necessary to form the militia, I wrote a dialogue stating and answering all the objections I could think of to such a militia, which was printed, and had, as I thought great effect. While the several companies in the city and country were forming and learning their exercise, the governor prevailed with me to take charge of our northwestern frontier, which was infested by the enemy, and provide for the defence of the inhabitants by raising troops and building a line of forts. I undertook this military business, though I did not conceive myself well qualified for it. He gave me a commission, with full powers, and a parcel of blank commissions for officers, to be given to whom I thought fit. I had but little difficulty in raising men, having soon five hundred and sixty under my command. My son, who had in the preceding war been an officer in the army raised against Canada, was my aiddecamp, and of great use to me. The Indians had burned Gnadenhutten, a village settled by the Moravians, and massacred the inhabitants; but the place was thought a good situation for one of the forts. In order to march thither, I assembled the companies at Bethlehem, the chief establishment of those people; I was surprised to find it in so good a posture of defence; the destruction of Gnadenhutten had made them apprehend danger. The principal buildings were defended by a stockade; they had purchased a quantity of arms and ammunition from New-York, and had even placed quantities of small paving stones between the windows of their high stone houses, for their women to throw them down upon the heads of any Indians that should attempt to force into them. The armed brethren, too, kept watch, and relieved each other on guard as methodically as in any garrison town. In conversation with the bishop,[Pg 167] Spangenberg, I mentioned my surprise; for, knowing that they had obtained an act of parliament exempting them from military duties in the colonies, I had supposed they were conscientiously scrupulous of bearing arms. He answered me, "That it was not one of their established principles; but that, at the time of their obtaining that act, it was thought to be a principle with many of their people. On this occasion, however, they, to their surprise, found it adopted by but a few." It seems they were either deceived in themselves or deceived the parliament; but common sense, aided by present danger, will sometimes be too strong for whimsical opinions.

It was the beginning of January when we set out upon this business of building forts; I sent one detachment towards the Minisink, with instructions to erect one for the security of that upper part of the country, and another to the lower part with similar instructions; and I concluded to go myself with the rest of my force to Gnadenhutten, where a fort was thought more immediately necessary. The Moravians procured me five wagons for our tools, stores, baggage, &c. Just before we left Bethlehem, eleven farmers, who had been driven from their plantations by the Indians, came to me requesting a supply of firearms, that they might go back and bring off their cattle. I gave them each a gun with suitable ammunition. We had not marched many miles before it began to rain, and it continued raining all day; there were no habitations on the road to shelter us till we arrived near night at the house of a German, where, and in his barn, we were all huddled together as wet as water could make us. It was well we were not attacked in our march, for our arms were of the most ordinary sort, and our men could not keep the locks of their guns dry. The Indians are dexterous in contrivances for that purpose, which we had not. They met[Pg 168] that day the eleven poor farmers above mentioned, and killed ten of them; the one that escaped informed us that his and his companions' guns would not go off, the priming being wet with the rain. The next day, being fair, we continued our march, and arrived at the desolate Gnadenhutten; there was a mill near, round which were left several pine boards, with which we soon hutted ourselves; an operation the more necessary at that inclement season, as we had no tents. Our first work was to bury more effectually the dead we found there, who had been half interred by the country people; the next morning our fort was planned and marked out, the circumference measuring four hundred and fifty-five feet, which would require as many palisades to be made, one with another, of a foot diameter each. Our axes, of which we had seventy, were immediately set to work to cut down trees; and our men being dexterous in the use of them, great despatch was made. Seeing the trees fall so fast, I had the curiosity to look at my watch when two men began to cut a pine; in six minutes they had it upon the ground, and I found it of fourteen inches diameter: each pine made three palisades of eighteen feet long, pointed at one end. While these were preparing our other men dug a trench all round of three feet deep, in which the palisades were to be planted; and the bodies being taken off our wagons, and the fore and hind wheels separated by taking out the pin which united the two parts of the perch, we had ten carriages, with two horses each, to bring the palisades from the woods to the spot. When they were set up, our carpenters built a platform of boards all round within, about six feet high, for the men to stand on when to fire through the loopholes. We had one swivel gun, which we mounted on one of the angles, and fired it as soon as fixed, to let the Indians know, if any were within hearing, that we had such pieces; and thus our fort[Pg 169] (if that name may be given to so miserable a stockade) was finished in a week, though it rained so hard every other day that the men could not well work.

This gave me occasion to observe, that when men are employed they are best contented, for on the days they worked they were good-natured and cheerful, and with the consciousness of having done a good day's work they spent the evening jollily; but on our idle days they were mutinous and quarrelsome, finding fault with the pork, the bread, &c., and we were continually in bad humour, which put me in mind of a sea-captain, whose rule it was to keep his men constantly at work; and when his mate once told him that they had done everything, and there was nothing farther to employ them about, "Oh," said he, "make them scour the anchor."

This kind of fort, however contemptible, is a sufficient defence against Indians who had no cannon. Finding ourselves now posted securely, and having a place to retreat to on occasion, we ventured out in parties to scour the adjacent country. We met with no Indians, but we found the places on the neighbouring hills where they had lain to watch our proceedings. There was an art in their contrivance of those places that seems worth mentioning. It being winter, a fire was necessary for them; but a common fire on the surface of the ground would, by its light, have discovered their position at a distance; they had therefore dug holes in the ground, about three feet in diameter and somewhat deeper; we found where they had, with their hatchets, cut off the charcoal from the sides of burnt logs lying in the woods. With these coals they had made small fires in the bottom of the holes, and we observed among the weeds and grass the prints of their bodies, made by their lying all round with their legs hanging down in the holes to keep their feet warm, which with them is an essential point.[Pg 170] This kind of fire, so managed, could not discover them either by its light, flame, sparks, or even smoke; it appeared that the number was not great, and it seems they saw we were too many to be attacked by them with prospect of advantage.

I had hardly got my fort well stored with provisions when I received a letter from the governor acquainting me that he had called the Assembly, and wished my attendance there, if the posture of affairs on the frontiers was such that my remaining there was no longer necessary. My friends, too, of the Assembly, pressing me by their letters to be, if possible, at the meeting; and my three intended forts being now completed, and the inhabitants contented to remain on their farms under that protection, I resolved to return, the more willingly, as a New-England officer, Colonel Clapham, experienced in Indian war, being on a visit to our establishment, consented to accept the command. I gave him a commission, and, parading the garrison, had it read before them, and introduced him to them as an officer who, from his skill in military affairs, was much more fit to command them than myself, and, giving them a little exhortation, took my leave. I was escorted as far as

Bethlehem, where I rested a few days to recover from the fatigue I had undergone. The first night, lying in a good bed, I could hardly sleep, it was so different from my hard lodging on the floor of a hut at Gnadenhutten, with only a blanket or two. While at Bethlehem I inquired a little into the practices of the Moravians; some of them had accompanied me, and all were very kind to me. I found that they worked for a common stock, ate at common tables, and slept in common dormitories, great numbers together. In the dormitories I observed loopholes at certain distances all along just under the ceiling, which I thought judiciously placed for change of air. I went to their church, where I was entertained with good music,[Pg 171] the organ being accompanied with violins, haut-boys, flutes, clarinets, &c. I understood their sermons were not usually preached to mixed congregations of men, women, and children, as is our common practice, but that they assembled sometimes the married men, at other times their wives, then the young men, the young women, and the little children, each division by itself. The sermon I heard was to the latter, who came in and were placed in rows on benches, the boys under the conduct of a young man, their tutor, and the girls conducted by a young woman. The discourse seemed well adapted to their capacities, and was delivered in a pleasing, familiar manner, coaxing them, as it were, to be good. They behaved very orderly, but looked pale and unhealthy, which made me suspect they were kept too much within doors, or not allowed sufficient exercise. I inquired concerning the Moravian marriages, whether the report was true that they were by lot; I was told that lots were used only in particular cases: that generally, when a young man found himself disposed to marry, he informed the elders of his class, who consulted the elder ladies that governed the young women. As these elders of the different sexes were well acquainted with the tempers and dispositions of their respective pupils, they could best judge what matches were suitable, and their judgments were generally acquiesced in. But if, for example, it should happen that two or three young women were found to be equally proper for the young man, the lot was then recurred to. I objected, if the matches are not made by the mutual choice of the parties, some of them may chance to be very unhappy. "And so they may," answered my informer, "if you let the parties choose for themselves:" which, indeed, I could not deny.

Being returned to Philadelphia, I found the association went on with great success, the inhabitants[Pg 172] that were not Quakers having pretty generally come into it, formed themselves into companies, and chose their captains, lieutenants, and ensigns, according to the new law. Dr. Bond visited me, and gave me an account of the pains he had taken to spread a general good-liking to the law, and ascribed much to those endeavours. I had the vanity to ascribe all to my dialogue; however, not knowing but that he might be in the right, I let him enjoy his opinion, which I take to be generally the best way in such cases. The officers meeting, chose me to be colonel of the regiment, which I this time accepted. I forget how many companies we had, but we paraded about twelve hundred well-looking men, with a company of artillery, who had been furnished with six brass field-pieces, which they had become so expert in the use of as to fire twelve times in a minute. The first time I reviewed my regiment, they accompanied me to my house, and would salute me with some rounds fired before my door, which shook down and broke several glasses of my electrical apparatus. And my new honour proved not much less brittle; for all our commissions were soon after broken by a repeal of the law in England.

During this short time of my colonelship, being about to set out on a journey to Virginia, the officers of my regiment took it into their heads that it would be proper for them to escort me out of town as far as the lower ferry; just as I was getting on horseback they came to my door, between thirty and forty, mounted, and all in their uniforms. I had not been previously acquainted with their project, or I should have prevented it, being naturally averse to the assuming of state on any occasion; and I was a good deal chagrined at their appearance, as I could not avoid their accompanying me. What made it worse was, that, as soon as we began to move, they drew their swords and rode with[Pg 173] them naked all the way. Somebody wrote an account of this to the proprietor, and it gave him great offence. No such honour had been paid him when in the province, nor to any of his governors; and he said it was only proper to princes of the blood royal, which may be true for aught I know, who was and still am ignorant of the etiquette in such cases. This silly affair, however, greatly increased his rancour against me, which was before considerable, on account of my conduct in the Assembly respecting the exemption of his estate from taxation, which I had always opposed very warmly, and not without severe reflections on the meanness and injustice in contending for it. He accused me to the ministry as being the great obstacle to the king's service, preventing, by my influence in the house, the proper form of the bills for raising money; and he instanced the parade with my officers as a proof of my having an intention to take the government of the province out of his hands by force. He also applied to Sir

Everard Faukener, the postmaster-general, to deprive me of my office; but it had no other effect than to procure from Sir Everard a gentle admonition.

Notwithstanding the continual wrangle between the governor and the house, in which I, as a member, had so large a share, there still subsisted a civil intercourse between that gentleman and myself, and we never had any personal difference. I have sometimes since thought, that his little or no resentment against me, for the answers it was known I drew up to his messages, might be the effect of professional habit, and that, being bred a lawyer, he might consider us both as merely advocates for contending clients in a suit; he for the proprietaries, and I for the Assembly: he would, therefore, sometimes call in a friendly way to advise with me on difficult points; and sometimes, though not often, take my advice. We acted in concert to supply[Pg 174] Braddock's army with provisions; and when the shocking news arrived of his defeat, the governor sent in haste for me, to consult with him on measures for preventing the desertion of the back counties. I forget now the advice I gave, but I think it was that Dunbar should be written to, and prevailed with, if possible, to post his troops on the frontiers for their protection, until, by re-enforcements from the colonies, he might be able to proceed in the expedition: and, after my return from the frontier, he would have had me undertake the conduct of such an expedition with provincial troops, for the reduction of Fort Duquesne (Dunbar and his men being otherwise employed); and he proposed to commission me as a general. I had not so good an opinion of my military abilities as he professed to have, and I believe his professions must have exceeded his real sentiments: but probably he might think that my popularity would facilitate the business with the men, and influence in the Assembly the grant of money to pay for it; and that, perhaps, without taxing the proprietary. Finding me not so forward to engage as he expected, the project was dropped; and he soon after left the government, being superseded by Captain Denny.

Before I proceed in relating the part I had in public affairs under this new governor's administration, it may not be amiss to give here some account of the rise and progress of my philosophical reputation.

In 1746, being at Boston, I met there with a Dr. Spence, who was lately arrived from Scotland, and showed me some electric experiments. They were imperfectly performed, as he was not very expert; but, being on a subject quite new to me, they equally surprised and pleased me. Soon after my return to Philadelphia, our library company received from Mr. Peter Collinson, F.R.S., of London, a present of a glass tube, with some account of the use of it[Pg 175] in making such experiments. I eagerly seized the opportunity of repeating what I had seen at Boston; and, by much practice, acquired great readiness in performing those also which we had an account of from England, adding a number of new ones. I say much practice, for my house was constantly full for some time with persons who came to see these new wonders. To divide a little this encumbrance among my friends, I caused a number of similar tubes to be blown in our glasshouse, with which they furnished themselves, so that we had at length several performers. Among these the principal was Mr. Kinnersly, an ingenious neighbour, who, being out of business, I encouraged to undertake showing the experiments for money, and drew up for him two lectures, in which the experiments were ranged in such order, and accompanied with explanations in such method, as that the foregoing should assist in comprehending the following. He procured an elegant apparatus for the purpose, in which all the little machines that I had roughly made for myself were neatly formed by instrument-makers. His lectures were well-attended and gave great satisfaction; and, after some time, he went through the colonies, exhibiting them in every capital town, and picked up some money. In the West India islands, indeed, it was with difficulty the experiments could be made, from the general moisture of the air.

Obliged as we were to Mr. Collinson for the present of the tube, &c., I thought it right he should be informed of our success in using it, and wrote him several letters containing accounts of our experiments. He got them read in the Royal Society, where they were not at first thought worth so much notice as to be printed in their transactions. One paper which I wrote for Mr. Kinnersly, on the sameness of lightning with electricity, I sent to Mr. Mitchel, an acquaintance of mine, and one of the members also of that society; who wrote me word[Pg 176] that it had been read, but was laughed at by the connoisseurs. The papers, however, being shown to Dr.

Fothergill, he thought them of too much value to be stifled, and advised the printing of them. Mr. Collinson then gave them to Cave for publication in his Gentleman's Magazine; but he chose to print them separately in a pamphlet, and Dr. Fothergill wrote the preface. Cave, it seems, judged rightly for his profession; for, by the additions that arrived afterward, they swelled to a quarto volume; which has had five editions, and cost him nothing for copy-money.

It was, however, some time before those papers were much taken notice of in England. A copy of them happening to fall into the hands of the Count de Buffon (a philosopher deservedly of great reputation in France, and, indeed, all over Europe), he prevailed with Monsieur Dubourg to translate them into French; and they were printed at Paris. The publication offended the Abbé Nollet, preceptor in Natural Philosophy to the royal family, and an able experimenter, who had formed and published a theory of electricity, which then had the general vogue. He could not at first believe that such a work came from America, and said it must have been fabricated by his enemies at Paris, to oppose his system. Afterward, having been assured that there really existed such a person as Franklin at Philadelphia (which he had doubted), he wrote and published a volume of letters, chiefly addressed to me, defending his theory, and denying the verity of my experiments, and of the positions deduced from them. I once purposed answering the abbé, and actually began the answer; but, on consideration that my writings contained a description of experiments which any one might repeat and verify, and, if not to be verified, could not be defended; or of observations offered as conjectures, and not delivered dogmatically, therefore not laying me under any[Pg 177] obligation to defend them; and reflecting that a dispute between two persons, written in different languages, might be lengthened greatly by mistranslations, and thence misconceptions of another's meaning, much of one of the abbé's letters being founded on an error in the translation, I concluded to let my papers shift for themselves, believing it was better to spend what time I could spare from public business in making new experiments than in disputing about those already made. I therefore never answered Monsieur Nollet, and the event gave me no cause to repent my silence; for my friend, Monsieur Le Roy, of the Royal Academy of Sciences, took up my cause and refuted him: my book was translated into the Italian, German, and Latin languages; and the doctrine it contained was, by degrees, generally adopted by the philosophers of Europe, in preference to that of the abbé; so that he lived to see himself the last of his sect, except Monsieur B——, of Paris, his eléve and immediate disciple.

What gave my book the more sudden and general celebrity, was the success of one of its proposed experiments, made by Messieurs Dalibard and Delor, at Marly, for drawing lightning from the clouds. This engaged the public attention everywhere. Monsieur Delor, who had an apparatus for experimental philosophy, and lectured in that branch of science, undertook to repeat what he called the Philadelphia experiments; and after they were performed before the king and court, all the curious of Paris flocked to see them. I will not swell this narrative with an account of that capital experiment, nor of the infinite pleasure I received in the success of a similar one I made soon after with a kite at Philadelphia, as both are to be found in the histories of electricity. Dr. Wright, an English physician, when at Paris, wrote to a friend, who was of the Royal Society, an account of the high esteem[Pg 178] my experiments were in among the learned abroad, and of their wonder that my writings had been so little noticed in England. The society, on this, resumed the consideration of the letters that had been read to them, and the celebrated Dr. Watson drew up a summary account of them, and of all I had afterward sent to England on the subject, which he accompanied with some praise of the writer. This summary was then printed in their transactions: and some members of the society in London, particularly the very ingenious Mr. Canton, having verified the experiment of procuring lightning from the clouds by a pointed rod, and acquainted them with the success, they soon made me more than amends for the slight with which they had before treated me. Without my having made any application for that honour, they chose me a member; and voted that I should be excused the customary payments, which would have amounted to twenty-five guineas; and ever since have given me their transactions gratis.[12] They also presented me with[Pg 179] the gold medal of Sir Godfrey Copley, for the year 1753, the delivery of which was accompanied by a very handsome speech of the president, Lord Macclesfield, wherein I was highly honoured.

Our new governor, Captain Denny, brought over for me the before-mentioned medal from the Royal Society, which he presented to me at an entertainment given him by the city. He accompanied it with very polite expressions of his esteem for me, having, as he said, been long acquainted with my character. After dinner, when the company, as was customary at that time, were engaged in drinking, he took me aside into another room, and acquainted me that he had been advised by his friends in England to cultivate a friendship with me, as one who was capable of giving him the best advice, and of contributing most effectually to render his administration easy. That he therefore desired of all things to have a good understanding with me, and he begged me to be assured of his readiness on all occasions to render me any service that might be in his power. He said much to me also of the proprietors' good disposition towards the province, and of the advantage it would be to us all, and to me in particular, if the opposition that had been so long[Pg 180] continued to his measures was dropped, and harmony restored between him and the people, in effecting which it was thought no one could be more serviceable than myself; and I might depend on adequate acknowledgments and recompenses, &c. The drinkers, finding we did not return immediately to the table, sent us a decanter of Madeira, which the governor made liberal use of, and, in proportion, became more profuse of his solicitations and promises. My answers were to this purpose; that my circumstances, thanks to God, were such as to make proprietary favours unnecessary to me; and that, being a member of the Assembly, I could not possibly accept of any; that, however, I had no personal enmity to the proprietary, and that, whenever the public measures he proposed should appear to be for the good of the people, no one would espouse and forward them more zealously than myself; my past opposition had been founded on this, that the measures which had been urged were evidently intended to serve the proprietary interest with great prejudice to that of the people. That I was much obliged to him (the governor) for his profession of regard to me, and that he might rely on everything in my power to render his administration as easy as possible, hoping, at the same time, that he had not brought the same unfortunate instructions his predecessors had been hampered with. On this he did not then explain himself; but when he afterward came to do business with the Assembly, they appeared again; the disputes were renewed, and I was as active as ever in the opposition, being the penman, first of the request to have a communication of the instructions, and then of the remarks upon them, which may be found in the Votes of the Times, and in the Historical Review I afterward published: but between us personally no enmity arose; we were often together; he was a man of letters, and had seen much of the world, and was[Pg 181] entertaining and pleasing in conversation. He gave me information that my old friend Ralph was still alive, that he was esteemed one of the best political writers in England; had been employed in the dispute between Prince Frederic and the king, and had obtained a pension of three hundred pounds a year; that his reputation was indeed small as a poet, but his prose was thought as good as any man's.

The Assembly finally finding the proprietary obstinately persisted in shackling the deputies with instructions, inconsistent not only with the privileges of the people, but with the service of the crown, resolved to petition the king against them, and appointed me their agent to go over to England to present and support the petition. The house had sent up a bill to the governor, granting a sum of sixty thousand pounds for the king's use (ten thousand pounds of which was subjected to the orders of the then general, Lord Loudon), which the governor, in compliance with his instructions, absolutely refused to pass. I had agreed with Captain Morris, of the packet at New-York, for my passage, and my stores were put on board; when Lord Loudon arrived at Philadelphia, expressly, as he told me, to endeavour an accommodation between the governor and Assembly, that his majesty's service might not be obstructed by their dissensions. Accordingly, he desired the governor and myself to meet him, that he might hear what was to be said on both sides. We met and discussed the business: in behalf of the Assembly, I urged the various arguments that may be found in the public papers of that time, which were of my writing, and are printed with the minutes of the Assembly; and the governor pleaded his instructions, the bond he had given to observe them, and his ruin if he disobeyed; yet seemed not unwilling to hazard himself if Lord Loudon would advise it. This his lordship did not choose to do, though I once thought I had nearly prevailed with[Pg 182] him to do it; but finally he rather chose to urge the compliance of the Assembly; and he entreated me to use my endeavours with them for that purpose, declaring that he would spare none of the king's troops for the defence of our frontiers, and that, if we did not continue to provide for that defence ourselves, they must remain exposed to the enemy. I acquainted the house with what had passed, and presenting them with a set of resolutions I had drawn up, declaring our rights, that we did not relinquish our claim to those rights, but only suspended the exercise of them on this occasion, through force, against which we protested, they at length agreed to drop the bill, and frame another conformably to the proprietary instructions; this, of course, the governor passed, and I was then at liberty to proceed on my voyage. But, in the mean time, the packet had sailed with my sea stores, which was some loss to me, and my only recompense was his lordship's thanks for my service, all the credit of obtaining the accommodation falling to his share.

He set out for New-York before me; and as the time for despatching the packet-boats was in his disposition, and there were two then remaining there, one of which, he said, was to sail very soon, I requested to know the precise time, that I might not miss her by any delay of mine. The answer was, "I have given out that she is to sail on Saturday next; but I may let you know, entre nous, that if you are there by Monday morning, you will be in time, but do not delay longer!" By some accidental hinderance at a ferry, it was Monday noon before I arrived, and I was much afraid she might have sailed, as the wind was fair; but I was soon made easy by the information that she was still in the harbour, and would not move till next day. One would imagine that I was now on the very point of departing for Europe; I thought so, but I was not then so well acquainted with his lordship's character,[Pg 183] of which indecision was one of the strongest features: I shall give some instances. It was about the beginning of April that I came to New-York, and I think it was near the end of June before we sailed. There were then two of the packet-boats which had been long in readiness, but were detained for the general's letters, which were always to be ready to-morrow. Another packet arrived; she too was detained, and before we sailed a fourth was expected. Ours was the first to be despatched, as having been there longest. Passengers were engaged for all, and some extremely impatient to be gone, and the merchants uneasy about their letters, and for the orders they had given for ensurance (it being war-time) and for autumnal goods; but their anxiety availed nothing; his lordship's letters were not ready: and yet, whoever waited on him found him always at his desk, pen in hand, and concluded he must needs write abundantly.

Going myself one morning to pay my respects, I found in his antechamber one Innis, a messenger of Philadelphia, who had come thence express, with a packet from Governor Denny for the general. He delivered to me some letters from my friends there, which occasioned my inquiring when he was to return, and where he lodged, that I might send some letters by him. He told me he was ordered to call to-morrow at nine for the general's answer to the governor, and should set off immediately; I put my letters into his hands the same day. A fortnight after I met him again in the same place. "So you are soon returned, Innis!" "Returned; no, I am not gone yet." "How so?" "I have called here this and every morning these two weeks past for his lordship's letters, and they are not yet ready." "Is it possible, when he is so great a writer; for I see him constantly at his escritoir." "Yes," said Innis, "but he is like St. George on the signs; always on horseback but never rides on." This observation[Pg 184] of the messenger was, it seems, well founded; for, when in England, I understood that Mr. Pitt (afterward Lord Chatham) gave it as one reason for removing this general and sending Generals Amherst and Wolf, that the minister never heard from him, and could not know what he was doing.

This daily expectation of sailing, and all the three packets going down to Sandy Hook to join the fleet there, the passengers thought it best to be on board, lest, by a sudden order, the ships should sail and they be left behind. There, if I remember, we were about six weeks, consuming our sea stores and obliged to procure more. At length the fleet sailed, the general and all his army on board bound to Louisburg, with intent to besiege and take that fortress; all the packet-boats in company ordered to attend the general's ship, ready to receive his despatches when they should be ready. We were out five days before we got a letter with leave to part, and then our ship quitted the fleet and steered for England. The other two packets he still detained, carried them with him to Halifax, where he stayed some time to exercise his men in sham attacks upon sham forts; then altered his mind as to besieging Louisburg, and returned to New-York with all his troops, together with the two packets above mentioned, and all their passengers! During his absence the French and savages had taken Fort George, on the frontier of that province, and the Indians had massacred many of the garrison after capitulation. I saw afterward in London Captain Bound, who commanded one of those packets; he told me that when he had been detained a month, he acquainted his lordship that his ship was grown foul to a degree that must necessarily hinder her fast sailing (a point of consequence for a packet-boat), and requested an allowance of time to heave her down and clean her bottom. His lordship asked how long a time that would require. He answered,[Pg 185] Three days. The general replied, "If you can do it in one day, I give leave, otherwise not; for you must certainly sail the day after to-morrow." So he never obtained leave, though detained afterward from day to day during full three months. I saw also in London one of Bonell's passengers, who was so enraged against his lordship for deceiving and detaining him so long at New-York, and then carrying him to Halifax and back again, that he swore he would sue him for damages. Whether he did or not I never heard; but, as he represented it, the injury to his affairs was very considerable. On the whole, I wondered much how such a man came to be intrusted with so important a business as the conduct of a great army: but having since seen more of the great world, and the means of obtaining, and motives for giving places and employments, my wonder is diminished. General Shirley, on whom the command of the army devolved upon the death of Braddock, would, in my opinion, if continued in place, have made a much better campaign than that of Loudon in 1756, which was frivolous, expensive, and disgraceful to our nation beyond conception. For though Shirley was not bred a soldier, he was sensible and sagacious in himself, and attentive to good advice from others, capable of forming judicious plans, and quick and active in carrying them into execution. Loudon, instead of defending the colonies with his great army, left them totally exposed, while he paraded idly at Halifax, by which means Fort George was lost; besides, he deranged all our mercantile operations, and distressed our trade by a long embargo on the exportation of provisions, on pretence of keeping supplies from being obtained by the enemy, but in reality for beating down their price in favour of the contractors, in whose profits, it was said (perhaps from suspicion only), he had a share; and when at length the embargo was taken off, neglected to send notice of it[Pg 186] to Charleston, where the Carolina fleet was detained near three months, and whereby their bottoms were so much damaged by the worm that a great part of them foundered in their passage home. Shirley was, I believe, sincerely glad of being relieved from so burdensome a charge as the conduct of an army must be to a man unacquainted with military business. I was at the entertainment given by the city of New-York to Lord Loudon, on his taking upon him the command. Shirley, though thereby superseded, was present also. There was a great company of officers, citizens, and strangers; and some chairs having been borrowed in the neighbourhood, there was one among them very low, which fell to the lot of Mr. Shirley. I sat by him, and perceiving it, I said, they have given you a very low seat. "No matter, Mr. Franklin," said he, "I find a low seat the easiest."

While I was, as before mentioned, detained at New-York, I received all the accounts of the provisions, &c., that I had furnished to Braddock, some of which accounts could not sooner be obtained from the different persons I had employed to assist in the business; I presented them to Lord Loudon, desiring to be paid the balance. He caused them to be examined by the proper officer, who, after comparing every article with its voucher, certified them to be right; and his lordship promised to give me an order on the paymaster for the balance due to me. This was, however, put off from time to time; and though I called often for it by appointment, I did not get it. At length, just before my departure, he told me he had, on better consideration, concluded not to mix his accounts with those of his predecessors. "And you," said he, "when in England, have only to exhibit your accounts to the treasury, and you will be paid immediately." I mentioned, but without effect, a great and unexpected expense I had been put to by being detained[Pg 187] so long at New-York, as a reason for my desiring to be presently paid; and on my observing that it was not right I should be put to any farther trouble or delay in obtaining the money I had advanced, as I charged no commission for my service, "Oh," said he, "you must not think of persuading us that you are no gainer: we understand better those matters, and know that every one concerned in supplying the army, finds means, in the doing it, to fill his own pockets." I assured him that was not my case, and that I had not pocketed a farthing; but he appeared clearly not to believe me; and, indeed, I afterward learned, that immense fortunes are often made in such employments: as to my balance, I am not paid it to this day, of which more hereafter.

Our captain of the packet boasted much before we sailed of the swiftness of his ship; unfortunately, when we came to sea, she proved the dullest of ninety-six sail, to his no small mortification. After many conjectures respecting the cause, when we were near another ship, almost as dull as ours, which, however, gained upon us, the captain ordered all hands to come aft, and stand as near the ensign staff as possible. We were, passengers included, about forty persons; while we stood there, the ship mended her pace, and soon left her neighbour far behind, which proved clearly what our captain suspected, that she was loaded too much by the head. The casks of water, it seems, had been placed forward; these he therefore ordered to be moved farther aft, on which the ship recovered her character, and proved the best sailer in the fleet. The captain said she had once gone at the rate of thirteen knots, which is accounted thirteen miles per hour. We had on board, as a passenger, Captain Archibald Kennedy, of the royal navy, afterward Earl of Cassilis, who contended that it was impossible, and that no ship ever sailed so fast, and that there must have been some error in the division[Pg 188] of the logline, or some mistake in heaving the log. A wager ensued between the two captains, to be decided when there should be sufficient wind: Kennedy therefore examined the logline, and, being satisfied with it, he determined to throw the log himself. Some days after, when the wind was very fair and fresh, and the captain of the packet (Lutwidge) said he believed she then went at the rate of thirteen knots, Kennedy made the experiment, and owned his wager lost. The foregoing fact I give for the sake of the following observation: it has been remarked, as an imperfection in the art of shipbuilding, that it can never be known till she is tried whether a new ship will or will not be a good sailer; for that the model of a good sailing ship has been exactly followed in a new one, which has been proved, on the contrary, remarkably dull. I apprehend that this may partly be occasioned by the different opinions of seamen respecting the modes of loading, rigging, and sailing of a ship; each has his method; and the same vessel, laden by the method and orders of one captain, shall sail worse than when by the orders of another. Besides, it scarce ever happens that a ship is formed, fitted for the sea, and sailed by the same person; one man builds the hull, another rigs her, a third loads and sails her. No one of these has the advantage of knowing all the ideas and experience of the others, and, therefore, cannot draw just conclusions from a combination of the whole. Even in the simple operation of sailing when at sea, I have often observed different judgments in the officers who commanded the successive watches, the wind being the same. One would have the sails trimmed sharper than another, so that they seemed to have no certain rule to govern by. Yet I think a set of experiments might be instituted, first, to determine the most proper form of the hull for swift sailing; next, the best dimensions and[Pg 189] most proper place for the masts; then the form and quantity of sails, and their position as the winds may be; and, lastly, the disposition of the lading. This is an age of experiments, and I think a set accurately made and combined would be of great use.

We were several times chased in our passage, but outsailed everything; and in thirty days had soundings. We had a good observation, and the captain judged himself so near our port (Falmouth), that if we made a good run in the night, we might be off the mouth of that harbour in the morning; and, by running in the night, might escape the notice of the enemy's privateers, who often cruised near the entrance of the channel. Accordingly all sail was set that we could possibly carry, and the wind being very fresh and fair, we stood right before it, and made great way. The captain, after his observation, shaped his course, as he thought, so as to pass wide of the Scilly rocks; but it seems there is sometimes a strong current setting up St. George's Channel, which formerly caused the loss of Sir Cloudesley Shovel's Squadron (in 1707): this was probably also the cause of what happened to us. We had a watchman placed in the bow, to whom they often called, "Look well out before there;" and he as often answered, "Ay, ay;" but perhaps had his eyes shut, and was half asleep at the time; they sometimes answering, as is said, mechanically: for he did not see a light just before us, which had been hid by the studding sails from the man at the helm and from the rest of the watch, but by an accidental yaw of the ship was discovered, and occasioned a great alarm, we being very near it; the light appearing to me as large as a cart wheel. It was midnight, and our captain fast asleep; but Captain Kennedy, jumping upon deck and seeing the danger, ordered the ship to wear round, all sails standing; an operation dangerous to the masts, but it carried us clear, and[Pg 190] we avoided shipwreck, for we were running fast on the rocks on which the light was erected. This deliverance impressed me strong with the utility of light-houses, and made me resolve to encourage the building some of them in America, if I should live to return thither.

In the morning it was found by our soundings, &c., that we were near our port, but a thick fog hid the land from our sight. About nine o'clock the fog began to rise, and seemed to be lifted up from the water like the curtain of a theatre, discovering underneath the town of Falmouth, the vessels in the harbour, and the fields that surround it. This was a pleasing spectacle to those who had been long without any other prospect than the uniform view of a vacant ocean! and it gave us the more pleasure, as we were now free from the anxieties which had arisen.[13]

I set out immediately, with my son,[14] for London, and we only stopped a little by the way to view Stonehenge, on Salisbury Plain; and Lord Pembroke's house and gardens, with the very curious antiquities at Wilton.

We arrived in London, July 27th, 1757.

[Conclusion of Memoirs written by himself.]

FOOTNOTES:

[10] This little book is dated Sunday, 1st July, 1773, and is in the possession of Mr. W. T. Franklin: a copy was also in the possession of the late B. T. Bache.

[11] Fothergill (John), F.R.S., an eminent physician, born in 1712, at Carr End, in Yorkshire, of Quaker parents, died in 1780.

[12] Dr. Franklin gives a farther account of his election in the following extract of a letter to his son, Governor Franklin.

"London, Dec. 19, 1767

"We have had an ugly affair at the Royal Society lately. One Dacosti, a Jew, who, as our clerk, was intrusted with collecting our moneys, has been so unfaithful as to embezzle near thirteen hundred pounds in four years. Being one of the council this year as well as the last, I have been employed all the last week in attending the inquiry into, and unravelling his accounts, in order to come at a full knowledge of his frauds. His securities are bound in one thousand pounds to the society, which they will pay, but we are like to lose the rest. He had this year received twenty-six admission payments of twenty-five guineas each, which he did not bring to account.

"While attending this affair, I had an opportunity of looking over the old council books and journals of the society; and having a curiosity to see how I came in (of which I had never been informed), I looked back for the minutes relating to it. You must know it is not usual to admit persons that have not requested to be admitted; and a recommendatory certificate in favour of the candidate, signed by at least three of the members is by our rule to be presented to the society, expressing that he is desirous of that honour, and is so and so qualified. As I had never asked or expected the honour, I was, as I said before, curious to see how the business was managed. I found that the certificate, worded very advantageously for me, was signed by Lord Macclesfield, then president, Lord Parker, and Lord Willoughby; that the election was by a unanimous vote; and the honour being voluntarily conferred by the society unsolicited by me, it was thought wrong to demand or receive the usual fees or composition; so that my name was entered on the list with a vote of council that I was not to pay anything. And, accordingly, nothing has ever been demanded of me. Those who are admitted in the common way pay five guineas as admission fees, and two guineas and a half yearly contribution, or twenty five guineas down in lieu of it. In my case a substantial favour accompanied the honour."

[13] In a letter from Dr. Franklin to his wife, dated at Falmouth, the 17th July, 1757, after giving her a similar account of his voyage, escape, and landing, he adds, "The bell ringing for church, we went thither immediately, and, with hearts full of gratitude, returned sincere thanks to God for the mercies we had received."

[14] William Franklin, afterward governor of New-Jersey.

PART III.

[Continuation by Dr. Stuber.[15]]

Dr. Franklin having mentioned his electrical discoveries only in a very transient manner in the preceding memoirs, some farther account of them cannot fail to be interesting.

He engaged in a course of electrical experiments with all the ardour and thirst for discovery which characterized the philosophers of that day. Of all the branches of experimental philosophy, electricity had been least explored. The attractive power of amber is mentioned by Theophrastus and Pliny, and from them by later naturalists. In the year 1600, Gilbert, an English physician, enlarged considerably the catalogue of substances which have the property[Pg 192] of attracting light bodies. Boyle, Otto Guericke, a burgomaster of Magdeburg, celebrated as the inventor of the airpump, Dr. Wall, and Sir Isaac Newton, added some facts. Guericke first observed the repulsive power of electricity, and the light and noise produced by it. In 1709, Hawkesbec communicated some important observations and experiments to the world. For several years electricity was entirely neglected, until Mr. Grey applied himself to it, in 1728, with great assiduity. He and his friend Mr. Wheeler made a great variety of experiments; in which they demonstrated that electricity may be communicated from one body to another, even without being in contact, and in this way may be conducted to a great distance. Mr. Grey afterward found that, by suspending rods of iron by silk or hair lines, and bringing an excited tube under them, sparks might be drawn, and a light perceived at the extremities in the dark. M. du Faye, intendant of the French king's gardens, made a number of experiments, which added not a little to the science. He made the discovery of two kinds of electricity, which he called vitreous and resinous; the former produced by rubbing glass, the latter from excited sulphur, sealing-wax, &c. But this idea he afterward gave up as erroneous. Between the year 1739 and 1742, Desauguliers made a number of experiments, but added little of importance. He first used the terms conductors and electrics per se. In 1742, several ingenious Germans engaged in this subject; of these the principal were, Professor Boze, of Wittemberg, Professor Winkler, of Leipsic, Gordon, a Scotch Benedictine monk, professor of philosophy at Erfurt, and Dr. Ludolf, of Berlin. The result of their researches astonished the philosophers of Europe. Their apparatus was large, and by means of it they were enabled to collect large quantities of the electric fluid, and thus to produce phenomena which had been hitherto unobserved.[Pg 193] They killed small birds, and set spirits on fire. Their experiments excited the curiosity of other philosophers. Collinson, about the year 1745, sent to the Library Company of Philadelphia an account of these experiments, together with a tube, and directions how to use it. Franklin, with some of his friends, immediately engaged in a course of experiments, the result of which is well known. He was enabled to make a number of important discoveries, and to propose theories to account for various phenomena; which have been universally adopted, and which bid fair to endure for ages. His observations he communicated in a series of letters, to his friend Collinson, the first of which is dated March 28, 1747. In these he shows the power of points in draining and throwing off the electrical matter, which had hitherto escaped the notice of electricians. He also made the grand discovery of a plus and minus, or of a positive and negative state of electricity. We give him the honour of this without hesitation, although the English have claimed it for their countryman, Dr. Watson. Watson's paper is dated January 21, 1748; Franklin's July 11, 1747; several months prior. Shortly after, Franklin, from his principles of the plus and minus state, explained, in a satisfactory manner, the phenomena of the Leyden vial, first observed by Mr. Cuneus, or by Professor Muschenbroeck, of Leyden, which had much perplexed philosophers. He showed clearly that the bottle, when charged, contained no more electricity than before, but that as much was taken from one side as was thrown on the other; and that, to discharge it, nothing was necessary but to produce a communication between the two sides by which the equilibrium might be restored, and that then no signs of electricity would remain. He afterward demonstrated, by experiments, that the electricity did not reside in the coating, as had been supposed, but in the pores of[Pg 194] the glass itself. After a vial was charged, he removed the coating, and found that, upon applying a new coating, the shock might still be received. In the year 1749, he first suggested his idea of explaining the phenomena of thunder-gusts, and of the aurora borealis, upon electrical principles. He points out many particulars in which lightning and electricity agree: and he adduces many facts, and reasonings from facts, in support of his positions. In the same year he conceived the astonishingly bold and grand idea of ascertaining the truth of his doctrine by actually drawing down the lightning, by means of sharp-pointed iron rods raised into the region of the clouds. Even in this uncertain state, his passion to be useful to mankind displays itself in a powerful manner. Admitting the identity of electricity and lightning, and knowing the power of points in repelling bodies charged with electricity, and in conducting their fire silently and imperceptibly, he suggested the idea of securing houses, ships, &c., from being damaged by lightning, by erecting pointed rods, that should rise some feet above the most elevated part, and descend some feet into the ground or the water. The effect of these, he concluded, would be either to prevent a stroke by repelling the cloud beyond the striking distance, or by drawing off the electrical fire which it contained; or, if they could not effect this, they would at least conduct the electric matter to the earth, without injury to the building.

It was not until the summer of 1752 that he was enabled to complete his grand and unparalleled discovery by experiment. The plan which he had originally proposed was to erect on some high tower or other elevated place a sentry-box, from which should rise a pointed iron rod, insulated by being fixed in a cake of resin. Electrified clouds passing over this would, he conceived, impart to it a portion of their electricity, which would be rendered[Pg 195] evident to the senses by sparks being emitted when a key, the knuckle, or other conductor was presented to it. Philadelphia at this time afforded no opportunity of trying an experiment of this kind. While Franklin was waiting for the erection of a spire, it occurred to him that he might have more ready access to the region of clouds by means of a common kite. He prepared one by fastening two cross sticks to a silk handkerchief, which would not suffer so much from the rain as paper. To the upright stick was affixed an iron point. The string was, as usual, of hemp, except the lower end, which was silk. Where the hempen string terminated a key was fastened. With this apparatus, on the appearance of a thunder-gust approaching, he went out into the commons, accompanied by his son, to whom alone he communicated his intentions, well knowing the ridicule which, too generally for the interest of science, awaits unsuccessful experiments in philosophy. He placed himself under a shade to avoid the rain; his kite was raised; a thunder-cloud passed over it; no sign of electricity appeared. He almost despaired of success, when, suddenly, he observed the loose fibres of his string to move towards an erect position. He now presented his knuckle to the key, and received a strong spark. How exquisite must his sensations have been at this moment! On this experiment depended the fate of his theory. If he succeeded, his name would rank high among those who had improved science; if he failed, he must inevitably be subjected to the derision of mankind, or, what is worse, their pity, as a well-meaning man, but a weak, silly projector. The anxiety with which he looked for the result of his experiment may be easily conceived. Doubts and despair had begun to prevail, when the fact was ascertained in so clear a manner, that even the most incredulous could no longer withhold their assent. Repeated sparks were drawn from the key,[Pg 196] a vial was charged, a shock given, and all the experiments made which are usually performed with electricity.

About a month before this period, some ingenious Frenchman had completed the discovery in the manner originally proposed by Dr. Franklin. The letters which he sent to Mr. Collinson, it is said, were refused a place in the Transactions of the Royal Society of London. However this may be, Collinson published them in a separate volume, under the title of "New Experiments and Observations on Electricity, made at Philadelphia, in America." They were read with avidity, and soon translated into different languages. A very incorrect French translation fell into the hands of the celebrated Buffon, who, notwithstanding the disadvantages under which the work laboured, was much pleased with it, and repeated the experiments with success. He prevailed on his friend, M. D'Alibard, to give his countrymen a more correct translation of the works of the American electrician. This contributed much towards spreading a knowledge of Franklin's principles in France. The king, Louis XV., hearing of these experiments, expressed a wish to be a spectator of them. A course of experiments was given at the seat of the Duc D'Ayen, at St. Germain, by M. de Lor. The applauses which the king bestowed upon Franklin excited in Buffon, D'Alibard, and De Lor, an earnest desire of ascertaining the truth of his theory of thunder-gust. Buffon erected his apparatus on the tower of Monthar, M. D'Alibard at Mary-la-ville, and De Lor at his house in the Estrapade at Paris, some of the highest ground in that capital. D'Alibard's machine first showed signs of electricity. On the 10th of May, 1752, a thunder-cloud passed it, in the absence of M'Alibard, and a number of sparks were drawn from it by Coiffier, a joiner, with whom D'Alibard had left directions how to proceed, and by M. Raulet[Pg 197] the prior of Mary-la-ville. An account of this experiment was given to the Royal Academy of Sciences, by M. D'Alibard, in a memoir, dated May 13, 1752. On the 18th of May, M. de Lor proved equally successful with the apparatus erected at his own house. These philosophers soon excited those of other parts of Europe to repeat the experiment, among whom none signalized themselves more than Father Beccaria, of Turin, to whose observations science is much indebted. Even the cold regions of Russia were penetrated by the ardour for discovery. Professor Richman bade fair to add much to the stock of knowledge on this subject, when an unfortunate flash from his conductor put a period to his existence. The friends of science will long remember with regret the amiable martyr to electricity.

By these experiments Franklin's theory was established in the most convincing manner. When the truth of it could no longer be doubted, envy and vanity endeavoured to detract from its merit. That an American, an inhabitant of the obscure city of Philadelphia, the name of which was hardly known, should be able to make discoveries and to frame theories which had escaped the notice of the enlightened philosophers of Europe, was too mortifying to be admitted. He must certainly have taken the idea from some one else. An American, a being of an inferior order, make discoveries! Impossible. It was said that the Abbé Nollet, 1748, had suggested the idea of the similarity of lightning and electricity in his Leçons de Physique. It is true that the abbé mentions the idea, but he throws it out as a bare conjecture, and proposes no mode of ascertaining the truth of it. He himself acknowledges that Franklin first entertained the bold thought of bringing lightning from the heavens, by means of pointed rods fixed in the air. The similarity of lightning and electricity is so strong, that we need[Pg 198] not be surprised at notice being taken of it as soon as electrical phenomena became familiar. We find it mentioned by Dr. Wall and Mr. Grey, while the science was in its infancy. But the honor of forming a regular theory of thunder-gusts, of suggesting a mode of determining the truth of it by experiments, and of putting these experiments in practice, and thus establishing the theory upon a firm and solid basis, is incontestibly due to Franklin. D'Alibard, who made the first experiments in France, says that he only followed the tract which Franklin had pointed out.

It has been of late asserted, that the honour of completing the experiment with the electrical kite does not belong to Franklin. Some late English paragraphs have attributed it to some Frenchman, whose name they do not mention: and the Abbé Bertholon gives it to M. de Romas, assessor to the presideal of Nerac: the English paragraphs probably refer to the same person. But a very slight attention will convince us of the injustice of this procedure: Dr. Franklin's experiment was made in June, 1752, and his letter, giving an account of it, is dated October 19, 1752. M. de Romas made his first attempt on the 14th of May, 1753, but was not successful until the 7th of June, a year after Franklin had completed the discovery, and when it was known to all the philosophers in Europe.

Besides these great principles, Franklin's letters on electricity contain a number of facts and hints which have contributed greatly towards reducing this branch of knowledge to a science. His friend, Mr. Kinnersley, communicated to him a discovery of the different kinds of electricity, excited by rubbing glass and sulphur. This, we have said, was first observed by M. du Faye, but it was for many years neglected. The philosophers were disposed to account for the phenomena rather from a difference in the quantity of electricity collected, and[Pg 199] even Du Faye himself seems at last to have adopted this doctrine. Franklin at first entertained the same idea; but, upon repeating the experiment, he perceived that Mr. Kinnersley was right; and that the vitreous and resinous electricity of Du Faye were nothing more than the positive and negative states which he had before observed; and that the glass globe charged positively, or increased the quantity of electricity on the prime conductor, while the globe of sulphur diminishes its natural quantity, or charged negatively. These experiments and observations opened a new field for investigation, upon which electricians entered with avidity, and their labours have added much to the stock of our knowledge.

In September, 1752, Franklin entered upon a course of experiments to determine the state of electricity in the clouds. From a number of experiments he formed this conclusion: "That the clouds of a thunder-gust are most commonly in a negative state of electricity, but sometimes in a positive state;" and from this it follows, as a necessary consequence, "that, for the most part, in thunder-strokes, it is the earth that strikes into the clouds, and not the clouds that strike into the earth." The letter containing these observations is dated in September, 1753; and yet the discovery of ascending thunder has been said to be of a modern date, and has been attributed to the Abbé Bertholon, who published his memoir on the subject in 1776.

Franklin's letters have been translated into most of the European languages and into Latin. In proportion as they have become known, his principles have been adopted. Some opposition was made to his theories, particularly by the Abbé Nollet, who was, however, feebly supported, while the first philosophers in Europe stepped forth in defence of Franklin's principles, among whom D'Alibard and[Pg 200] Beccaria were the most distinguished. The opposition has gradually ceased, and the Franklinian system is now universally adopted where science flourishes.

The important practical use which Franklin made of his discoveries, the securing of houses from injury by lightning, has been already mentioned. Pointed conductors are now very common in America; but prejudice has hitherto prevented their general introduction into Europe, notwithstanding the most undoubted proofs of their utility have been given. But mankind can with difficulty be brought to lay aside established practices, or to adopt new ones. And perhaps we have more reason to be surprised that a practice, however rational, which was proposed about forty years ago, should in that time have been adopted in so many places, than that it has not universally prevailed. It is only by degrees that the great body of mankind can be led into new practices, however salutary their tendency. It is now nearly eighty years since inoculation was introduced into Europe and America; and it is so far from being general at present, that it will require one or two centuries to render it so.

The disputes between the proprietaries and the people of the province continued in full force, although a war was raging on the frontiers. Not even the sense of danger was sufficient to reconcile, for ever so short a time, their jarring interests. The Assembly still insisted upon the justice of taxing the proprietary estates; but the governors constantly refused their assent to this measure, without which no bill could pass into a law. Enraged at the obstinacy, and what they conceived to be the unjust proceedings of their opponents, the Assembly at length determined to apply to the mother country for relief. A petition was addressed to the king in council, stating the inconveniences under which the inhabitants laboured, from the attention of the proprietaries to their[Pg 201] private interest, to the neglect of the general welfare of the community, and praying for redress. Franklin was appointed to present this address, as agent for the province of Pennsylvania, and departed from America in June, 1757. In conformity to the instructions which he had received from the legislature, he held a conference with the proprietaries who then resided in England, and endeavoured to prevail upon them to give up the long-contested point. Finding that they would hearken to no terms of accommodation, he laid his petition before the council. During this time Governor Denny assented to a law imposing a tax, in which no discrimination was made in favour of the estates of the Penn family. They, alarmed at this intelligence and Franklin's exertions, used their utmost endeavours to prevent the royal sanction being given to this law, which they represented as highly iniquitous, designed to throw the burden of supporting government upon them, and calculated to produce the most ruinous consequences to them and their posterity. The cause was amply discussed before the privy council. The Penns found here some strenuous advocates; nor were there wanting some who warmly espoused the side of the people. After some time spent in debate, a proposal was made that Franklin should solemnly engage that the assessment of the tax should be so made as that the proprietary estates should pay no more than a due proportion. This he agreed to perform, the Penn family withdrew their opposition, and tranquillity was thus once more restored to the province.

The mode in which this dispute was terminated is a striking proof of the high opinion entertained of Franklin's integrity and honour, even by those who considered him as inimical to their views. Nor was their confidence ill-founded. The assessment was made upon the strictest principle of equity;[Pg 202] and the proprietary estates bore only a proportionable share of the expenses of supporting government.

After the completion of this important business, Franklin remained at the court of Great Britain as agent for the province of Pennsylvania. The extensive knowledge which he possessed of the situation of the colonies, and the regard which he always manifested for their interests, occasioned his appointment to the same office by the colonies of Massachusetts, Maryland, and Georgia. His conduct, in this situation, was such as rendered him still more dear to his countrymen.

He had now an opportunity of indulging in the society of those friends whom his merits had procured him while at a distance. The regard which they had entertained for him was rather increased by a personal acquaintance. The opposition which had been made to his discoveries in philosophy gradually ceased, and the rewards of literary merit were abundantly conferred upon him. The Royal Society of London, which had at first refused his performances admission into its transactions, now thought it an honour to rank him among its fellows. Other societies of Europe were equally ambitious of calling him a member. The University of St. Andrew, in Scotland, conferred upon him the degree of Doctor of Laws. Its example was followed by the Universities of Edinburgh and Oxford. His correspondence was sought for by the most eminent philosophers of Europe. His letters to these abound with true science, delivered in the most simple, unadorned manner.

The province of Canada was at this time in the possession of the French, who had originally settled it. The trade with the Indians, for which its situation was very convenient, was exceedingly lucrative. The French traders here found a market for their commodities, and received in return large quantities of rich furs, which they disposed of at a[Pg 203] high price in Europe. While the possession of this country was highly advantageous to France, it was a grievous inconvenience to the inhabitants of the British colonies. The Indians were almost generally desirous to cultivate the friendship of the French, by whom they were abundantly supplied with arms and ammunition. Whenever a war happened, the Indians were ready to fall upon the frontiers; and this they frequently did, even when Great Britain and France were at peace. From these considerations, it appeared to be the interest of Great Britain to gain the possession of Canada. But the importance of such an acquisition was not well understood in England. Franklin about this time published his Canada pamphlet, in which he, in a very forcible manner, pointed out the advantages which would result from the conquest of this province.

An expedition against it was planned, and the command given to General Wolfe. His success is well known. At the treaty in 1762, France ceded Canada to Great Britain; and by her cession of Louisiana, at the same time, relinquished all her possessions on the continent of America.

Although Dr. Franklin was now principally occupied with political pursuits, he found time for philosophical studies. He extended his electrical researches, and made a variety of experiments, particularly on the tourmalin. The singular properties which this stone possesses, of being electrified on one side positively, and on the other negatively, by heat alone, without friction, had been but lately observed.

Some experiments on the cold produced by evaporation, made by Dr. Cullen, had been communicated to Dr. Franklin by Professor Simpson, of Glasgow. These he repeated, and found that, by the evaporation of ether in the exhausted receiver of an airpump, so great a degree of cold was produced in a summer's day, that water was converted[Pg 204] into ice. This discovery he applied to the solution of a number of phenomena, particularly a single fact, which philosophers had endeavoured in vain to account for, viz., that the temperature of the human body, when in health, never exceeds 96 degrees of Fahrenheit's thermometer, although the atmosphere which surrounds it may be heated to a much greater degree. This he attributed to the increased perspiration and consequent evaporation produced by the heat.

In a letter to Mr. Small, of London, dated in May, 1760, Dr. Franklin makes a number of observations, tending to show that, in North America, northeast storms begin in the southwest parts. It appears, from actual observations, that a northeast storm, which extended a considerable distance, commenced at Philadelphia nearly four hours before it was felt at Boston. He endeavoured to account for this by supposing that, from heat, some rarefication takes place about the Gulf of Mexico; that the air farther north, being cooler, rushes in, and is succeeded by the cooler and denser air still farther north, and that thus a continued current is at length produced.

The tone produced by rubbing the brim of a drinking-glass with a wet finger had been generally known. A Mr. Puckeridge, an Irishman, by placing on a table a number of glasses of different sizes, and tuning them, by partly filling them with water, endeavoured to form an instrument capable of playing tunes. He was prevented, by an untimely end, from bringing his invention to any degree of perfection. After his death some improvements were made upon his plan. The sweetness of the tones induced Dr. Franklin to make a variety of experiments; and he at length formed that elegant instrument which he has called the Armonica.

In the summer of 1762 he returned to America. On his passage he observed the singular effect produced by the agitation of a vessel containing oil[Pg 205] floating on water. The surface of the oil remains smooth and undisturbed, while the water is agitated with the utmost commotion. No satisfactory explanation of this appearance has, we believe, ever been given.

Dr. Franklin received the thanks of the Assembly of Pennsylvania, "as well for the faithful discharge of his duty to that province in particular, as for the many and important services done to America in general during his residence in Great Britain." A compensation of 5000l., Pennsylvania currency, was also decreed him for his service during six years.

During his absence he had been annually elected member of the Assembly. On his return to Pennsylvania he again took his seat in this body, and continued a steady defender of the liberties of the people.

In December, 1762, a circumstance which caused great alarm in the province took place. A number of Indians had resided in the county of Lancaster, and conducted themselves uniformly as friends to the white inhabitants. Repeated depredations on the frontiers had exasperated the inhabitants to such a degree, that they determined on revenge upon every Indian. A number of persons, to the amount of about 120, principally inhabitants of Donegal and Peckstang, or Paxton, townships, in the county of York, assembled, and, mounted on horseback, proceeded to the settlement of these harmless and defenceless Indians, whose number had now been reduced to about twenty. The Indians received intelligence of the attack which was intended against them, but disbelieved it. Considering the white people as their friends, they apprehended no danger from them. When the party arrived at the Indian settlement, they found only some women and children, and a few old men, the rest being absent at work. They murdered all whom[Pg 206] they found, and among others the chief Shaheas, who had been always distinguished for his friendship to the whites. This bloody deed excited much indignation in the well-disposed part of the community.

The remainder of these unfortunate Indians, who, by absence, had escaped the massacre, were conducted to Lancaster, and lodged in the jail as a place of security. The governor issued a proclamation, expressing the strongest disapprobation of the action, offering a reward for the discovery of the perpetrators of the deed, and prohibiting all injuries to the peaceable Indians in future. But, notwithstanding this, a party of the same men shortly after marched to Lancaster, broke open the jail, and inhumanly butchered the innocent Indians who had been placed there for security. Another proclamation was issued, but it had no effect. A detachment marched down to Philadelphia for the express purpose of murdering some friendly Indians, who had been removed to the city for safety. A number of the citizens armed in their defence. The Quakers, whose principles are opposed to fighting, even in their own defence, were most active upon this occasion. The rioters came to Germantown. The governor fled for safety to the house of Dr. Franklin, who, with some others, advanced to meet the Paxton boys, as they were called, and had influence enough to prevail upon them to relinquish their undertaking and return to their homes.

The disputes between the proprietaries and the Assembly, which for a time had subsided, were again revived. The proprietaries were dissatisfied with the concessions made in favour of the people, and made great struggles to recover the privilege of exempting their estates from taxation, which they had been induced to give up.

In 1763 the Assembly passed a militia bill, to which the governor refused to give his assent, unless[Pg 207] the Assembly would agree to certain amendments which he proposed. These consisted in increasing the fines, and, in some cases, substituting death for fines. He wished, too, that the officers should be appointed altogether by himself, and not be nominated by the people, as the bill had proposed. These amendments the Assembly considered as inconsistent with the spirit of liberty. They would not adopt them; the governor was obstinate, and the bill was lost.

These, and various other circumstances, increased the uneasiness which subsisted between the proprietaries and the Assembly, to such a degree that, in 1764, a petition to the king was agreed to by the house, praying an alteration from a proprietary to a regal government. Great opposition was made to this measure, not only in the house, but in the public prints. A speech of Mr. Dickenson on the subject was published, with a preface by Dr. Smith, in which great pains were taken to show the impropriety and impolicy of this proceeding. A speech of Mr. Golloway, in reply to Mr. Dickenson, was published, accompanied with a preface by Dr. Franklin, in which he ably opposed the principles laid down in the preface to Mr. Dickenson's speech. This application to the throne produced no effect. The proprietary government was still continued.

At the election for a new Assembly, in the fall of 1764, the friends of the proprietaries made great exertions to exclude those of the adverse party; and they obtained a small majority in the city of Philadelphia. Franklin now lost his seat in the house, which he had held for fourteen years. On the meeting of the Assembly it appeared that there was still a decided majority of Franklin's friends. He was immediately appointed provincial agent, to the great chagrin of his enemies, who made a solemn protest against this appointment: which was refused admission upon the minutes, as being unprecedented.[Pg 208] It was, however, published in the papers, and produced a spirited reply from him, just before his departure for England.

The disturbances produced in America by Mr. Grenville's stamp-act, and the opposition made to it, are well known. Under the Marquis of Rockingham's administration, it appeared expedient to endeavour to calm the minds of the colonists, and the repeal of the odious tax was contemplated. Among other means of collecting information on the disposition of the people to submit to it, Dr. Franklin was called to the bar of the House of Commons. The examination which he here underwent was published, and contains a striking proof of the extent and accuracy of his information, and the facility with which he communicated his sentiments. He represented facts in so strong a point of view, that the expediency of the act must have appeared clear to every unprejudiced mind. The act, after some opposition, was repealed, about a year after it was enacted, and before it had ever been carried into execution.

In the year 1766, he made a visit to Holland and Germany, and received the greatest marks of attention from men of science. In his passage through Holland, he learned from the watermen the effect which a diminution of the quantity of water in canals has in impeding the progress of boats. Upon his return to England, he was led to make a number of experiments, all of which tended to confirm the observation. These, with an explanation of the phenomenon, he communicated in a letter to his friend, Sir John Pringle, which is among his philosophical pieces.

In the following year he travelled into France, where he met with a no less favourable reception than he had experienced in Germany. He was introduced to a number of literary characters, and to the king, Louis XV.[Pg 209]

Several letters, written by Hutchinson, Oliver, and others, to persons in eminent stations in Great Britain, came into the hands of Dr. Franklin. These contained the most violent invectives against the leading characters of the State of Massachusetts, and strenuously advised the prosecution of vigorous measures to compel the people to obedience to the measures of the ministry. These he transmitted to the legislature, by whom they were published. Attested copies of them were sent to Great Britain, with an address, praying the king to discharge from office persons who had rendered themselves obnoxious to the people, and who had shown themselves so unfriendly to their interests. The publication of these letters produced a duel between Mr. Whately and Mr. Temple; each of whom was suspected of having been instrumental in procuring them. To prevent any farther disputes on this subject, Dr. Franklin, in one of the public papers, declared that he had sent them to America, but would give no information concerning the manner in which he had obtained them; nor was this ever discovered.

Shortly after, the petition of the Massachusetts Assembly was taken up for examination before the privy council. Dr. Franklin attended as agent for the Assembly; and here a torrent of the most violent and unwarranted abuse was poured upon him by the solicitor-general, Wedderburne, who was engaged as counsel for Oliver and Hutchinson. The petition was declared to be scandalous and vexatious, and the prayer of it refused.

Although the parliament of Great Britain had repealed the stamp-act, it was only upon the principle of expediency. They still insisted upon their right to tax the colonies; and, at the same time that the stamp-act was repealed, an act was passed declaring the right of parliament to bind the colonies in all cases whatever. This language was used even by most strenuous opposers of the stamp-act, and,[Pg 210] among others, by Mr. Pitt. This right was never recognised by the colonists; but, as they flattered themselves that it would not be exercised, they were not very active in remonstrating against it. Had this pretended right been suffered to remain dormant, the colonists would cheerfully have furnished their quota of supplies, in the mode to which they had been accustomed; that is, by acts of their own assemblies, in consequence of requisitions from the secretary of state. If this practice had been pursued, such was the disposition of the colonies towards their mother country, that, notwithstanding the disadvantages under which they laboured, from restraints upon their trade, calculated solely for the benefit of the commercial and manufacturing interests of Great Britain, a separation of the two countries might have been a far distant event. The Americans, from their earliest infancy, were taught to venerate a people from whom they were descended; whose language, laws, and manners were the same as their own. They looked up to them as models of perfection; and, in their prejudiced minds, the most enlightened nations of Europe were considered as almost barbarians in comparison with Englishmen. The name of an Englishman conveyed to an American the idea of everything good and great. Such sentiments instilled into them in early life, what but a repetition of unjust treatment could have induced them to entertain the most distant thought of separation! The duties on glass, paper, leather, painters' colours, tea, &c., the disfranchisement of some of the colonies, the obstruction to the measures of the legislature in others by the king's governors, the contemptuous treatment of their humble remonstrances, stating their grievances, and praying a redress of them, and other violent and oppressive measures, at length excited an ardent spirit of opposition. Instead of endeavouring to allay this by a more lenient[Pg 211] conduct, the ministry seemed resolutely bent upon reducing the colonies to the most slavish obedience to their decrees. But this only tended to aggravate. Vain were all the efforts made use of to prevail upon them to lay aside their designs, to convince them of the impossibility of carrying them into effect, and of the mischievous consequences which must ensue from the continuance of the attempt. They persevered with a degree of inflexibility scarcely paralleled.

The advantages which Great Britain derived from her colonies was so great, that nothing but a degree of infatuation little short of madness could have produced a continuance of measures calculated to keep up a spirit of uneasiness, which might occasion the slightest wish for a separation. When we consider the great improvements in the science of government, the general diffusion of the principles of liberty among the people of Europe, the effects which these have already produced in France, and the probable consequences which will result from them elsewhere, all of which are the offspring of the American revolution, it cannot but appear strange that events of so great moment to the happiness of mankind should have been ultimately occasioned by the wickedness or ignorance of a British ministry.

Dr. Franklin left nothing untried to prevail upon the ministry to consent to a change of measures. In private conversations, and in letters to persons in government, he continually expatiated upon the impolicy and injustice of their conduct towards America; and stated that, notwithstanding the attachment of the colonists to the mother country, a repetition of ill-treatment must ultimately alienate their affections. They listened not to his advice. They blindly persevered in their own schemes, and left to the colonists no alternative but opposition or unconditional submission. The latter accorded[Pg 212] not with the principles of freedom which they had been taught to revere. To the former they were compelled, though reluctantly, to have recourse.

Dr. Franklin finding all efforts to restore harmony between Great Britain and her colonies useless, returned to America in the year 1775, just after the commencement of hostilities. The day after his return, he was elected by the legislature of Pennsylvania a delegate to Congress. Not long after his election, a committee was appointed, consisting of Mr. Lynch, Mr. Harrison, and himself, to visit the camp at Cambridge, and, in conjunction with the commander-in-chief, to endeavour to convince the troops, whose term of enlistment was about to expire, of the necessity of their continuing in the field, and persevering in the cause of their country.

In the fall of the same year he visited Canada, to endeavour to unite them in the common cause of liberty; but they could not be prevailed upon to oppose the measures of the British government. M. le Roy, in a letter annexed to Abbé Fauchett's eulogium of Dr. Franklin, states that the ill success of this negotiation was occasioned in a great degree by religious animosities, which subsisted between the Canadians and their neighbours, some of whom had, at different times, burned their chapels.

When Lord Howe came to America in 1776, vested with power to treat with the colonists, a correspondence took place between him and Dr. Franklin on the subject of a reconciliation. Dr. Franklin was afterward appointed, together with John Adams and Edward Rutledge, to wait upon the commissioners, in order to learn the extent of their powers. These were found to be only to grant pardons upon submission. These were terms which could not be accepted, and the object of the commissioners could not be obtained.

The momentous question of independence was shortly after brought into view, at a time when the[Pg 213] fleets and armies which were sent to enforce obedience were truly formidable. With an army, numerous indeed, but ignorant of discipline, and entirely unskilled in the art of war, without money, without a fleet, without allies, and with nothing but the love of liberty to support them, the colonists determined to separate from a country from which they had experienced a repetition of injury and insult. In this question Dr. Franklin was decidedly in favour of the measure proposed, and had great influence in bringing others over to his sentiments.

The public mind had been already prepared for this event by Mr. Paine's celebrated pamphlet, Common Sense. There is good reason to believe that Dr. Franklin had no inconsiderable share at least in furnishing materials for this work.

In the convention which assembled at Philadelphia in 1776, for the purpose of establishing a new form of government for the State of Pennsylvania, Dr. Franklin was chosen president. The late constitution of this state, which was the result of their deliberations, may be considered as a digest of his principles of government. The single legislature and the plural executive seem to have been his favourite tenets.

In the latter end of 1776, Dr. Franklin was appointed to assist at the negotiation which had been set on foot by Silas Deane, at the court of France. A conviction of the advantages of a commercial intercourse with America, and a desire of weakening the British empire by dismembering it, first induced the French court to listen to proposals of an alliance. But they showed rather a reluctance to the measure, which, by Dr. Franklin's address, and particularly by the success of the American arms against General Burgoyne, was at length overcome; and in February, 1778, a treaty of alliance, offensive and defensive, was concluded; in consequence of which,[Pg 214] France became involved in the war with Great Britain.

Perhaps no person could have been found more capable of rendering essential services to the United States at the court of France than Dr. Franklin. He was well known as a philosopher, and his character was held in the highest estimation. He was received with the greatest marks of respect by all the literary characters, and this respect was extended among all classes of men. His personal influence was hence very considerable. To the effects of this were added those of various performances which he published, tending to establish the credit and character of the United States. To his exertions in this way may, in no small degree, be ascribed the success of the loans negotiated in Holland and France, which greatly contributed to bringing the war to a happy conclusion.

The repeated ill success of their arms, and more particularly the capture of Cornwallis and his army, at length convinced the British nation of the impossibility of reducing the Americans to subjection. The trading interest particularly became clamorous for peace. The ministry were unable longer to oppose their wishes. Provisional articles of peace were agreed to, and signed at Paris, on the 30th of November, 1782, by Dr. Franklin, Mr. Adams, Mr. Jay, and Mr. Laurens, on the part of the United States, and by Mr. Oswald on the part of Great Britain. These formed the basis of the definitive treaty, which was concluded the 3d of September, 1783, and signed by Dr. Franklin, Mr. Adams, and Mr. Jay on the one part, and by Mr. David Hartly on the other.

On the 3rd of April, 1783, a treaty of Amity and Commerce between the United States and Sweden, was concluded at Paris by Dr. Franklin and the Count Von Krutz.

A similar treaty with Prussia was concluded in[Pg 215] 1785, not long before Dr. Franklin's departure from Europe.

Dr. Franklin did not suffer his political pursuits to engross his whole attention. Some of his performances made their appearance in Paris. The objects of these were generally the promotion of industry and economy.

In the year 1784, when animal magnetism made great noise in the world, particularly at Paris, it was thought a matter of such importance that the king appointed commissioners to examine into the foundation of this pretended science. Dr. Franklin was one of the number. After a fair and diligent examination, in the course of which Mesmer repeated a number of experiments, in the presence of the commissioners, some of which were tried upon themselves, they determined that it was a mere trick, intended to impose upon the ignorant and credulous. Mesmer was thus interrupted in his career to wealth and fame, and a most insolent attempt to impose upon the human understanding baffled.

The important ends of Dr. Franklin's mission being completed by the establishment of American independence, and the infirmities of age and disease coming upon him, he became desirous of returning to his native country. Upon application to Congress to be recalled, Mr. Jefferson was appointed to succeed him in 1785. Some time in September of the same year Dr. Franklin arrived in Philadelphia. He was shortly after chosen a member of the supreme executive council for the city, and soon after was elected president of the same.

When a convention was called to meet in Philadelphia, in 1787, for the purpose of giving more energy to the government of the union, by revising and amending the articles of confederation, Dr. Franklin was appointed a delegate from the State of Pennsylvania. He signed the constitution which[Pg 216] they proposed for the union, and gave it the most unequivocal marks of his approbation.

A society for political inquiries, of which Dr. Franklin was president, was established about this period. The meetings were held at his house. Two or three essays read in this society were published. It did not long continue.

In the year 1787, two societies were established in Philadelphia, founded on the principles of the most liberal and refined humanity: The Philadelphia Society for alleviating the miseries of public prisons: and the Pennsylvania Society for promoting the abolition of slavery, the relief of free negroes unlawfully held in bondage, and the improvement of the condition of the African race. Of each of these Dr. Franklin was president. The labours of these bodies have been crowned with great success; and they continue to prosecute, with unwearied diligence, the laudable designs for which they were established.

Dr. Franklin's increasing infirmities prevented his regular attendance at the council chamber, and in 1788 he retired wholly from public life.

His constitution had been a remarkably good one. He had been little subject to disease, except an attack of the gout occasionally, until about the year 1781, when he was first attacked with symptoms of the calculous complaint, which continued during his life. During the intervals of pain from this grievous disease, he spent many cheerful hours, conversing in the most agreeable and instructive manner. His faculties were entirely unimpaired, even to the hour of his death.

His name, as president of the abolition society, was signed to the memorial presented to the House of Representatives of the United States, on the 12th of February, 1789, praying them to exert the full extent of power vested in them by the constitution in discouraging the traffic in the human species. This was his last public act. In the debates to which[Pg 217] this memorial gave rise, several attempts were made to justify the trade. In the Federal Gazette of March 25, there appeared an essay, signed Historicus, written by Dr. Franklin, in which he communicated a speech, said to have been delivered in the Divan of Algiers, in 1687, in opposition to the prayer of the petition of a sect called Erika, or purists, for the abolition of piracy and slavery. This pretended African speech was an excellent parody of one delivered by Mr. Jackson, of Georgia. All the arguments urged in favour of negro slavery are applied with equal force to justify the plundering and enslaving of Europeans. It affords, at the same time, a demonstration of the futility of the arguments in defence of the slave-trade, and of the strength of mind and ingenuity of the author, at his advanced period of life. It furnished, too, a no less convincing proof of his power of imitating the style of other times and nations than his celebrated parable against persecution. And as the latter led many persons to search the scriptures with a view to find it, so the former caused many persons to search the bookstores and libraries for the work from which it was said to be extracted.

During the greatest part of his life Dr. Franklin had enjoyed an almost uninterrupted state of good health, and this he entirely attributed to his exemplary temperance.

In the year 1735, indeed, he had been seized with a pleurisy, which ended in a suppuration of the left lobe of the lungs, so that he was almost suffocated by the quantity of matter thrown up. But from this, as well as from another attack of the same kind, he recovered so completely, that his breathing was not in the least affected.

As he advanced in years, however, he became subject to fits of the gout, to which, in 1782, a nephritic cholic was superadded. From this time he was also affected with the stone as well as the gout; and for[Pg 218] the last twelve months of his life these complaints almost entirely confined him to his bed.

Notwithstanding his distressed situation, neither his mental faculties nor his natural cheerfulness ever forsook him. His memory was tenacious to the very last; and he seemed to be an exception to the general rule, that, at a certain period of life, the organs which are subservient to this faculty become callous; a remarkable instance of which is, that he learned to speak French after he had attained the age of seventy!

In the beginning of April following, he was attacked with a fever and complaint of his breast, which terminated his existence. The following account of his last illness was written by his friend and physician, Dr. Jones.

"The stone, with which he had been afflicted for several years, had for the last twelve months confined him chiefly to his bed; and during the extreme painful paroxysms, he was obliged to take large doses of laudanum to mitigate his tortures; still, in the intervals of pain, he not only amused himself with reading and conversing cheerfully with his family, and a few friends who visited him, but was often employed in doing business of a public as well as private nature, with various persons who waited on him for that purpose; and in every instance displayed not only that readiness and disposition of doing good which was the distinguishing characteristic of his life, but the fullest and clearest possession of his uncommon mental abilities, and not unfrequently indulged himself in those jeux d'esprit and entertaining anecdotes which were the delight of all who heard him.

"About sixteen days before his death, he was seized with a feverish indisposition, without any particular symptoms attending it, till the third or fourth day, when he complained of a pain in his left breast, which increased till it became extremely[Pg 219] acute, attended with a cough and labourious breathing. During this state, when the severity of his pain sometimes drew forth a groan of complaint, he would observe, that he was afraid he did not bear them as he ought, acknowledged his grateful sense of the many blessings he had received from that Supreme Being who had raised him from small and low beginnings to such high rank and consideration among men, and made no doubt but his present afflictions were kindly intended to wean him from a world in which he was no longer fit to act the part assigned him. In this frame of body and mind he continued till five days before his death, when his pain and difficulty of breathing entirely left him, and his family were flattering themselves with the hopes of his recovery, when an imposthumation, which had formed itself in his lungs, suddenly burst, and discharged a great quantity of matter, which he continued to throw up while he had sufficient strength to do it; but as that failed, the organs of respiration became gradually oppressed, a calm lethargic state succeeded, and, on the 17th of April, 1790, about eleven o'clock at night, he quietly expired, closing a long and useful life of eighty-four years and three months."[16]

The following account of his funeral, and the honours paid to his memory, is derived from an anonymous source, but is correct.

"All that was mortal of this great man was interred on the 21st of April, in the cemetery of Christ Church, Philadelphia, in that part adjoining to Arch-street, N. W. corner, in order that, if a monument[Pg 220] should be erected over his grave, it might be seen to more advantage.

"Never was any funeral so numerously and so respectably attended in any part of the States of America. The concourse of people assembled upon this occasion was immense. All the bells in the city were muffled, and the very newspapers were published with black borders. The body was interred amid peals of artillery; and nothing was omitted that could display the veneration of the citizens for such an illustrious character.

"The Congress ordered a general mourning for one month throughout America; the National Assembly of France paid the same compliment for three days; and the commons of Paris, as an extraordinary tribute of honour to his memory, assisted in a body at the funeral oration, delivered by the Abbé Fauchet, in the rotunda of the corn-market, which was hung with black, illuminated with chandeliers, and decorated with devices analogous to the occasion.

"Dr. Smith, provost of the college of Philadelphia, and David Rittenhouse, one of its members, were selected by the Philosophical Society to prepare a eulogium to the memory of its founder; and the subscribers to the City Library, who had just erected a handsome building for containing their books, left a vacant niche for a statue of their benefactor.

"This has since been placed there by the munificence of an estimable citizen of Philadelphia. It was imported from Italy; the name of the artist is Francis Lazzarini; it is composed of Carara marble, and cost 500 guineas.

"It was the first piece of sculpture of that size which had been seen in America. Franklin is represented in a standing posture; one arm is supported by means of some books, in his right hand he holds an inverted sceptre, an emblem of anti-monarchical[Pg 221] principles, and in his left a scroll of paper. He is dressed in a Roman toga. The resemblance is correct; the head is a copy from the excellent bust produced by the chisel of Houdon. The following inscription is engraven on the pedestal:

THIS STATUE

OF

DR. BENJAMIN FRANKLIN,

WAS PRESENTED BY

WILLIAM BINGHAM, Esq.,

1792.

"Franklin's life," says the anonymous writer of the foregoing, "affords one of the finest moral lessons that can be offered up to the admiration, the applause, or the imitation of mankind.

"As a man, we have beheld him practising and inculcating the virtues of frugality, temperance, and industry.

"As a citizen, we have seen him repelling the efforts of tyranny, and ascertaining the liberty of his countrymen.

"As a legislator, he affords a bright example of a genius soaring above corruption, and continually aiming at the happiness of his constituents.

"As a politician, we survey him, on one hand, acquiring the aid of a powerful nation, by means of his skilful negotiations; and on the other, calling forth the common strength of a congress of republics, by fixing a central point to which they could all look up, and concentrating their common force for the purposes of union, harmony, legislation, and defence.

"As a philosopher, his labours and his discoveries are calculated to advance the interests of humanity:[Pg 222] he might, indeed, have been justly termed the friend of man, the benefactor of the universe!

"The pursuits and occupations of his early youth afford a most excellent and instructive example to the young; his middle life, to the adult; his advanced years, to the aged. From him the poor may learn to acquire wealth, and the rich to adapt it to the purposes of beneficence.

"In regard to his character, he was rather sententious than fluent; more disposed to listen than to talk; a judicious rather than an imposing companion. He was what, perhaps, every able man is, impatient of interruption; for he used to mention the custom of the Indians with great applause, who, after listening with a profound attention to the observations of each other, preserve a respectful silence for some minutes before they begin their own reply.

"He was polite in his manners, and never gave a pointed contradiction to the assertions of his friends or his antagonists, but treated every argument with great calmness, and conquered his adversaries rather by the force of reason than assertion."

The advice of his death reached France at a period well adapted to excite great emotions; and in the National Assembly, 11th June, 1790, Mr. Mirabeau the elder addressed the assembly as follows:

"Franklin is dead!"

[A profound silence reigned throughout the hall.]

"The genius which gave freedom to America and scattered torrents of light upon Europe, is returned to the bosom of the Divinity!

"The sage whom two worlds claim; the man, disputed by the history of the sciences and the history of empires, holds, most undoubtedly, an elevated rank among the human species.

"Political cabinets have but too long notified the death of those who were never great but in their funeral[Pg 223] orations; the etiquette of courts has but too long sanctioned hypocritical grief. Nations ought only to mourn for their benefactors; the representatives of free men ought never to recommend any other than the heroes of humanity to their homage.

"The Congress hath ordered a general mourning for one month throughout the fourteen confederated states, on account of the death of Franklin; and America hath thus acquitted her tribute of admiration in behalf of one of the fathers of her constitution.

"Would it not be worthy of you, fellow-legislators, to unite yourselves in this religious act, to participate in this homage rendered in the face of the universe to the rights of man, and to the philosopher who has so eminently propagated the conquest of them throughout the world?

"Antiquity would have elevated altars to that mortal who, for the advantage of the human race, embracing both heaven and earth in his vast and extensive mind, knew how to subdue thunder and tyranny!

"Enlightened and free, Europe at least owes its remembrance and its regret to one of the greatest men who has ever served the cause of philosophy and of liberty.

"I propose that a decree do now pass, enacting that the National Assembly shall wear mourning during three days for Benjamin Franklin."

MM. de la Rochefoucault and Lafayette immediately rose in order to second this motion.

The assembly adopted it, at first by acclamation; and afterward decreed, by a large majority, amid the plaudits of all the spectators, that on Monday 14th of June, it should go into mourning for three days; that the discourse of M. Mirabeau should be printed; and that the president should write a letter[Pg 224] of condolence upon the occasion to the Congress of America.[17]

The following character of Dr. Franklin, by one of his intimate friends, is so ably and accurately drawn, that we cannot refrain adding it to the foregoing.

"There is in the character of every distinguished person something to admire and something to imitate. The incidents that have marked the life of a great man always excite curiosity and often afford improvement. If there be talents which we can never expect to equal, if there be a series of good fortune which we can never expect to enjoy, we still need not lose the labour of our biographical inquiries. We may probably become acquainted with habits which it may be prudent to adopt, and discover virtues which we cannot fail to applaud. It will be easy for the reader to make a full application of these remarks in his contemplations upon the late celebrated Dr. Franklin. By his death one of the best lights of the world may be said to be extinguished. I shall not attempt any historical details of the life of this illustrious patriot and philosopher,[Pg 225] as I have nothing farther in view than to make a few comments upon the most striking traits of his character.

"Original genius was peculiarly his attribute. The native faculties of his mind qualified him to penetrate into every science: and his unremitted diligence left no field of knowledge unexplored. There were no limits to his curiosity. His inquiries were spread over the whole face of nature. But the study of man seemed to be his highest delight: and if his genius had any special bias, it lay in discovering those things that made men wiser and happier. As truth was the sole object of his researches, he was, of course, no sectary: and as reason was his guide, he embraced no system which that did not authorize. In short, he laid the whole volume of nature open before him, and diligently and faithfully perused it.

"Nor were his political attainments less conspicuous than his philosophical. The ancients usually ranked good fortune among those circumstances of life which indicate merit. In this view Dr. Franklin is almost unrivalled, having seldom undertaken more than he accomplished. The world are too well acquainted with the events of his political career to require, at this time, a particular enumeration of them. It may be presumed the historians of the American revolution will exhibit them in proper colours.

"If Dr. Franklin did not aspire after the splendour of eloquence, it was only because the demonstrative plainness of his manner was superior to it. Though he neither loved political debate nor excelled in it, he still preserved much influence in public assemblies, and discovered an aptitude in his remarks on all occasions. He was not fond of taking a leading part in such investigations as could never terminate in any degree of certainty. To come forward in questions which, in their nature, are indefinite, and[Pg 226] in their issue problematical, does not comport with the caution of a man who has taught himself to look, for demonstration. He reserved his observations for those cases which science could enlighten and common sense approve. The simplicity of his style was well adapted to the clearness of his understanding. His conceptions were so bright and perfect, that he did not choose to involve them in a cloud of expressions. If he used metaphors, it was to illustrate, and not to embellish the truth. A man possessing such a lively imagery of ideas should never affect the arts of a vain rhetorician, whose excellence consists only in a beautiful arrangement of words.

"But whatever claims to eminence Dr. Franklin may have as a politician or a scholar, there is no point of light in which his character shines with more lustre than when we view him as a man or a citizen. He was eminently great in common things. Perhaps no man ever existed whose life can, with more justice, be denominated useful. Nothing ever passed through his hands without receiving improvement, and no person ever went into his company without gaining wisdom. His sagacity was so sharp and his science so various, that, whatever might be the profession or occupation of those with whom he conversed, he could meet every one upon his own ground. He could enliven every conversation with an anecdote, and conclude it with a moral.

"The whole tenour of his life was a perpetual lecture against the idle, the extravagant, and the proud. It was his principal aim to inspire mankind with a love of industry, temperance, and frugality, and to inculcate such duties as promote the important interests of humanity. He never wasted a moment of time, or lavished a farthing of money in folly or dissipation. Such expenses as the dignity of his station required he readily sustained, limiting[Pg 227] them by the strictest rules of propriety. Many public institutions experienced his well-timed liberality, and he manifested a sensibility of heart by numerous acts of private charity.

"By a judicious division of time, Dr. Franklin acquired the art of doing everything to advantage, and his amusements were of such a nature as could never militate with the main objects of his pursuit. In whatever situation he was placed by chance or design, he extracted something useful for himself or others. His life was remarkably full of incident. Every circumstance of it turned to some valuable account. The maxims which his discerning mind has formed apply to innumerable cases and characters. Those who move in the lowest, equally with those who move in the most elevated rank in society, may be guided by his instructions. In the private deportment of his life, he in many respects has furnished a most excellent model. His manners were easy and accommodating, and his address winning and respectful. All who knew him speak of him as a most agreeable man, and all who have heard of him applaud him as a very useful one. A man so wise and so amiable could not but have many admirers and many friends."

The following are extracts from the will and codicil of Dr. Franklin:

FRANKLIN

"With regard to my books, those I had in France and those I left in Philadelphia being now assembled together here, and a catalogue made of them, it is my intention to dispose of the same as follows: My 'History of the Academy of Sciences,' in sixty or seventy volumes quarto, I give to the Philosophical Society of Philadelphia, of which I have the honour to be president. My collection in folio, of 'Les Arts et les Metiers' [Arts and Trade], I give to the American Philosophical Society, established[Pg 228] in New-England, of which I am a member. My quarto edition of the same, 'Arts et Metiers', I give to the Library Company of Philadelphia. Such and so many of my books as I shall mark on the said catalogue with the name of my grandson Benjamin Franklin Bache, I do hereby give to him: and such and so many of my books as I shall mark on the said catalogue with the name of my grandson William Bache, I do hereby give to him: and such as shall be marked with the name of Jonathan Williams, I hereby give to my cousin of that name. The residue and remainder of all my books, manuscripts, and papers, I do give to my grandson William Temple Franklin. My share in the Library Company of Philadelphia I give to my grandson Benjamin Franklin Bache, confiding that he will permit his brothers and sisters to share in the use of it.

"I was born in Boston, New-England, and owe my first instructions in literature to the free grammar-schools established there. I therefore give one hundred pounds sterling to my executors, to be by them, the survivers or surviver of them, paid over to the managers or directors of the freeschools in my native town of Boston, to be by them, or those persons or person who shall have the superintendance and management of the said schools, put out to interest, and so continued at interest for ever; which interest annually shall be laid out in silver medals, and given as honorary rewards annually by the directors of the said freeschools, for the encouragement of scholarship in the said schools, belonging to the said town, in such manner as to the discretion of the selectmen of the said town shall seem meet. Out of the salary that may remain due to me as president of the state, I do give the sum of two thousand pounds to my executors, to be by them, the survivers or surviver of them, paid over to such person or persons as the legislature of this state, by an act of Assembly, shall appoint to receive[Pg 229] the same, in trust, to be employed for making the Schuylkill navigable.

"During the number of years I was in business as a stationer, printer, and postmaster, a great many small sums became due to me, for books, advertisements, postage of letters, and other matters, which were not collected, when, in 1757, I was sent by the Assembly to England as their agent, and by subsequent appointments continued there till 1775; when, on my return, I was immediately engaged in the affairs of Congress, and sent to France in 1776, where I remained nine years, not returning till 1785; and the said debts not being demanded in such a length of time, have become in a manner obsolete, yet are nevertheless justly due. These, as they are stated in my great folio leger E, I bequeath to the contributors of the Pennsylvania Hospital, hoping that those debtors, and the descendants of such as are deceased, who now, as I find, make some difficulty of satisfying such antiquated demands as just debts, may, however, be induced to pay or give them as charity to that excellent institution. I am sensible that much must inevitably be lost, but I hope something considerable may be received. It is possible, too, that some of the parties charged may have existing old unsettled accounts against me: in which case the managers of the said hospital will allow and deduct the amount, or pay the balances, if they find it against me.

"I request my friends, Henry Hill, Esq., John Jay, Esq., Francis Hopkinson, Esq., and Mr. Edward Duffield, of Benfield, in Philadelphia county, to be the executors of this my last will and testament, and I hereby nominate and appoint them for that purpose.

"I would have my body buried with as little expense or ceremony as may be.

"Philadelphia, July 17, 1788."

CODICIL.

"I, Benjamin Franklin, in the foregoing or annexed last will and testament named, having farther considered the same, do think proper to make and publish the following codicil or addition thereto:

"It having long been a fixed political opinion of mine, that in a democratical state there ought to be no offices of profit, for the reasons I had given in an article of my drawing in our constitution, it was my intention, when I accepted the office of president, to devote the appointed salary to some public uses: accordingly, I had, before I made my will in July last, given large sums of it to colleges, schools, building of churches, &c.; and in that will I bequeathed two thousand pounds more to the state, for the purpose of making the Schuylkill navigable; but understanding since that such a sum will do but little towards accomplishing such a work, and that the project is not likely to be undertaken for many years to come; and having entertained another idea, that I hope may be more extensively useful, I do hereby revoke and annul that bequest, and direct that the certificates I have for what remains due to me of that salary be sold towards raising the sum of two thousand pounds sterling, to be disposed of as I am now about to order.

"It has been an opinion, that he who receives an estate from his ancestors is under some kind of obligation to transmit the same to his posterity. This obligation does not lie on me, who never inherited a shilling from any ancestor or relation. I shall, however, if it is not diminished by some accident before my death, leave a considerable estate among my descendants and relations. The above observation is made merely as some apology to my family[Pg 231] for my making bequests that do not appear to have any immediate relation to their advantage.

"I was born in Boston, New-England, and owe my first instructions in literature to the free grammar-schools established there. I have, therefore, already considered those schools in my will. But I am also under obligations to the state of Massachusetts for having, unasked, appointed me formerly their agent in England, with a handsome salary, which continued some years; and although I accidentally lost in their service, by transmitting Governor Hutchinson's letters, much more than the amount of what they gave me, I do not think that ought in the least to diminish my gratitude. I have considered that among artisans, good apprentices are most likely to make good citizens; and having myself been bred to a manual art, printing, in my native town, and afterward assisted to set up my business in Philadelphia by kind loans of money from two friends there, which was the foundation of my fortune, and of all the utility in life that may be ascribed to me, I wish to be useful, even after my death, if possible, in forming and advancing other young men, that may be serviceable to their country in both these towns. To this end I devote two thousand pounds sterling, which I give, one thousand thereof to the inhabitants of the town of Boston, in Massachusetts, and the other thousand to the inhabitants of the city of Philadelphia, in trust, to and for the uses, intents, and purposes herein after mentioned and declared. The said sum of one thousand pounds sterling, if accepted by the inhabitants of the town of Boston, shall be managed under the direction of the selectmen, united with the ministers of the oldest Episcopalian, Congregational, and Presbyterian churches in that town, who are to let out the same upon interest at five per cent. per annum, to such young married artificers, under the age of twenty-five[Pg 232] years, as have served an apprenticeship in the said town, and faithfully fulfilled the duties required in their indentures, so as to obtain a good moral character from at least two respectable citizens, who are willing to become their sureties in a bond, with the applicants, for the repayment of the money so lent, with interest, according to the terms hereinafter prescribed; all which bonds are to be taken for Spanish milled dollars, or the value thereof in current gold coin: and the managers shall keep a bound book or books, wherein shall be entered the names of those who shall apply for and receive the benefit of this institution, and of their sureties, together with the sums lent, the dates, and other necessary and proper records respecting the business and concerns of this institution: and as these loans are intended to assist young married artificers in setting up their business, they are to be proportioned by the discretion of the managers, so as not to exceed sixty pounds sterling to one person, nor to be less than fifteen pounds. And if the number of appliers so entitled should be so large as that the sum will not suffice to afford to each as much as might otherwise not be improper, the proportion to each shall be diminished, so as to afford every one some assistance. These aids may, therefore, be small at first; but as the capital increases by the accumulated interest, they will be more ample. And in order to serve as many as possible in their turn, as well as to make the repayment of the principal borrowed more easy, each borrower shall be obliged to pay, with the yearly interest, one tenth part of the principal; which sums of principal and interest so paid in shall be again let out to fresh borrowers. And as it is presumed that there will always be found in Boston virtuous and benevolent citizens willing to bestow a part of their time in doing good to the rising generation, by superintending and managing this institution gratis, it is hoped[Pg 233] that no part of the money will at any time be dead or diverted to other purposes, but be continually augmenting by the interest, in which case there may, in time, be more than the occasion in Boston shall require: and then some may be spared to the neighbouring or other towns in the said state of Massachusetts, which may desire to have it, such towns engaging to pay punctually the interest, and the proportions of the principal annually to the inhabitants of the town of Boston. If this plan is executed, and succeeds, as is projected, without interruption for one hundred years, the sum will then be one hundred and thirty-one thousand pounds, of which I would have the managers of the donation to the town of Boston then lay out, at their discretion, one hundred thousand pounds in public works, which may be judged of most general utility to the inhabitants, such as fortifications, bridges, aqueducts, public buildings, baths, pavements, or whatever may make living in the town more convenient to its people, and render it more agreeable to strangers resorting thither for health or a temporary residence. The remaining thirty-one thousand pounds I would have continued to be let out on interest, in the manner above directed, for another hundred years; as I hope it will have been found that the institution has had a good effect on the conduct of youth, and been of service to many worthy characters and useful citizens. At the end of this second term, if no unfortunate accident has prevented the operation, the sum will be four millions and sixty-one thousand pounds sterling, of which I leave one million and sixty-one thousand pounds to the disposition and management of the inhabitants of the town of Boston, and three millions to the disposition of the government of the state, not presuming to carry my views farther.

"All the directions herein given respecting the disposition and management of the donation to the inhabitants[Pg 234] of Boston, I would have observed respecting that to the inhabitants of Philadelphia; only, as Philadelphia is incorporated, I request the corporation of that city to undertake the management agreeably to the said directions, and I do hereby vest them with full and ample powers for that purpose. And having considered that the covering its ground-plat with buildings and pavements, which carry off most of the rain, and prevent its soaking into the earth, and renewing and purifying the springs, whence the water of the wells must gradually grow worse, and, in time, be unfit for use, as I find has happened in all old cities, I recommend that, at the end of the first hundred years, if not done before, the corporation of the city employ a part of the hundred thousand pounds in bringing by pipes the water of Wissahiccon Creek into the town, so as to supply the inhabitants, which I apprehend may be done without great difficulty, the level of that creek being much above that of the city, and may be made higher by a dam. I also recommend making the Schuylkill completely navigable. At the end of the second hundred years, I would have the disposition of the four millions and sixty-one thousand pounds divided between the inhabitants of the city of Philadelphia and the government of Pennsylvania, in the same manner as herein directed with respect to that of the inhabitants of Boston and the government of Massachusetts. It is my desire that this institution should take place and begin to operate within one year after my decease; for which purpose due notice should be publicly given previous to the expiration of that year, that those for whose benefit this establishment is intended may make their respective applications; and I hereby direct my executor, the survivers or surviver of them, within six months after my decease, to pay over the said sum of two thousand pounds sterling to such persons as shall be duly appointed[Pg 235] by the selectmen of Boston and the corporation of Philadelphia to receive and take charge of their respective sums of one thousand pounds each for the purposes aforesaid. Considering the accidents to which all human affairs and projects are subject in such a length of time, I have, perhaps, too much flattered myself with a vain fancy that these dispositions, if carried into execution, will be continued without interruption, and have the effects proposed; I hope, however, that if the inhabitants of the two cities should not think fit to undertake the execution, they will at least accept the offer of these donations as a mark of my good-will, a token of my gratitude, and a testimony of my earnest desire to be useful to them even after my departure. I wish, indeed, that they may both undertake to endeavour the execution of the project, because

I think that, though unforeseen difficulties may arise, expedients will be found to remove them, and the scheme be found practicable. If one of them accepts the money with the conditions and the other refuses, my will then is that both sums be given to the inhabitants of the city accepting, the whole to be applied to the same purpose and under the same regulations directed for the separate parts; and if both refuse, the money remains, of course, in the mass of my estate, and it is to be disposed of therewith, according to my will made the seventeenth day of July, 1788. I wish to be buried by the side of my wife, if it may be, and that a marble stone, to be made by Chambers, six feet long, four feet wide, plain, with only a small moulding round the upper edge, and this inscription,

Benjamin

and

Deborah

}   Franklin,

178-, be placed over us both.

"My fine crabtree walking-stick, with a gold head, curiously wrought in the form of the Cap of Liberty,[Pg 236] I give to my friend and the friend of mankind, General Washington. If it were a sceptre, he has merited it, and would become it. It was a present to me from that excellent woman Madame de Forbach, the Dowager Duchess of Deux Ponts, connected with some verses which should go with it.

"Philadelphia, 23d June, 1789."

The following epitaph was written by Dr. Franklin for himself when he was only twenty-three years of age, as appears by the original (with various corrections), found among his papers, and from which this is a faithful copy:

[Epitaph, written 1728.]

"THE BODY

OF

BENJAMIN FRANKLIN,

PRINTER,

FRANKLIN

(like the cover of an old book,

its contents torn out,

and stripped of its lettering and gilding),

lies here food for worms;

yet the work itself shall not be lost,

for it will (as he believed) appear once more

in a new and more elegant edition,

revised and corrected

by

THE AUTHOR."

FOOTNOTES:

[15] Dr. Stuber was born in Philadelphia, of German parents. He was sent at an early age to the university, where his genius, diligence, and amiable temper soon acquired him the particular notice and favour of those under whose immediate direction he was placed. After passing through the common course of study in a much shorter time than usual, he left the university at the age of sixteen, with great reputation. Not long after, he entered on the study of physic; and the zeal with which he pursued it, and the advances he made, gave his friends reason to form the most flattering prospects of his future eminence and usefulness in the profession. As Dr. Stuber's circumstances were very moderate, he did not think this pursuit well calculated to answer them. He therefore relinquished it after he had obtained a degree in the profession, and qualified himself to practice with credit and success, and immediately entered on the study of the law. While in the pursuit of the last-mentioned object, he was prevented, by a premature death, from reaping the fruit of those talents with which he was endowed, and of a youth spent in the ardent and successful pursuit of useful and elegant literature.

[16] Three days previous to his decease, he desired his daughter, Mrs. Sarah Bache, to have his bed made, "in order that he might die in a decent manner," as was his expression: an idea probably suggested by an acquaintance with the custom of the ancients. Mrs. Bache having replied that she hoped he would recover, and live many years longer, he instantly rejoined, "I hope not."

[17] The Congress of the United States thus expressed their sentiments in return.

Resolved, by the Senate and House of Representatives of the United States of America, in Congress assembled, That the President of the United States be requested to cause to be communicated to the National Assembly of France, the peculiar sensibility of Congress to the tribute paid to the memory of Benjamin Franklin by the enlightened and free representatives of a great nation, in their decree of the eleventh June, one thousand seven hundred and ninety.

Signed,

Fred. Aug. Muhlenberg,

Speaker of the House of Representatives.

John Adams,

Vice-President of the United States

and President of the Senate.

Approved, March the 2d, 1791.

Signed,

GEORGE WASHINGTON,

President of the United States.

[Pg 237]

WRITINGS OF FRANKLIN.

The Examination of Dr. Franklin before the British House of Commons, relative to the Repeal of the American Stamp-act.[18]

1766, Feb. 3. Benjamin Franklin, Esq., and a number of other persons, were "ordered to attend the committee of the whole House of Commons, to whom it was referred to consider farther the several papers relative to America, which were presented to the House by Mr. Secretary Conway, &c."[Pg 238]

Q. What is your name and place of abode?

A. Franklin, of Philadelphia.

Q. Do the Americans pay any considerable taxes among themselves?

A. Certainly, many, and very heavy taxes.

Q. What are the present taxes in Pennsylvania, laid by the laws of the colony?

A. There are taxes on all estates, real and personal; a poll tax; a tax on all offices, professions, trades, and businesses, according to their profits; an excise on all wine, rum, and other spirits; and a duty of ten pounds per head on all negroes imported, with some other duties.

Q. For what purposes are those taxes laid?

A. For the support of the civil and military establishments of the country, and to discharge the heavy debt contracted in the last war.

Q. How long are those taxes to continue?

A. Those for discharging the debt are to continue till 1772, and longer if the debt should not be then all discharged. The others must always continue.

Q. Was it not expected that the debt would have been sooner discharged?

A. It was, when the peace was made with France and Spain. But a fresh war breaking out with the Indians, a fresh load of debt was incurred; and the taxes, of course, continued longer by a new law.

Q. Are not all the people very able to pay those taxes?

A. No. The frontier counties all along the continent having been frequently ravaged by the enemy, and greatly impoverished, are able to pay very little[Pg 239] tax. And therefore, in consideration of their distresses, our late tax laws do expressly favour those counties, excusing the sufferers; and I suppose the same is done in other governments.

Q. Are not you concerned in the management of the postoffice in America?

A. Yes. I am deputy postmaster-general of North America.

Q. Don't you think the distribution of stamps by post to all the inhabitants very practicable, if there was no opposition?

A. The posts only go along the seacoasts; they do not, except in a few instances, go back into the country; and if they did, sending for stamps by post would occasion an expense of postage, amounting, in many cases, to much more than that of the stamps themselves. * * * *

Q. From the thinness of the back settlements, would not the stamp-act be extremely inconvenient to the inhabitants, if executed?

A. To be sure it would; as many of the inhabitants could not get stamps when they had occasion for them, without taking long journeys, and spending perhaps three or four pounds, that the crown might get sixpence.

Q. Are not the colonies, from their circumstances, very able to pay the stamp duty?

A. In my opinion there is not gold and silver enough in the colonies to pay the stamp duty for one year.

Q. Don't you know that the money arising from the stamps was all to be laid out in America?

A. I know it is appropriated by the act to the American service; but it will be spent in the conquered colonies, where the soldiers are; not in the colonies that pay it.

Q. Is there not a balance of trade due from the colonies where the troops are posted, that will bring back the money to the old colonies?[Pg 240]

A. I think not. I believe very little would come back. I know of no trade likely to bring it back. I think it would come from the colonies where it was spent directly to England; for I have always observed, that in every colony, the more plenty the means of remittance to England, the more goods are sent for and the more trade with England carried on.

Q. What number of white inhabitants do you think there are in Pennsylvania?

A. I suppose there may be about one hundred and sixty thousand?

Q. What number of them are Quakers?

A. Perhaps a third.

Q. What number of Germans?

A. Perhaps another third; but I cannot speak with certainty.

Q. Have any number of the Germans seen service as soldiers in Europe?

A. Yes, many of them, both in Europe and America.

Q. Are they as much dissatisfied with the stamp duty as the English?

A. Yes, and more; and with reason, as their stamps are, in many cases, to be double.

Q. How many white men do you suppose there are in North America?

A. About three hundred thousand, from sixteen to sixty years of age?

Q. What may be the amount of one year's imports into Pennsylvania from Britain?

A. I have been informed that our merchants compute the imports from Britain to be above £500,000.

Q. What may be the amount of the produce of your province exported to Britain?

A. It must be small, as we produce little that is wanted in Britain. I suppose it cannot exceed £40,000.

Q. How, then, do you pay the balance?[Pg 241]

A. The balance is paid by our produce carried to the West Indies (and sold in our own islands, or to the

French, Spaniards, Danes, and Dutch); by the same produce carried to other colonies in North America (as to New-England, Nova Scotia, Newfoundland, Carolina, and Georgia); by the same, carried to different parts of Europe (as Spain, Portugal, and Italy). In all which places we receive either money, bills of exchange, or commodities that suit for remittance to Britain; which, together with all the profits on the industry of our merchants and mariners, arising in those circuitous voyages, and the freights made by their ships, centre finally to Britain to discharge the balance, and pay for British manufactures continually used in the provinces, or sold to foreigners by our traders.

Q. Have you heard of any difficulties lately laid on the Spanish trade?

A. Yes, I have heard that it has been greatly obstructed by some new regulations, and by the English men-of-war and cutters stationed all along the coast in America.

Q. Do you think it right that America should be protected by this country, and pay no part of the expense?

A. That is not the case. The colonies raised, clothed, and paid, during the last war, near twenty-five thousand men, and spent many millions.

Q. Were you not reimbursed by Parliament?

A. We were only reimbursed what, in your opinion, we had advanced beyond our proportion, or beyond what might reasonably be expected from us; and it was a very small part of what we spent. Pennsylvania, in particular, disbursed about £500,000; and the reimbursements, in the whole, did not exceed £60,000.

Q. You have said that you pay heavy taxes in Pennsylvania; what do they amount to in the pound?

A. The tax on all estates, real and personal, is[Pg 242] eighteen pence in the pound, fully rated; and the tax on the profits of trades and professions, with other taxes, do, I suppose, make full half a crown in the pound.

Q. Do you know anything of the rate of exchange in Pennsylvania, and whether it has fallen lately?

A. It is commonly from one hundred and seventy to one hundred and seventy-five. I have heard that it has fallen lately from one hundred and seventy-five to one hundred and sixty-two and a half, owing, I suppose, to their lessening their orders for goods; and when their debts to this country are paid, I think the exchange will probably be at par.

Q. Do not you think the people of America would submit to pay the stamp duty if it was moderated?

A. No, never, unless compelled by force of arms.

Q. What was the temper of America towards Great Britain before the year 1763?

A. The best in the world. They submitted willingly to the government of the crown, and paid in their courts obedience to acts of Parliament. Numerous as the people are in the several old provinces, they cost you nothing in forts, citadels, garrisons, or armies, to keep them in subjection. They were governed by this country at the expense only of a little pen, ink, and paper: they were led by a thread. They had not only a respect, but an affection for Great Britain; for its laws, its customs, and manners; and even a fondness for its fashions, that greatly increased the commerce. Natives of Britain were always treated with particular regard; to be an Old England-man was, of itself, a character of some respect, and gave a kind of rank among us. * * *
*

Q. And what is their temper now?

A. Oh, very much altered.

Q. Did you ever hear the authority of Parliament to make laws for America questioned till lately?

A. The authority of Parliament was allowed to[Pg 243] be valid in all laws, except such as should lay internal taxes. It was never disputed in laying duties to regulate commerce.

Q. In what proportion had population increased in America?

A. I think the inhabitants of all the provinces together, taken at a medium, double in about twenty-five years. But their demand for British manufactures increases much faster; as the consumption is not merely in proportion to their numbers, but grows with the growing abilities of the same numbers to pay for them. In 1723, the whole importation from Britain to Pennsylvania was but about £15,000 sterling; it is now near half a million.

Q. In what light did the people of America use to consider the Parliament of Great Britain?

A. They considered the Parliament as the great bulwark and security of their liberties and privileges, and always spoke of it with the utmost respect and veneration. Arbitrary ministers, they thought, might possibly, at times, attempt to oppress them; but they relied on it that the Parliament, on application, would always give redress. They remembered, with gratitude, a strong instance of this, when a bill was brought into Parliament, with a clause to make royal instructions laws in the colonies, which the House of Commons would not pass, and it was thrown out.

Q. And have they not still the same respect for Parliament?

A. No, it is greatly lessened.

Q. To what cause is that owing?

A. To a concurrence of causes; the restraints lately laid on their trade, by which the bringing of foreign gold and silver into the colonies was prevented; the prohibition of making paper money among themselves,[19] and then demanding a new and[Pg 244] heavy tax by stamps, taking away, at the same time, trials by juries, and refusing to receive and hear their humble petitions.

Q. Don't you think they would submit to the stamp-act if it was modified, the obnoxious parts taken out, and the duty reduced to some particulars of small moment?

A. No, they will never submit to it.

Q. What do you think is the reason that the people in America increase faster than in England?

A. Because they marry younger and more generally.

Q. Why so?

A. Because any young couple that are industrious may easily obtain land of their own, on which they can raise a family.

Q. Are not the lower rank of people more at their ease in America than in England?

A. They may be so if they are sober and diligent, as they are better paid for their labour.

Q. What is your opinion of a future tax, imposed on the same principle with that of the stamp-act? How would the Americans receive it?

A. Just as they do this. They would not pay it.

Q. Have you not heard of the resolutions of this house and of the House of Lords, asserting the right of Parliament relating to America, including a power to tax the people there?

A. Yes, I have heard of such resolutions.

Q. What will be the opinion of the Americans on those resolutions?

A. They will think them unconstitutional and unjust.

Q. Was it an opinion in America before 1763, that the Parliament had no right to lay taxes and duties there?

A. I never heard any objection to the right of laying duties to regulate commerce, but a right to lay[Pg 245] internal taxes was never supposed to be in Parliament, as we are not represented there.

Q. On what do you found your opinion, that the people in America made any such distinction?

A. I know that whenever the subject has occurred in conversation where I have been present, it has appeared to be the opinion of every one, that we could not be taxed by a Parliament wherein we were not represented. But the payment of duties laid by an act of Parliament as regulations of commerce was never disputed.

Q. But can you name any act of Assembly, or public act of any of your governments, that made such distinction?

A. I do not know that there was any; I think there was never an occasion to make any such act, till now that you have attempted to tax us: that has occasioned resolutions of Assembly declaring the distinction, in which I think every Assembly on the continent, and every member in every Assembly, have been unanimous. * * * *

Q. You say the colonies have always submitted to external taxes, and object to the right of Parliament only, in laying internal taxes; now, can you show that there is any kind of difference between the two taxes to the colony on which they may be laid?

A. I think the difference is very great. An external tax is a duty laid on commodities imported; that duty is added to the first cost and other charges on the commodity, and, when it is offered for sale, makes a part of the price. If the people do not like it at that price, they refuse it; they are not obliged to pay it. But an internal tax is forced from the people without their consent, if not laid by their own representatives. The stamp-act says we shall have no commerce, make no exchange of property with each other, neither purchase nor grant, nor recover debts; we shall neither marry nor make our wills, unless we pay such and such sums; and[Pg 246] thus it is intended to extort our money from us, or ruin us by the consequences of refusing to pay it.

Q. But supposing the external tax or duty to be laid on the necessaries of life imported into your colony, will not that be the same thing in its effects as an internal tax?

A. I do not know a single article imported into the northern colonies but what they can either do without or make themselves.

Q. Don't you think cloth from England absolutely necessary to them?

A. No, by no means absolutely necessary; with industry and good management, they may well supply themselves with all they want.

Q. Will it not take a long time to establish that manufacture among them; and must they not, in the mean while, suffer greatly?

A. I think not. They have made a surprising progress already; and I am of opinion that, before their old clothes are worn out, they will have new ones of their own making.

Q. Can they possibly find wool enough in North America?

A. They have taken steps to increase the wool. They entered into general combinations to eat no more lamb; and very few lambs were killed last year. This course, persisted in, will soon make a prodigious difference in the quantity of wool. And the establishing of great manufactories, like those in the clothing towns here, is not necessary, as it is where the business is to be carried on for the purposes of trade. The people will all spin and work for themselves, in their own houses.

Q. Can there be wool and manufacture enough in one or two years?

A. In three years I think there may.

Q. Does not the severity of the winter in the northern colonies occasion the wool to be of bad quality?[Pg 247]

A. No, the wool is very fine and good. * * * *

Q. Considering the resolution of Parliament[20] as to the right, do you think, if the stamp-act is repealed, that the North Americans will be satisfied?

A. I believe they will.

Q. Why do you think so?

A. I think the resolutions of right will give them very little concern if they are never attempted to be carried into practice. The colonies will probably consider themselves in the same situation in that respect with Ireland: they know you claim the same right with regard to Ireland, but you never exercise it. And they may believe you never will exercise it in the colonies any more than in Ireland, unless on some very extraordinary occasion.

Q. But who are to be the judges of that extraordinary occasion? Is not the Parliament?

A. Though the Parliament may judge of the occasion, the people will think it can never exercise such right till representatives from the colonies are admitted into Parliament; and that, whenever the occasion arises, representatives will be ordered. * *

Q. Can anything less than a military force carry the stamp-act into execution?

A. I do not see how a military force can be applied to that purpose.

Q. Why may it not?

A. Suppose a military force sent into America, they will find nobody in arms; what are they then to do? They cannot force a man to take stamps who chooses to do without them. They will not find a rebellion: they may indeed make one.

Q. If the act is not repealed, what do you think will be the consequence?

A. A total loss of the respect and affection the people of America bear to this country, and of all the commerce that depends on that respect and affection.[Pg 248]

Q. How can the commerce be affected?

A. You will find that, if the act is not repealed, they will take very little of your manufactures in a short time.

Q. Is it in their power to do without them?

A. I think they may very well do without them.

Q. Is it their interest not to take them?

A. The goods they take from Britain are either necessaries, mere conveniences, or superfluities. The first, as cloth, &c., with a little industry they can make at home; the second they can do without till they are able to provide them among themselves; and the last, which are much the greatest part, they will strike off immediately. They are mere articles of fashion, purchased and consumed because the fashion in a respected country; but will now be detested and rejected. The people have already struck-off, by general agreement, the use of all goods fashionable in mournings, and many thousand pounds worth are sent back as unsaleable.

Q. Is it their interest to make cloth at home?

A. I think they may at present get it cheaper from Britain, I mean of the same fineness and neatness of workmanship; but when one considers other circumstances, the restraints on their trade, and the difficulty of making remittances, it is their interest to make everything.

Q. Suppose an act of internal regulations connected with a tax, how would they receive it?

A. I think it would be objected to.

Q. Then no regulation with a tax would be submitted to?

A. Their opinion is, that when aids to the crown are wanted, they are to be asked of the several assemblies, according to the old established usage; who will, as they always have done, grant them freely. And that their money ought not to be given away without their consent, by persons at a distance,[Pg 249] unacquainted with their circumstances and abilities. The granting aids to the crown is the only means they have of recommending themselves to their sovereign; and they think it extremely hard and unjust that a body of men, in which they have no representatives, should make a merit to itself of giving and granting what is not their own, but theirs; and deprive them of a right they esteem of the utmost importance, as it is the security of all their other rights.

Q. But is not the postoffice, which they have long received, a tax as well as a regulation?

A. No; the money paid for the postage of a letter is not of the nature of a tax; it is merely a quantum meruit for a service done: no person is compellable to pay the money if he does not choose to receive the service. A man may still, as before the act, send his letter by a servant, a special messenger, or a friend, if he thinks it cheaper and safer.

Q. But do they not consider the regulations of the postoffice, by the act of last year, as a tax?

A. By the regulations of last year, the rate of postage was generally abated near thirty per cent. through all America; they certainly cannot consider such abatement as a tax.

Q. If an excise was laid by Parliament, which they might likewise avoid paying by not consuming the articles excised, would they then not object to it?

A. They would certainly object to it, as an excise is unconnected with any service done, and is merely an aid, which they think ought to be asked of them and granted by them, if they are to pay it, and can be granted for them by no others whatsoever, whom they have not empowered for that purpose.

Q. You say they do not object to the right of Parliament in laying duties on goods to be paid on their importation: now, is there any kind of difference[Pg 250] between a duty on the importation of goods and an excise on their consumption?

A. Yes, a very material one: an excise, for the reasons I have just mentioned, they think you can have no right to lay within their country. But the sea is yours: you maintain, by your fleets, the safety of navigation in it, and keep it clear of pirates: you may have, therefore, a natural and equitable right to some toll or duty on merchandises carried through that part of your dominions, towards defraying the expense you are at in ships to maintain the safety of that carriage.

Q. Does this reasoning hold in the case of a duty laid on the produce of their lands exported? And would they not then object to such a duty?

A. If it tended to make the produce so much dearer abroad as to lessen the demand for it, to be sure they would object to such a duty: not to your right of laying it, but they would complain of it as a burden, and petition you to lighten it. * * *

Q. Supposing the stamp-act continued and enforced, do you imagine that ill-humour will induce the Americans to give as much for worse manufactures of their own, and use them preferable to better of ours?

A. Yes, I think so. People will pay as freely to gratify one passion as another, their resentment as their pride.

Q. Would the people at Boston discontinue their trade?

A. The merchants are a very small number compared with the body of the people, and must discontinue their trade if nobody will buy their goods.

Q. What are the body of the people in the colonies?

A. They are farmers, husbandmen, or planters.

Q. Would they suffer the produce of their lands to rot?

A. No; but they would not raise so much. They would manufacture more and plough less.[Pg 251]

Q. Would they live without the administration of justice in civil matters, and suffer all the inconveniences of such a situation for any considerable time, rather than take the stamps, supposing the stamps were protected by a sufficient force, where every one might have them?

A. I think the supposition impracticable, that the stamps should be so protected as that every one might have them. The act requires sub-distributors to be appointed in every county town, district, and village, and they would be necessary. But the principal distributors, who were to have had a considerable profit on the whole, have not thought it worth while to continue in the office; and I think it impossible to find sub-distributors fit to be trusted, who, for the trifling profit that must come to their share, would incur the odium and run the hazard that would attend it; and if they could be found, I think it impracticable to protect the stamps in so many distant and remote places.

Q. But in places where they could be protected, would not the people use them rather than remain in such a situation, unable to obtain any right, or recover by law any debt?

A. It is hard to say what they would do. I can only judge what other people will think and how they will act by what I feel within myself. I have a great many debts due to me in America, and I had rather they should remain unrecoverable by any law, than submit to the stamp-act. They will be debts of honour. It is my opinion, the people will either continue in that situation, or find some way to extricate themselves, perhaps by generally agreeing to proceed in the courts without stamps.

Q. What do you think a sufficient military force to protect the distribution of the stamps in every part of America?

A. A very great force, I can't say what, if the disposition of America is for a general resistance[Pg 252]

Q. What is the number of men in America able to bear arms, or of disciplined militia?

A. There are I suppose, at least....

[Question objected to. He withdrew. Called in again.]

Q. Is the American stamp-act an equal tax on the country?

A. I think not.

Q. Why so?

A. The greatest part of the money must arise from lawsuits for the recovery of debts, and be paid by the lower sort of people, who were too poor easily to pay their debts. It is, therefore, a heavy tax on the poor, and a tax upon them for being poor.

Q. But will not this increase of expense be a means Of lessening the number of lawsuits?

A. I think not; for as the costs all fall upon the debtor, and are to be paid by him, they would be no discouragement to the creditor to bring his action.

Q. Would it not have the effect of excessive usury?

A. Yes; as an oppression of the debtor. * * * *

Q. Are there any slitting-mills in America?

A. I think there are three, but I believe only one at present employed. I suppose they will all be set to work if the interruption of the trade continues.

Q. Are there any fulling-mills there?

A. A great many.

Q. Did you never hear that a great quantity of stockings were contracted for, for the army, during the war, and manufactured in Philadelphia?

A. I have heard so.

Q. If the stamp-act should be repealed, would not the Americans think they could oblige the Parliament to repeal every external tax-law now in force?

A. It is hard to answer questions of what people at such a distance will think.[Pg 253]

Q. But what do you imagine they will think were the motives of repealing the act?

A. I suppose they will think that it was repealed from a conviction of its inexpediency; and they will rely upon it, that, while the same inexpediency subsists, you will never attempt to make such another.

Q. What do you mean by its inexpediency?

A. I mean its inexpediency on several accounts: the poverty and inability of those who were to pay the tax, the general discontent it has occasioned, and the impracticability of enforcing it.

Q. If the act should be repealed, and the Legislature should show its resentment to the opposers of the stamp-act, would the colonies acquiesce in the authority of the Legislature? What is your opinion they would do?

A. I don't doubt at all that, if the Legislature repeal the stamp-act, the colonies will acquiesce in the authority.

Q. But if the Legislature should think fit to ascertain its right to lay taxes, by any act laying a small tax contrary to their opinion, would they submit to pay the tax?

A. The proceedings of the people in America have been considered too much together. The proceedings of the assemblies have been very different from those of the mobs, and should be distinguished, as having no connexion with each other. The assemblies have only peaceably resolved what they take to be their rights: they have taken no measures for opposition by force; they have not built a fort, raised a man, or provided a grain of ammunition, in order to such opposition. The ringleaders of riots, they think, ought to be punished: they would punish them themselves if they could. Every sober, sensible man would wish to see rioters punished, as otherwise peaceable people have no security of person or estate; but as to an internal[Pg 254] tax, how small soever, laid by the Legislature here on the people there, while they have no representatives in this Legislature, I think it will never be submitted to: they will oppose it to the last: they do not consider it as at all necessary for you to raise money on them by your taxes; because they are, and always have been, ready to raise money by taxes among themselves, and to grant large sums, equal to their abilities, upon requisition from the crown. They have not only granted equal to their abilities, but, during all the last war, they granted far beyond their abilities, and beyond their proportion with this country (you yourselves being judges) to the amount of many hundred thousand pounds; and this they did freely and readily, only on a sort of promise from the secretary of state that it should be recommended to Parliament to make them compensation. It was accordingly recommended to Parliament in the most honourable manner for them. America has been greatly misrepresented and abused here, in papers, and pamphlets, and speeches, as ungrateful, and unreasonable, and unjust, in having put this nation to immense expense for their defence, and refusing to bear any part of that expense. The colonies raised, paid, and clothed near twenty-five thousand men during the last war; a number equal to those sent from Britain, and far beyond their proportion: they went deeply into debt in doing this, and all their taxes and estates are mortgaged, for many years to come, for discharging that debt. Government here was at that time very sensible of this. The colonies were recommended to Parliament. Every year the king sent down to the house a written message to this purpose, "That his majesty, being highly sensible of the zeal and vigour with which his faithful subjects in North America had exerted themselves in defence of his majesty's just rights and possessions, recommended it to the house to take the[Pg 255] same into consideration, and enable him to give them a proper compensation." You will find those messages on your own journals every year of the war to the very last; and you did accordingly give £200,000 annually to the crown, to be distributed in such compensation to the colonies. This is the strongest of all proofs that the colonies, far from being unwilling to bear a share of the burden, did exceed their proportion; for if they had done less, or had only equalled their proportion, there would have been no room or reason for compensation. Indeed, the sums reimbursed them were by no means adequate to the expense they incurred beyond their proportion: but they never murmured at that; they esteemed their sovereign's approbation of their zeal and fidelity, and the approbation of this house, far beyond any other kind of compensation; therefore there was no occasion for this act to force money from a willing people: they had not refused giving money for the purposes of the act, no requisition had been made, they were always willing and ready to do what could reasonably be expected from them, and in this light they wish to be considered.

Q. But suppose Great Britain should be engaged in a war in Europe, would North America contribute to the support of it?

A. I do think they would, as far as their circumstances would permit. They consider themselves as a part of the British empire, and as having one common interest with it: they may be looked on here as foreigners, but they do not consider themselves as such. They are zealous for the honour and prosperity of this nation; and, while they are well used, will always be ready to support it, as far as their little power goes. In 1739 they were called upon to assist in the expedition against Carthagena, and they sent three thousand men to join your army. It is true Carthagena is in America,[Pg 256] but as remote from the northern colonies as if it had been in Europe. They make no distinction of wars as to their duty of assisting in them. I know the last war is commonly spoken of here as entered into for the defence, or for the sake of the people in America. I think it is quite misunderstood. It began about the limits between Canada and Nova Scotia; about territories to which the crown indeed laid claim, but which were not claimed by any British colony; none of the lands had been granted to any colonist; we had, therefore, no particular concern or interest in that dispute. As to the Ohio, the contest there began about your right of trading in the Indian country; a right you had by the treaty of Utrecht, which the French infringed; they seized the traders and their goods, which were your manufactures; they took a fort which a company of your merchants, and their factors and correspondents, had erected there, to secure that trade. Braddock was sent with an army to retake that fort (which was looked on here as another encroachment on the king's territory) and to protect your trade. It was not till after his defeat that the colonies were attacked.[21] They were before in perfect peace with both French and Indians; the troops were not, therefore, sent for their defence. The trade with the Indians, though carried on in America, is not an American interest. The people of America are chiefly farmers and planters; scarce anything that they raise or produce is an article of commerce with the Indians. The Indian trade is a British interest; it is carried on with British manufactures, for the profit of British merchants and[Pg 257] manufacturers; therefore the war, as it commenced for the defence of territories of the crown (the property of no American) and for the defence of a trade purely British, was really a British war, and yet the people of America made no scruple of contributing their utmost towards carrying it on and bringing it to a happy conclusion.

Q. Do you think, then, that the taking possession of the king's territorial rights, and strengthening the frontiers, is not an American interest?

A. Not particularly, but conjointly a British and an American interest.

Q. You will not deny that the preceding war, the war with Spain, was entered into for the sake of America; was it not occasioned by captures made in the American seas?

A. Yes; captures of ships carrying on the British trade there with British manufactures.

Q. Was not the late war with the Indians, since the peace with France, a war for America only?

A. Yes; it was more particularly for America than the former; but it was rather a consequence or remains of the former war, the Indians not having been thoroughly pacified; and the Americans bore by much the greatest share of the expense. It was put an end to by the army under General Bouquet; there were not above three hundred regulars in that army, and above one thousand Pennsylvanians.

Q. Is it not necessary to send troops to America, to defend the Americans against the Indians?

A. No, by no means; it never was necessary. They defended themselves when they were but a handful, and the Indians much more numerous. They continually gained ground, and have driven the Indians over the mountains, without any troops sent to their assistance from this country. And can it be thought necessary now to send troops for their defence from those diminished Indian tribes,[Pg 258] when the colonies are become so populous and so strong? There is not the least occasion for it; they are very able to defend themselves. * *
*

Q. Do you think the assemblies have a right to levy money on the subject there, to grant to the crown?

A. I certainly think so; they have always done it.

Q. Are they acquainted with the declaration of rights? And do they know that, by that statute, money is not to be raised on the subject but by consent of Parliament?

A. They are very well acquainted with it.

Q. How, then, can they think they have a right to levy money for the crown, or for any other than local purposes?

A. They understand that clause to relate to subjects only within the realm; that no money can be levied on them for the crown but by consent of Parliament. The colonies are not supposed to be within the realm; they have assemblies of their own, which are their parliaments, and they are, in that respect, in the same situation with Ireland. When money is to be raised for the crown upon the subject in Ireland or in the colonies, the consent is given in the Parliament of Ireland or in the assemblies of the colonies. They think the Parliament of Great Britain cannot properly give that consent till it has representatives from America; for the petition of right expressly says, it is to be by common consent in Parliament; and the people of America have no representatives in Parliament to make a part of that common consent.

Q. If the stamp-act should be repealed, and an act should pass ordering the assemblies of the colonies to indemnify the sufferers by the riots, would they do it?

A. That is a question I cannot answer.

Q. Suppose the king should require the colonies to grant a revenue, and the Parliament should be[Pg 259] against their doing it, do they think they can grant a revenue to the king without the consent of the Parliament of Great Britain?

A. That is a deep question. As to my own opinion, I should think myself at liberty to do it, and should do it if I liked the occasion.

Q. When money has been raised in the colonies upon requisition, has it not been granted to the king?

A. Yes, always; but the requisitions have generally been for some service expressed, as to raise, clothe, and pay troops, and not for money only.

Q. If the act should pass requiring the American assemblies to make compensation to the sufferers, and they should disobey it, and then the Parliament should, by another act, lay an internal tax, would they then obey it?

A. The people will pay no internal tax; and I think an act to oblige the assemblies to make compensation is unnecessary; for I am of opinion that, as soon as the present heats are abated, they will take the matter into consideration, and, if it is right to be done, they will do it themselves.

Q. Do not letters often come into the postoffices in America directed to some inland town where no post goes?

A. Yes.

Q. Can any private person take up those letters, and carry them as directed?

A. Yes; any friend of the person may do it, paying the postage that has accrued.

Q. But must not he pay an additional postage for the distance to such inland town?

A. No.

Q. Can the postmaster answer delivering the letter, without being paid such additional postage?

A. Certainly he can demand nothing where he does no service.

Q. Suppose a person, being far from home, finds[Pg 260] a letter in a postoffice directed to him, and he lives in a place to which the post generally goes, and the letter is directed to that place, will the postmaster deliver him the letter without his paying the postage receivable at the place to which the letter is directed?

A. Yes; the office cannot demand postage for a letter that it does not carry, or farther than it does carry it.

Q. Are not ferrymen in America obliged, by act of Parliament, to carry over the posts without pay?

A. Yes.

Q. Is not this a tax on the ferrymen?

A. They do not consider it as such, as they have an advantage from persons travelling with the post.

Q. If the stamp-act should be repealed, and the crown should make a requisition to the colonies for a sum of money, would they grant it?

A. I believe they would.

Q. Why do you think so?

A. I can speak for the colony I live in: I have it in instruction from the Assembly to assure the ministry, that as they always had done, so they should always think it their duty to grant such aids to the crown as were suitable to their circumstances and abilities, whenever called upon for that purpose, in the usual constitutional manner; and I had the honour of communicating this instruction to that honourable gentleman then minister.

Q. Would they do this for a British concern, as suppose a war in some part of Europe that did not affect them?

A. Yes, for anything that concerned the general interest. They consider themselves as part of the whole.

Q. What is the usual constitutional manner of calling on the colonies for aids?

A. A letter from the secretary of state.[Pg 261]

Q. Is this all you mean; a letter from the secretary of state?

A. I mean the usual way of requisition, in a circular letter from the secretary of state, by his majesty's command, reciting the occasion, and recommending it to the colonies to grant such aid as became their loyalty, and were suitable to their abilities.

Q. Did the secretary of state ever write for money for the crown?

A. The requisitions have been to raise, clothe, and pay men, which cannot be done without money.

Q. Would they grant money alone, if called on?

A. In my opinion they would, money as well as men, when they have money, or can make it.

Q. If the Parliament should repeal the stamp-act, will the Assembly of Pennsylvania rescind their resolutions?

A. I think not.

Q. Before there was any thought of the stamp-act, did they wish for a representation in Parliament?

A. No.

Q. Don't you know that there is, in the Pennsylvania charter, an express reservation of the right of Parliament to lay taxes there?

A. I know there is a clause in the charter by which the king grants that he will levy no taxes on the inhabitants, unless it be with the consent of the Assembly or by act of Parliament.

Q. How, then, could the Assembly of Pennsylvania assert, that laying a tax on them by the stamp-act was an infringement of their rights?

A. They understand it thus: by the same charter, and otherwise, they are entitled to all the privileges and liberties of Englishmen; they find in the great charters, and the petition and declaration of rights, that one of the privileges of English subjects is, that they are not to be taxed but by their common[Pg 262] consent; they have therefore relied upon it, from the first settlement of the province, that the Parliament never would nor could, by colour of that clause in the charter, assume a right of taxing them, till it had qualified itself to exercise such right, by admitting representatives from the people to be taxed, who ought to make a part of that common consent.

Q. Are there any words in the charter that justify that construction?

A. The common rights of Englishmen, as declared by Magna Charta and the Petition of Right, all justify it. *
* * *

Q. Are all parts of the colonies equally able to pay taxes?

A. No, certainly; the frontier parts, which have been ravaged by the enemy, are greatly disabled by that means; and, therefore, in such cases, are usually favoured in our tax-laws.

Q. Can we, at this distance, be competent judges of what favours are necessary?

A. The Parliament have supposed it, by claiming a right to make tax-laws for America; I think it impossible.

Q. Would the repeal of the stamp-act be any discouragement of your manufactures? Will the people that have begun to manufacture decline it?

A. Yes, I think they will; especially if, at the same time, the trade is open again, so that remittances can be easily made. I have known several instances that make it probable. In the war before last, tobacco being low, and making little remittance, the people of Virginia went generally into family manufactures. Afterward, when tobacco bore a better price, they returned to the use of British manufactures. So fulling-mills were very much disused in the last war in Pennsylvania, because bills were then plenty, and remittances could easily be made to Britain for English cloth and other goods.[Pg 263]

Q. If the stamp-act should be repealed, would it induce the assemblies of America to acknowledge the rights of Parliament to tax them, and would they erase their resolutions?

A. No, never.

Q. Are there no means of obliging them to erase those resolutions?

A. None that I know of; they will never do it, unless compelled by force of arms.

Q. Is there a power on earth that can force them to erase them?

A. No power, how great soever, can force men to change their opinions.

Q. Do they consider the postoffice as a tax or as a regulation?

A. Not as a tax, but as a regulation and convenience; every assembly encouraged it, and supported it in its infancy by grants of money, which they would not otherwise have done; and the people have always paid the postage.

Q. When did you receive the instructions you mentioned?

A. I brought them with me when I came to England, about fifteen months since.

Q. When did you communicate that instruction to the minister?

A. Soon after my arrival; while the stamping of America was under consideration, and before the bill was brought in.

Q. Would it be most for the interest of Great Britain to employ the hands of Virginia in tobacco or in manufactures?

A. In tobacco, to be sure.

Q. What used to be the pride of the Americans?

A. To indulge in the fashions and manufactures of Great Britain.

Q. What is now their pride?

A. To wear their old clothes over again, till they can make new ones.[Pg 264]

Feb. 13. Benjamin Franklin, Esq., having passed through his examination, was exempted from farther attendance.

He withdrew.

Feb. 24. The resolutions of the committee were reported by the chairman, Mr. Fuller, their seventh and last resolution setting forth, "that it was their opinion that the House be moved, that leave be given to bring in a bill to repeal the stamp-act." A proposal for recommitting this resolution was negatived by 240 votes to 133.—Journals of the House of Commons.

Narrative of the Massacre of Friendly Indians in Lancaster County, Pennsylvania, 1764.

These Indians were the remains of a tribe of the Six Nations, settled at Conestogo, and thence called Conestogo Indians. On the first arrival of the English in Pennsylvania, messengers from this tribe came to welcome them, with presents of venison, corn, and skins; and the whole tribe entered into a treaty of friendship with the first proprietor, William Penn, which was to last "as long as the sun should shine, or the waters run in the rivers."

This treaty has been since frequently renewed, and the chain brightened, as they express it, from time to time. It has never been violated, on their part or ours, till now. As their lands by degrees were mostly purchased, and the settlements of the white people began to surround them, the proprietor assigned them lands on the manor of Conestogo, which they might not part with; there they have lived many years in friendship with their white[Pg 265] neighbours, who loved them for their peaceable, inoffensive behaviour.

It has always been observed, that Indians settled in the neighbourhood of white people do not increase, but diminish continually. This tribe accordingly went on diminishing, till there remained in their town on the manor but twenty persons, viz., seven men, five women, and eight children, boys and girls.

Of these, Shehaes was a very old man, having assisted at the second treaty held with them, by Mr. Penn, in 1701, and ever since continued a faithful and affectionate friend to the English. He is said to have been an exceeding good man, considering his education, being naturally of a most kind, benevolent temper.

Peggy was Shehaes's daughter; she worked for her aged father, continuing to live with him, though married, and attended him with filial duty and tenderness.

John was another good old man; his son Harry helped to support him.

George and Will Soc were two brothers, both young men.

John Smith, a valuable young man of the Cayuga nation, who became acquainted with Peggy, Shehaes's daughter, some few years since, married and settled in that family. They had one child, about three years old.

Betty, a harmless old woman; and her son Peter, a likely young lad.

Sally, whose Indian name was Wyanjoy, a woman much esteemed by all that knew her, for her prudent and good behaviour in some very trying situations of life. She was a truly good and an amiable woman, had no children of her own; but, a distant relation dying, she had taken a child of that relation's to bring up as her own, and performed towards it all the duties of an affectionate parent.[Pg 266]

The reader will observe that many of their names are English. It is common with the Indians, that have an affection for the English, to give themselves and their children the names of such English persons as they particularly esteem.

This little society continued the custom they had begun, when more numerous, of addressing every new governor and every descendant of the first proprietor, welcoming him to the province, assuring him of their fidelity, and praying a continuance of that favour and protection they had hitherto experienced. They had accordingly sent up an address of this kind to our present governor on his arrival; but the same was scarce delivered when the unfortunate catastrophe happened which we are about to relate.

On Wednesday, the 14th of December, 1763, fifty-seven men from some of our frontier townships, who had projected the destruction of this little commonwealth, came, all well mounted, and armed with firelocks, hangers, and hatchets, having travelled through the country in the night, to Conestogo manor. There they surrounded the small village of Indian huts, and just at break of day broke into them all at once. Only three men, two women, and a young boy were found at home, the rest being out among the neighbouring white people, some to sell the baskets, brooms, and bowls they manufactured, and others on other occasions. These poor defenceless creatures were immediately fired upon, stabbed, and hatcheted to death! The good Shehaes, among the rest, cut to pieces in his bed. All of them were scalped and otherwise horribly mangled. Then their huts were set on fire, and most of them burned down. When the troop, pleased with their own conduct and bravery, but enraged that any of the poor Indians had escaped the massacre, rode off, and in small parties, by different roads, went home.[Pg 267]

The universal concern of the neighbouring white people on hearing of this event, and the lamentations of the younger Indians when they returned and saw the desolation, and the butchered, half-burned bodies of their murdered parents and other relations, cannot well be expressed.

The magistrates of Lancaster sent out to collect the remaining Indians, brought them into the town for their better security against any farther attempt, and, it is said, condoled with them on the misfortune that had happened, took them by the hand, comforted, and promised them protection. They were all put into the workhouse, a strong building as the place of greatest safety.

When the shocking news arrived in town, a proclamation was issued by the governor, detailing the particulars of this horrible outrage, and calling earnestly upon the people of the province to use all possible means to apprehend and bring to condign punishment its savage perpetrators.

Notwithstanding this proclamation, those cruel men again assembled themselves, and, hearing that the remaining fourteen Indians were in the workhouse at Lancaster, they suddenly appeared in that town on the 27th of December. Fifty of them, armed as before, dismounting, went directly to the workhouse, and by violence broke open the door, and entered with the utmost fury in their countenances. When the poor wretches saw they had no protection nigh, nor could possibly escape, and being without the least weapon for defence, they divided into their little families, the children clinging to the parents; they fell on their knees, protested their innocence, declared their love to the English, and that, in their whole lives, they had never done them injury; and in this posture they all received the hatchet! Men, women, and little children were every one inhumanly murdered in cold blood!

The barbarous men who committed the atrocious[Pg 268] fact, in defiance of government, of all laws human and divine, and to the eternal disgrace of their country and colour, then mounted their horses, huzzaed in triumph, as if they had gained a victory, and rode off unmolested!

The bodies of the murdered were then brought out and exposed in the street, till a hole could be made in the earth to receive and cover them.

But the wickedness cannot be covered; the guilt will lie on the whole land, till justice is done on the murderers. The blood of the innocent will cry to Heaven for vengeance.

It is said that Shehaes, being before told that it was to be feared some English might come from the frontier into the country and murder him and his people, he replied, "It is impossible; there are Indians, indeed, in the woods, who would kill me and mine, if they could get at us, for my friendship to the English; but the English will wrap me in their matchcoat and secure me from all danger." How unfortunately was he mistaken!

Another proclamation has been issued, offering a great reward for apprehending the murderers.

But these proclamations have as yet produced no discovery; the murderers having given out such threatenings against those that disapprove their proceedings, that the whole country seems to be in terror, and no one dares speak what he knows; even the letters from thence are unsigned, in which any dislike is expressed of the rioters.

There are some (I am ashamed to hear it) who would extenuate the enormous wickedness of these actions, by saying, "The inhabitants of the frontiers are exasperated with the murder of their relations by the enemy Indians in the present war." It is possible; but, though this might justify their going out into the woods to seek for those enemies, and avenge upon them those murders, it can never[Pg 269] justify their turning into the heart of the country to murder their friends.

If an Indian injures me, does it follow that I may revenge that injury on all Indians? It is well known that Indians are of different tribes, nations, and languages, as well as the white people. In Europe, if the French, who are white people, should injure the Dutch, are they to revenge it on the English, because they too are white people? The only crime of these poor wretches seems to have been, that they had a reddish-brown skin and black hair; and some people of that sort, it seems, had murdered some of our relations. If it be right to kill men for such a reason, then, should any man with a freckled face and red hair kill a wife or child of mine, it would be right for me to revenge it by killing all the freckled, red-haired men, women, and children I could afterward anywhere meet with.

But it seems these people think they have a better justification; nothing less than the Word of God. With the Scriptures in their hands and mouths, they can set at naught that express command, Thou shalt do no murder; and justify their wickedness by the command given Joshua to destroy the heathen. Horrid perversion of Scripture and of religion! To father the worst of crimes on the God of peace and love! Even the Jews, to whom that particular commission was directed, spared the Gibeonites on account of their faith once given. The faith of this government has been frequently given to those Indians, but that did not avail them with people who despise government.

We pretend to be Christians, and, from the superior light we enjoy, ought to exceed heathens, Turks, Saracens, Moors, negroes, and Indians in the knowledge and practice of what is right. I will endeavour to show, by a few examples from books and history, the sense those people have had of such actions.[Pg 270]

Homer wrote his poem, called the Odyssey, some hundred years before the birth of Christ. He frequently speaks of what he calls not only the duties, but the sacred rites of hospitality, exercised towards strangers while in our house or territory, as including, besides all the common circumstances of entertainment, full safety and protection of person from all danger of life, from all injuries, and even insults. The rites of hospitality were called sacred, because the stranger, the poor, and the weak, when they applied for protection and relief, were, from the religion of those times, supposed to be sent by the Deity to try the goodness of men, and that he would avenge the injuries they might receive, where they ought to have been protected. These sentiments, therefore, influenced the manners of all ranks of people, even the meanest; for we find, that when Ulysses came as a poor stranger to the hut of Eumæus the swineherd, and his great dogs ran out to tear the ragged man, Eumæus drove them away with stones; and

"'Unhappy stranger!' (thus the faithful swain

Began, with accent gracious and humane),

'What sorrow had been mine, if at my gate,

Thy reverend age had met a shameless fate!

But enter this my homely roof, and see

Our woods not void of hospitality.'

He said, and seconding the kind request,

With friendly step precedes the unknown guest;

A shaggy goat's soft hide beneath him spread,

And with fresh rushes heaped an ample bed.

Joy touched the hero's tender soul, to find

So just reception from a heart so kind;

And 'Oh, ye gods, with all your blessings grace'

(He thus broke forth) 'this friend of human race!'

The swain replied: 'It never was our guise

To slight the poor, or aught humane despise.

For Jove unfolds the hospitable door,

'Tis Jove that sends the strangers and the poor.'"

These heathen people thought that, after a breach of the rites of hospitality, a curse from Heaven[Pg 271] would attend them in everything they did, and even their honest industry in their callings would fail of success. Thus when Ulysses tells Eumæus, who doubted the truth of what he related, "If I deceive you in this, I should deserve death, and I consent that you should put me to death;" Eumæus rejects the proposal, as what would be attended with both infamy and misfortune, saying ironically,

"Doubtless, oh guest, great laud and praise were mine,

If, after social rites and gifts bestowed,

I stained my hospitable hearth with blood.

How would the gods my righteous toils succeed,

And bless the hand that made a stranger bleed?

No more."

Even an open enemy, in the heat of battle, throwing down his arms, submitting to the foe, and asking life and protection, was supposed to acquire an immediate right to that protection. Thus one describes his being saved when his party was defeated:

"We turned to flight; the gathering vengeance spread

On all parts round, and heaps on heaps lie dead.

The radiant helmet from my brows unlaced,

And lo, on earth my shield and javelin cast,

I meet the monarch with a suppliant's face,

Approach his chariot, and his knees embrace.

He heard, he saved, he placed me at his side;

My state he pitied, and my tears he dried;

Restrained the rage the vengeful foe expressed,

And turned the deadly weapons from my breast.

Pious to guard the hospitable rite,

And fearing Jove, whom mercy's works delight."

The suiters of Penelope are, by the same ancient poet, described as a set of lawless men, who were regardless of the sacred rites of hospitality. And, therefore, when the queen was informed they were slain, and that by Ulysses, she, not believing that Ulysses was returned, says,

"Ah no! some god the suiters' deaths decreed,

Some god descends, and by his hand they bleed;[Pg 272]

Blind, to contemn the stranger's righteous cause

And violate all hospitable laws!

... The powers they defied;

But Heaven is just, and by a god they died."

Thus much for the sentiments of the ancient heathens. As for the Turks, it is recorded in the Life of Mohammed, the founder of their religion, that Khaled, one of his captains, having divided a number of prisoners between himself and those that were with him, he commanded the hands of his own prisoners to be tied behind them, and then, in a most cruel and brutal manner, put them to the sword; but he could not prevail on his men to massacre their captives, because, in fight, they had laid down their arms, submitted, and demanded protection. Mohammed, when the account was brought to him, applauded the men for their humanity; but said to Khaled, with great indignation, "Oh Khaled, thou butcher, cease to molest me with thy wickedness. If thou possessedst a heap of gold as large as Mount Obod, and shouldst expend it all in God's cause, thy merit would not efface the guilt incurred by the murder of the meanest of these poor captives."

Among the Arabs or Saracens, though it was lawful to put to death a prisoner taken in battle, if he had made himself obnoxious by his former wickedness, yet this could not be done after he had once eaten bread or drunk water while in their hands. Hence we read in the history of the wars of the Holy Land, that when the Franks had suffered a great defeat from Saladin, and among the prisoners were the King of Jerusalem, and Arnold, a famous Christian captain, who had been very cruel to the Saracens; these two being brought before the sultan, he placed the king on his right hand and Arnold on his left, and then presented the king with a cup of water, who immediately drank to Arnold; but when Arnold was about to receive the cup, the sultan interrupted, saying, "I will not suffer this wicked[Pg 273] man to drink, as that, according to the laudable and generous custom of the Arabs, would secure him his life."

That the same laudable and generous custom still prevails among the Mohammedans, appears from the account, but last year published, of his travels by Mr. Bell, of Antermony, who accompanied the Czar, Peter the Great, in his journey to Derbent, through Daggestan. "The religion of the Daggestans," says he, "is generally Mohammedan, some following the sect of Osman, others that of Haly. Their language, for the most part, is Turkish, or, rather, a dialect of the Arabic, though many of them speak also the Persian language. One article I cannot omit concerning their laws of hospitality, which is, if their greatest enemy comes under their roof for protection, the landlord, of what condition soever, is obliged to keep him safe from all manner of harm or violence during his abode with him, and even to conduct him safely through his territories to a place of security."

From the Saracens this same custom obtained among the Moors of Africa; was by them brought into Spain, and there long sacredly observed. The Spanish historians record with applause one famous instance of it. While the Moors governed there, and the Spanish mixed with them, a Spanish cavalier, in a sudden quarrel, slew a young Moorish gentleman, and fled. His pursuers soon lost sight of him, for he had, unperceived, thrown himself over a garden wall. The owner, a Moor, happening to be in his garden, was addressed by the Spaniard on his knees, who acquainted him with his case, and implored concealment. "Eat this," said the Moor, giving him half a peach; "you now know that you may confide in my protection." He then locked him up in his garden apartment, telling him that, as soon as it was night, he would provide for his escape to a place of more safety. The Moor[Pg 274] then went into his house, where he had scarce seated himself when a great crowd, with loud lamentations, came to the gate bringing the corpse of his son, that had just been killed by a Spaniard. When the first shock of surprise was a little over, he learned, from the description given, that the fatal deed was done by the person then in his power. He mentioned this to no one; but, as soon as it was dark, retired to his garden apartment, as if to grieve alone, giving orders that none should follow him. There accosting the Spaniard, he said, "Christian, the person you have killed is my son; his body is in my house. You ought to suffer; but you have eaten with me, and I have given you my faith, which must not be broken. Follow me." He then led the astonished Spaniard to his stables, mounted him on one of his fleetest horses, and said, "Fly far while the night can cover you. You will be safe in the morning. You are, indeed, guilty of my son's blood; but God is just and good, and I thank him that I am innocent of yours, and that my faith given is preserved."

The Spaniards caught from the Moors this punto of honour, the effects of which remain, in a degree, to this day. So that, when there is fear of a war about to break out between England and Spain, an English merchant there, who apprehends the confiscation of his goods as the goods of an enemy, thinks them safe if he can get a Spaniard to take charge of them; for the Spaniard secures them as his own, and faithfully redelivers them, or pays the value whenever the Englishman can safely demand it.

Justice to that nation, though lately our enemies and hardly yet our cordial friends, obliges me, on this occasion, not to omit mentioning an instance of Spanish honour, which cannot but be still fresh in the memory of many yet living. In 1746, when we were in hot war with Spain, the Elizabeth, of[Pg 275] London, Captain William Edwards, coming through the Gulf from Jamaica, richly laden, met with a most violent storm, in which the ship sprung a leak, that obliged them, for the saving of their lives, to run her into the Havana. The captain went on shore, directly waited on the governor, told the occasion of his putting in, and that he surrendered his ship as a prize, and himself and his men as prisoners of war, only requesting good quarter. "No, sir," replied the Spanish governor; "if we had taken you in fair war at sea, or approaching our coast with hostile intentions, your ship would then have been a prize, and your people prisoners. But when, distressed by a tempest, you come into our ports for the safety of your lives, we, though enemies, being men, are bound as such, by the laws of humanity, to afford relief to distressed men who ask it of us. We cannot, even against our enemies, take advantage of an act of God. You have leave, therefore, to unload the ship, if that be necessary to stop the leak; you may refit here, and traffic so far as shall be necessary to pay the charges; you may then depart, and I will give you a pass, to be in force till you are beyond Bermuda. If after that you are taken, you will then be a prize; but now you are only a stranger, and have a stranger's right to safety and protection." The ship accordingly departed and arrived safe in London.

Will it be permitted me to adduce, on this occasion, an instance of the like honour in a poor, unenlightened

African negro. I find it in Captain Seagrave's account of his Voyage to Guinea. He relates, that a New-England sloop, trading there in 1752, left their second mate, William Murray, sick on shore, and sailed without him. Murray was at the house of a black, named Cudjoe, with whom he had contracted an acquaintance during their trade. He recovered, and the sloop being gone, he continued with his black friend till some other opportunity[Pg 276] should offer of his getting home. In the mean while, a Dutch ship came into the road, and some of the blacks, going on board her, were treacherously seized and carried off as slaves. Their relations and friends, transported with sudden rage, ran to the house of Cudjoe to take revenge by killing Murray. Cudjoe stopped them at the door, and demanded what they wanted. "The white men," said they, "have carried away our brothers and sons, and we will kill all white men; give us the white man you keep in your house, for we will kill him." "Nay," said Cudjoe, "the white men that carried away your brothers are bad men; kill them when you can catch them; but this white man is a good man, and you must not kill him." "But he is a white man," they cried; "the white men are all bad, and we will kill them all." "Nay," said he, "you must not kill a man that has done no harm, only for being white. This man is my friend, my house is his fort, and I am his soldier. I must fight for him. You must kill me before you can kill him. What good man will ever come again under my roof if I let my floor be stained with a good man's blood!" The negroes, seeing his resolution, and being convinced, by his discourse, that they were wrong, went away ashamed. In a few days Murray ventured abroad again with Cudjoe, when several of them took him by the hand, and told him they were glad they had not killed him; for, as he was a good (meaning an innocent) man, their God would have been angry, and would have spoiled their fishing. "I relate this," says Captain Seagrave, "to show that some among these dark people have a strong sense of justice and honour, and that even the most brutal among them are capable of feeling the force of reason, and of being influenced by a fear of God (if the knowledge of the true God could be introduced among them), since even[Pg 277] the fear of a false God, when their rage subsided, was not without its good effect."

Now I am about to mention something of Indians, I beg that I may not be understood as framing apologies for all Indians. I am far from desiring to lessen the laudable spirit of resentment in my countrymen against those now at war with us, so far as it is justified by their perfidy and inhumanity. I would only observe, that the Six Nations, as a body, have kept faith with the English ever since we knew them, now near a hundred years; and that the governing part of those people have had notions of honour, whatever may be the case of the rum-debauched, trader-corrupted vagabonds and thieves on the Susquehanna and Ohio at present in arms against us. As a proof of that honour, I shall only mention one well-known recent fact. When six Catawba deputies, under the care of Colonel Bull, of Charlestown, went, by permission, into the Mohawk's country to sue for, and treat of peace for their nation, they soon found the Six Nations highly exasperated, and the peace at that time impracticable. They were therefore in fear of their own persons, and apprehended that they should be killed in their way back to New-York; which, being made known to the Mohawk chiefs by Colonel Bull, one of them, by order of the council, made this speech to the Catawbas:

"Strangers and Enemies,

"While you are in this country, blow away all fear out of your breasts; change the black streak of paint on your cheeks for a red one, and let your faces shine with bear's grease. You are safer here than if you were at home. The Six Nations will not defile their own land with the blood of men that come unarmed to ask for peace. We shall send a guard with you, to see you safe out of our territories. So far you shall have peace, but no farther. Get home to your own country, and there take care[Pg 278] of yourselves, for there we intend to come and kill you."

The Catawbas came away unhurt accordingly.

It is also well known, that just before the late war broke out, when our traders first went among the

Piankeshaw Indians, a tribe of the Twigtwees, they found the principle of giving protection to strangers in full force; for, the French coming with their Indians to the Piankeshaw town, and demanding that those traders and their goods should be delivered up, the Piankeshaws replied, the English were come there upon their invitation, and they could not do so base a thing. But the French insisting on it, the Piankeshaws took arms in defence of their guests, and a number of them, with their old chief, lost their lives in the cause; the French at last prevailing by superior force only.

I will not dissemble that numberless stories have been raised and spread abroad, against not only the poor wretches that are murdered, but also against the hundred and forty Christianized Indians still threatened to be murdered; all which stories are well known, by those who know the Indians best, to be pure inventions, contrived by bad people, either to excite each other to join in the murder, or, since it was committed, to justify it, and believed only by the weak and credulous. I call thus publicly on the makers and venders of these accusations to produce their evidence. Let them satisfy the public that even Will Soc, the most obnoxious of all that tribe, was really guilty of those offences against us which they lay to his charge. But, if he was, ought he not to have been fairly tried? He lived under our laws, and was subject to them; he was in our hands, and might easily have been prosecuted; was it English justice to condemn and execute him unheard? Conscious of his own innocence, he did not endeavour to hide himself when the door of the workhouse, his sanctuary, was[Pg 279] breaking open. "I will meet them," says he, "for they are my brothers." These brothers of his shot him down at the door, while the word "brothers" was between his teeth.

But if Will Soc was a bad man, what had poor old Shehaes done? What could he or the other poor old men and women do? What had little boys and girls done! What could children of a year old, babes at the breast, what could they do, that they too must be shot and hatcheted? Horrid to relate! And in their parents' arms! This is done by no civilized nation in Europe. Do we come to America to learn and practise the manners of barbarians? But this, barbarians as they are, they practice against their enemies only, not against their friends. These poor people have been always our friends. Their fathers received ours, when strangers here, with kindness and hospitality. Behold the return we have made them! When we grew more numerous and powerful, they put themselves under our protection. See, in the mangled corpses of the last remains of the tribe, how effectually we have afforded it to them.

Unhappy people! to have lived in such times and by such neighbours. We have seen that they would have been safer among the ancient heathens, with whom the rites of hospitality were sacred. They would have been considered as guests of the public, and the religion of the country would have operated in their favour. But our frontier people call themselves Christians! They would have been safer if they had submitted to the Turks; for ever since Mohammed's reproof to Khaled, even the cruel Turks never kill prisoners in cold blood. These were not even prisoners. But what is the example of Turks to Scripture Christians! They would have been safer, though they had been taken in actual war against the Saracens, if they had once drank water with them. These were not taken in[Pg 280] war against us, and have drunk with us, and we with them, for fourscore years. But shall we compare Saracens to Christians?

They would have been safer among the Moors in Spain, though they had been murderers of sons, if faith had once been pledged to them, and a promise of protection given. But these have had the faith of the English given to them many times by the government, and, in reliance on that faith, they lived among us, and gave us the opportunity of murdering them. However, what was honourable in Moors may not be a rule to us; for we are Christians! They would have been safer, it seems, among popish Spaniards, even if enemies, and delivered into their hands by a tempest. These were not enemies; they were born among us, and yet we have killed them all. But shall we imitate idolatrous papists, we that are enlightened Protestants? They would even have been safer among the negroes of Africa, where at least one manly soul would have been found, with sense, spirit, and humanity enough to stand in their defence. But shall white men and Christians act like a pagan negro? In short, it appears that they would have been safe in any part of the known world, except in the neighbourhood of the Christian white savages of Peckstang and Donegall!

Oh ye unhappy perpetrators of this horrid wickedness! reflect a moment on the mischief ye have done, the disgrace ye have brought on your country, on your religion and your Bible, on your families and children. Think on the destruction of your captivated countryfolks (now among the wild Indians), which probably may follow, in resentment of your barbarity! Think on the wrath of the United Five Nations, hitherto our friends, but now provoked by your murdering one of their tribes, in danger of becoming our bitter enemies. Think of the mild and good government you have so audaciously[Pg 281] insulted; the laws of your king, your country, and your God, that you have broken; the infamous death that hangs over your heads; for justice, though slow, will come at last. All good people everywhere detest your actions. You have imbrued your hands in innocent blood; how will you make them clean? The dying shrieks and groans of the murdered will often sound in your ears. Their spectres will sometimes attend you, and affright even your innocent children. Fly where you will, your consciences will go with you. Talking in your sleep shall betray you; in the delirium of a fever you yourselves shall make your own wickedness known.

One hundred and forty peaceable Indians yet remain in this government. They have, by Christian missionaries, been brought over to a liking, at least, of our religion; some of them lately left their nation, which is now at war with us, because they did not choose to join in their depredations; and to show their confidence in us, and to give us an equal confidence in them, they have brought and put into our hands their wives and children. Others have lived long among us in Northampton county, and most of their children have been born there. These are all now trembling for their lives. They have been hurried from place to place for safety, now concealed in corners, then sent out of the province, refused a passage through a neighbouring colony, and returned, not unkindly, perhaps, but disgracefully, on our hands. Oh Pennsylvania! Once renowned for kindness to strangers, shall the clamours of a few mean niggards about the expense of this public hospitality, an expense that will not cost the noisy wretches sixpence a piece (and what is the expense of the poor maintenance we afford them, compared to the expense they might occasion if in arms against us?), shall so senseless a clamour, I say, force you to turn out of your own doors these unhappy guests,[Pg 282] who have offended their own countryfolks by their affection for you; who, confiding in your goodness, have put themselves under your protection? Those whom you have disarmed to satisfy groundless suspicions, will you leave them exposed to the armed madmen of your country? Unmanly men! who are not ashamed to come with weapons against the unarmed, to use the sword against women, and the bayonet against your children, and who have already given such bloody proofs of their inhumanity and cruelty.

Let us rouse ourselves for shame, and redeem the honour of our province from the contempt of its neighbours; let all good men join heartily and unanimously in support of the laws, and in strengthening the hands of government, that justice may be done, the wicked punished, and the innocent protected; otherwise we can, as a people, expect no blessing from Heaven; there will be no security for our persons or properties; anarchy and confusion will prevail over all; and violence, without judgment, dispose of everything.

Introduction to Historical Review of the Constitution and Government of Pennsylvania.[22]

To obtain an infinite variety of purposes by a few plain principles, is the characteristic of nature. As the eye is affected, so is the understanding; objects at a distance strike us according to their dimensions, or the quantity of light thrown upon them; near, according to their novelty or familiarity,[Pg 283] as they are in motion or at rest. It is the same with actions. A battle is all motion, a hero all glare: while such images are before us, we can attend to nothing else. Solon and Lycurgus would make no figure in the same scene with the king of Prussia; and we are at present so lost in the military scramble on the continent next us, in which, it must be confessed, we are deeply interested, that we have scarce time to throw a glance towards America, where we have also much at stake, and where, if anywhere, our account must be made up at last.

FRANKLIN

We love to stare more than to reflect; and to be indolently amused at our leisure rather than commit the smallest trespass on our patience by winding a painful, tedious maze, which would pay us in nothing but knowledge.

But then, as there are some eyes which can find nothing marvellous but what is marvellously great, so there are others which are equally disposed to marvel at what is marvellously little, and who can derive as much entertainment from their microscope in examining a mite, as Dr. —— in ascertaining the geography of the moon or measuring the tail of a comet.

Let this serve as an excuse for the author of these sheets, if he needs any, for bestowing them on the transactions of a colony till of late hardly mentioned in our annals; in point of establishment one of the last upon the British list, and in point of rank one of the most subordinate; as being not only subject, in common with the rest, to the crown, but also to the claims of a proprietary, who thinks he does them honour enough in governing them by deputy; consequently so much farther removed from the royal eye, and so much the more exposed to the pressure of self-interested instructions.

Considerable, however, as most of them for happiness of situation, fertility of soil, product of valuable[Pg 284] commodities, number of inhabitants, shipping amount of exportations, latitude of rights and privileges, and every other requisite for the being and well-being of society, and more considerable than any of them all for the celerity of its growth, unassisted by any human help but the vigour and virtue of its own excellent constitution.

A father and his family, the latter united by interest and affection, the former to be revered for the wisdom of his institutions and the indulgent use of his authority, was the form it was at first presented in. Those who were only ambitious of repose, found it here; and as none returned with an evil report of the land, numbers followed, all partook of the leaven they found; the community still wore the same equal face; nobody aspired, nobody was oppressed; industry was sure of profit, knowledge of esteem, and virtue of veneration.

An assuming landlord, strongly disposed to convert free tenants into abject vassals, and to reap what he did not sow, countenanced and abetted by a few desperate and designing dependants on the one side, and on the other, all who have sense enough to know their rights and spirit enough to defend them, combined as one man against the said landlord and his encroachments, is the form it has since assumed.

And surely, to a nation born to liberty like this, bound to leave it unimpaired, as they received it from their fathers, in perpetuity to their heirs, and interested in the conservation of it in every appendage of the British empire, the particulars of such a contest cannot be wholly indifferent.

On the contrary, it is reasonable to think the first workings of power against liberty, and the natural efforts of unbiased men to secure themselves against the first approaches of oppression, must have a captivating power over every man of sensibility and discernment among us.[Pg 285]

Liberty, it seems, thrives best in the woods. America best cultivates what Germany brought forth. And were it not for certain ugly comparisons, hard to be suppressed, the pleasure arising from such a research would be without alloy.

In the feuds of Florence, recorded by Machiavel, we find more to lament and less to praise. Scarce can we believe the first citizens of the ancient republics had such pretensions to consideration, though so highly celebrated in ancient story. And as to ourselves, we need no longer have recourse to the late glorious stand of the French parliaments to excite our emulation.

It is a known custom among farmers to change their corn from season to season for the sake of filling the bushel; and in case the wisdom of the age should condescend to make the like experiment in another shape, from hence we may learn whither to repair for the proper species.

It is not, however, to be presumed, that such as have long been accustomed to consider the colonies in general as only so many dependencies on the council-board, the board of trade, and the board of customs; or as a hotbed for causes, jobs, and other pecuniary emoluments, and as bound as effectually by instructions as by laws, can be prevailed upon to consider these patriot rustics with any degree of respect.

Derision, on the contrary, must be the lot of him who imagines it in the power of the pen to set any lustre upon them; and indignation theirs for daring to assert and maintain the independence interwoven in their constitution, which now, it seems, is become an improper ingredient, and, therefore, to be excised away.

But how contemptibly soever these gentlemen may talk of the colonies, how cheap soever they may hold their assemblies, or how insignificant the[Pg 286] planters and traders who compose them, truth will be truth, and principle principle, notwithstanding.

Courage, wisdom, integrity, and honour are not to be measured by the sphere assigned them to act in, but by the trials they undergo and the vouchers they furnish; and, if so manifested, need neither robes nor titles to set them off.

Dr. Franklin's motion for Prayers in the Convention assembled at Philadelphia, 1787, to revise the then existing Articles of Confederation.

Mr. President,

The small progress we have made after four or five weeks' close attendance and continual reasonings with each other, our different sentiments on almost every question, several of the last producing as many Noes as Ayes, is, methinks, a melancholy proof of the imperfection of the human understanding. We indeed seem to feel our own want of political wisdom, since we have been running all about in search of it. We have gone back to ancient history for models of government, and examined the different forms of those republics which, having been originally formed with the seeds of their own dissolution, now no longer exist; and we have viewed modern states all round Europe, but find none of their constitutions suitable to our circumstances.

In this situation of this Assembly, groping, as it were, in the dark, to find political truth, and scarce able to distinguish it when presented to us, how has it happened, sir, that we have not hitherto once thought of humbly applying to the Father of Lights to illuminate our understandings? In the beginning of the contest with Britain, when we were[Pg 287] sensible of danger, we had daily prayers in this room for the Divine protection! Our prayers, sir, were heard; and they were graciously answered. All of us who were engaged in the struggle must have observed frequent instances of a superintending Providence in our favour. To that kind Providence we owe this happy opportunity of consulting in peace on the means of establishing our future national felicity. And have we now forgotten that powerful friend? or do we imagine we no longer need its assistance? I have lived, sir, a long time: and the longer I live, the more convincing proofs I see of this truth, That God governs in the affairs of men! And if a sparrow cannot fall to the ground without his notice, is it probable that an empire can rise without his aid? We have been assured, sir, in the Sacred Writings, that "except the Lord build the house, they labour in vain that build it." I firmly believe this; and I also believe, that without his concurring aid, we shall succeed in this political building no better than the building of Babel: we shall be divided by our little partial local interests, our projects will be confounded, and we ourselves shall become a reproach and a byword down to future ages. And, what is worse, mankind may hereafter, from this unfortunate instance, despair of establishing government by human wisdom, and leave it to chance, war, and conquest.

I therefore beg leave to move,

That henceforth prayers, imploring the assistance of Heaven and its blessing on our deliberations, be held in this Assembly every morning before we proceed to business; and that one or more of the clergy of this city be requested to officiate in that service.

Made in the USA
Las Vegas, NV
07 April 2022

47025676R00079